SFP

Calling

This book was professionally typeset on Reedsy.
Find out more at reedsy.com

Acknowledgement

I would like to take this opportunity to thank the following: Anna, Anne, Brian, Helena, Leanne, Mike, Peter, Rebecca, Ruth, Stephanie, Steve, Verity and last but certainly not least, my far better half, Katy who can probably recite the novel word for word by now! All your help is very much appreciated.

Chapter 1

Heading along one of Hassel on the Hill's leafy lanes is chartered accountant, Roger Masters. He is jubilant. His brilliant head for figures has fended off the all too physical figures his questionable client might have faced inside.

As always when feeling victorious, he drives his big black wagon in a manner suggesting tomorrow may not come to pass. He bought it originally with his wife in mind. She instantly rejected it as far too large but Roger loves it. In an instant it transports him from ledger to Lone Ranger. Behind the wheel he wears a cowboy hat slung over his thick rimmed glasses and greying beard. Invariably though, his high spirits are lowered when he approaches his neighbour's house and observes what is parked outside. When he bought his current truck, he made sure it was bigger than the one owned by his neighbour, a builder. It was not long before Roger saw *him* next door arriving in a vehicle even bigger than Roger's. The wagon war has by no means ended.

Roger swings into his driveway which is long enough to be a leaflet deliverer's nightmare - no letterbox at the gate. On either side of the drive are vast, recently mowed lawns. These are flanked by hedges high enough to hide from their neighbours.

Roger's wife, Vicky Masters, can hear her husband's arrival as the large wheels crunch down the gravel. The sound reminds her of his words "I bought it to protect your physical being."

"Trying to park it does little for my mental well-being." she replied.

He pulls up at the open front door, grabs his laptop and other items but leaves his hat on the seat, and walks into his green-foliage-clad mock Tudor property.

In the kitchen the radio is playing the minuet of Beethoven's so-called *Easy* Sonata Op 49. Roger does not like this piece. It's the last one he tried to learn in his youth before his parents decided to abandon his piano lessons, and it always reminds him of that fateful day. He places a low-calorie energy drink on the worktop. "Here you are Portia," says Roger to his daughter.

"Awesome!" replies Portia who is about to take the bottle but her father withdraws it.

"Portia. The Grand Canyon is awesome, the Swiss Alps are awesome, some might say the ceiling of the Sistine Chapel is awesome. But while receivership of a bottle of pop may indeed be good, I think awesome is going a bit far," replies Roger.

"Dad - it's what we guys say these days," says Portia as she tucks back her straight, long black hair.

"There we go again... *guys*," says Roger making his last word sound like a loud GIZE. "I do not spend a fortune on your school fees for you to speak like a third-rate American chat show host."

"We've had political correctness," interrupts Roger's wife Vicky, finally turning from the sink. "Roger, maybe you should start a movement of *Britical* correctness. It's becoming an obsession."

"I may well do," says Roger noticing his wife and daughter sniggering. "I suppose they'll speak like that at the wannabe school you hope to go to."

"Roger it's not a stage school, it's a music college and her dream."

"Exactly, *dream* – and one big *dream* at that. Why Portia wants to snub my perfectly sensible offer of joining our firm with a junior partnership pending, for something that for many just turns into a dead end, I do not know."

"No but Mrs English says she has a future as a dramatic soprano," says Vicky.

"Oh, that teacher will say anything to keep fifty pounds an hour coming her way," says Roger.

Portia, wounded by those words rushes outside almost in tears. There is a long silence between Roger and his wife, broken by Portia saying "Dad, I think you might want to see something," in a tone which turns on a tap running something cold through her father's veins. Stepping out of the front door Roger reads emblazoned across his vehicle: BIG DOG – SMALL KNOB. "But I don't have a dog," he says.

"You don't get it, do you Roger?" says Vicky from behind. Portia comes to her side. She secretly agrees with the graffiti and has always thought of her Dad's vehicle as nothing but a penis extension. But the mists of symbolism now begin to clear in Roger's mind.

"Who? Who? Cretins, mindless cretins whoever it is. Goodness knows how I'll get it off," he says, looking at his wife.

"Don't ask me, I've no idea," says Vicky trying to think of possible suspects. "Probably an ex-client or some type of activist who might consider the truck a selfish indulgence."

"Just whose side are you on Mrs Masters?" Vicky shrugs. "Anyway – is there a mobile service? I'm not going to be seen driving *that* to the garage," says Roger pointing at the graffiti.

"Does it matter? Half of Hassledon and Hassel on the Hill have probably seen it by now. I'm sure another trip to the garage won't hurt."

"Okay, in that case, I'll borrow your car and you can take it."

"What? You know I'm hopeless at driving that thing."

"Well, maybe now is the time to hone your manoeuvring skills."

"No way."

"Vicky! Portia! You've got to listen to this. You'll love it!" calls Elaine from the Masters' gate. She is waving a CD in the air with one hand and has a glass of wine in the other. Elaine is the last person Roger wants to see. If she discovers and tells her husband about the graffiti, it will give his neighbours a two point lead in the one-upmanship stakes.

"Oh no Roger," says Vicky. "She's all we need."

"Too true" says Roger under his breath.

"The neighbour who can spread banter better than butter." For Vicky, the vision of Elaine the builder's wife, negotiating their gravel drive in her gleaming yet impractical stilettos, is like watching a flickering spark approach a gunpowder keg. Vicky walks towards her and stops directly in front of Elaine. She must *not* see the graffiti on her husband's vehicle "What's this?" says Vicky taking the CD out of Elaine's hand.

"Darius Dalloway, you know, the opera star. You love opera, don't you?" Vicky looks at the CD. She has seen Darius advertised on TV. In her opinion he is nothing more than a crooner masquerading as an opera singer.

4

"Yes, we do. But we like to see whole operas all the way though. Proper productions in a proper theatre in a private box. Not what some might call picnic opera. Look - my husband and I were about to go out. Can we talk about this another time? Elaine takes another sip on her wine.

"Oh, my hubby and I love going to those. Maybe your daughter…" says Elaine, grabbing back her CD and spilling wine on to Vicky's shoes. She sidesteps her and walks towards Portia who is standing in front of Roger's wagon. Portia notices Elaine advancing and tries to ignore her by thumbing her mobile.

Elaine sends ice through Roger's veins as she gets nearer. He only has seconds to re-park his vehicle to hide the graffiti against a hedge. He treads round to the driver's door, pausing to nod at Elaine coming behind him but then realises he has left the vehicle's keys next to where he placed that *awesome* bottle.

"Heard this Portia? Darius is wonderful! I'm sure you'll appreciate him - you know, being an opera singer and that," says Elaine standing next to Portia.

Portia then remembers what her singing teacher had to say about Darius Dalloway. *A charlatan! A marketing exercise - absolutely nothing more. Seen those adverts promoting him? More like soft porn with so-called opera in the background and I use the word opera very generously. Poor Verdi! Poor Puccini! Poor music! What do they say? Not bel canto – more, can belto.* "Mmm, wonderful," says Portia giving a quick glance at the CD Elaine presents to her.

Roger slinks back into the house. He does not want to be there when *it* happens. Vicky now having caught up with Elaine tries to goad her into the house but her neighbour takes out the CD inlay to show Vicky. "Mmm" says Vicky, pointing to one of the pictures in a bid to re-direct Elaine's gaze.

Elaine replies with "Bit o' alright int he? Sure you don't fancy going to see him?" Tickets have just gone on sale for a concert he's doing up at Hassel Manor. It's in three months time - Sunday evening, I think," says Elaine. Her attention is still drawn towards Vicky's pointing finger as they both gaze at the various images of Darius Dalloway.

"Well maybe it could be a possibility. Come inside and we can check the calendar, and top that up too," says Vicky pointing at her neighbour's nearly empty glass.

Vicky, finding Elaine so far compliant, hands her CD booklet back. Mistake. Elaine's tipsy fingers allow a whole line of Darius Dalloway colour photos to concertina to the ground: Darius smiling on stage at an outdoor event – union flags aplenty. Darius with his mouth wide open, tongue visible, punting a gondola. Darius sat on a regency sofa in palatial splendour with his hand placed strategically over his crotch. The album is called *Magnifico!*

"Oh dear!" says Elaine as she bends down to gather up the CD inlay. "Oh No!" Vicky turns to her daughter who was about to follow her mother and neighbour into the house. "Who did that?" says Elaine, catching sight of the word Vicky most dreaded her to see: *knob*. Elaine holds her hand to her mouth to prevent further blushing but releases a sound which Vicky cannot decide would best belong at a funeral or a comedy night. Vicky feels like a cat has just jumped all the way from her stomach and out through her mouth. Infection strikes as laughter erupts and Portia also explodes. In seconds a deep pan of emotion boils over into a trio of giggles.

"Don't know about your husband... but mine..." says Elaine

using a gap between her forefinger and thumb to explain the rest. Vicky is sent into further convulsions of laughter which, in turn gives her daughter Portia much-relieved permission to do the same.

Roger Masters is in the kitchen and hears the laughter and words delivered by Elaine – a lexicon he feels could only be produced on the most debauched of hen nights. What is worse, each of Elaine's comments is answered by shrill laughter from his wife and worst of all, to his horror, Portia. Those lessons he has been paying for have not only taught his daughter how to sing but also to shriek at an annoyingly loud pitch too. Each bellow of laughter hits him straight in the face. He cannot take any more, marches straight upstairs to his office and yanks open a drawer where a green cardboard *Easylite* file rests. Not a day passes without Roger saying the words *I'm old school*. With the file he returns downstairs.

"But Portia, look at you," says Elaine, "So tall, so beautiful, and those eyes, they're the colour of the ocean and such wonderful long black hair. You'll be duetting with Darius Dalloway before you know it. As I said, from small acorns... " The three of them laugh with even more abandon as Roger appears at the doorway. Elaine sees him and drops her glass. But Roger's presence can only reduce the laughter to the hissing of an ill-snuffed fuse.

"I'll get the dustpan," says Vicky trying to compose herself. Yet Roger blocks the doorway with clenched fists on each side of his torso.

"Sorry to spoil your fun Elaine but I need a word with these two," says Roger, using his foot to rake away splinters of glass to one side of the porch. He grabs Vicky's arm and adds "That can wait Vicky."

7

"Roger," says Elaine seeing the gravity on Roger's countenance, "I know someone who can get rid of that graffiti." But the words still tickle her.

"Bet you do," says Roger as he turns to his red-faced daughter. He cannot decide if her face carries shame or resembles a balloon about to burst. "Portia" he says. Portia turns to see a look on her father's face she has not seen since her early years. "Elaine, if you can excuse us, we'll arrange the removal of this...vandalism, eventually."

"Portia, remember the proviso we made?" says Roger slamming the contract onto the kitchen table. The radio is playing John Adams' *Shaker Loops.* Roger turns it off for the first time since all three could remember. "This contract is supposedly due for exchange in a few days time."

"Yes, I think we are aware...so?" says Vicky whose bracelets make more sound than usual when she raises her arms. The jingling of his wife's jewellery is a noise Roger has always found irritating, not least now. His wife continues "As we planned, Portia's going to manage the property during her college course by sharing it with student lodgers, who will in effect, be paying for your investment – and, in turn, save you forking out for your daughter's maintenance. Maybe even return a profit eventually. Remember Roger?"

"Yes, profit-wise we're looking very much at the long term. However, after the appalling shenanigans outside I'm seriously wondering if Portia deserves such an arrangement. From what I heard it seems she still has lot of growing up to do. I'd doubt she's able to manage a drunken session in the proverbial..."

"But Dad it was agreed. And as you said it would be a sound

8

investment even beyond my college days," says Portia.

"It may well be, but then if you find me such an object of ridicule maybe I should withdraw from this whole project as of now. And it's not the first time I've been put down. Is it Vicky?" There is a moment's silence as Roger looks at his wife and daughter. The great provider meets the great pretenders.

"We don't put you down Roger," says Vicky with remorse.

"Don't you now?"

"No, your daughter respects you and always has. There's elements of you I can see in her already," says Vicky.

"Not from all that filth I heard outside just now - much of it pointed at me! That's not what I call respect. And what about you?"

"Okay Roger. We're sorry. It was just us girls letting our hair down," says Vicky who realises her short brown hair has not much to let down.

"If Portia hadn't the ambition of becoming an opera singer, Elaine would probably not come round in the first place. She brought that disc probably thinking it would interest you, Portia."

"Oh, please Dad, don't insult me. That Darius whatshisname isn't a real opera singer anyway," says Portia.

"Look Roger, your daughter doesn't need all this upset with her A levels only a month away," says Vicky.

"Well, she could make it all very easy for herself by doing what I originally proposed: continue her lessons with her singing teacher, which I'd be willing to foot the bill for, but all the while work towards something she can fall back on if her singing so-called career doesn't happen - which it most probably will not," says Roger.

"Oh, great Dad. Thanks for showing so much faith in me.

But that's precisely the reason I want to go to college, to gain contacts and get more experience. *Then* I might have a chance to make that money you think is so important. But how on earth am I to do it stuck in this boring place? It's ridiculous."

"Oh, ridiculous hey? I was the one being ridiculed. It was bad enough having my vehicle vandalised and then you just act as if you were part of it. The whole neighbourhood could hear your squealing laughter all aimed at me. Well maybe what I'm about to say is equally as amusing.

"What's that?" say Vicky and Portia in unison.

"I met this singer who performed at a do I was at the other week. She also went to music college and guess what?

"What?" says Portia.

"When she's not singing, she cleans. Did you hear that Portia, *cleans* offices like mine for the minimum wage. Do you seriously want to end up like that?"

"Of course not Dad. But which college did she go to?"

"I didn't ask her that. But I suppose she's making *some* income - unlike *you* so far."

"Roger, has everything got to boil down to money? I remember the time your daughter sang at that concert a year ago. You were so proud of her and even *you* said she was as good as any other singer. Don't let the mindless morons who put that graffiti on your truck upset you," says Vicky.

"Ah yes, that concert where at the interval I queued all that time for the coffees, only to return to you in time to hear you say your husband's just *a boring old accountant.*"

"Sorry Roger."

"Yes. My whole pride in my daughter was deflated in seconds. And yes, Portia went down a storm but applause has not yielded hard cash yet, has it?

"Here we go again" says Vicky.

"Portia, I'd love it if you could prove to me in some way that singing might be able to work for you financially. When I first started..."

"Oh, and here comes the next record: *when I first started accounting, I was busy balancing study with winning future clients,*" says Vicky.

"And I *was.*"

"Well done *you!*"

"Okay, as I said, the contract's still here on the table. Five days to go before it's due for exchange - I'm still prepared to go ahead with it."

"Yes," mouths Portia.

"*But* what I'd like from you, Portia, is to show me how your singing might make *some* kind of return. We've spent so much on lessons I want to see something coming the other way."

"You're not proposing Portia does something *now* are you, so close to her A-levels?

"As I said, I managed to win clients while preparing for my finals. Oh - and what about all the students who have to work in menial jobs while studying? You've had it pretty easy so far Portia."

"But we're talking about your daughter Roger. Most parents strive to make things better for their children."

"That's okay Mum - don't want to feel my A-level success was all down to privilege." To which her father nods in agreement. "But I think you might be underestimating me, Dad. Remember that time you wouldn't let me go to see that rock band with that boy a few years ago because you thought I was too young?"

"Yes, I remember that well," says Roger.

"Yes, she organised a school trip. Talk about thinking outside the box. Ingenious!" says Vicky.

"And do you know what Dad? I'll gladly take your challenge. In fact, I have an idea already." says Portia.

"Ker-ching," says Vicky winking at her daughter while raising a thumb causing her jewellery to rattle again. Roger quickly throws the contract for the house purchase back in the file and closes the lid with enough force to suggest he is slamming the door of the property which the paperwork represents, and heads back upstairs.

Chapter 2

The chequered squares of Hassledon's estates are framed by streets that pay tribute to the New York grid system. Pathways within the estates slither and dither and occasionally bisect their border roads. A skydiver shoved out of an aircraft might mistake the aerial view of the town for a snakes and ladders board.

The snakes and the ladders are better known as green routes for pedestrians and cyclists. A fantastic idea in principle, yet in practice soon prove to be quite the contrary. The helpfully-intended pathways - enabling non car users to traverse the entire town without even touching a road - start to carry their own venom.

Before long, these paths become littered with assorted debris turning them into assault courses for nocturnal creatures. All too often, their failure to negotiate the obstacles leads to slow and agonising deaths. It's a hazardville for humans too. The relative seclusion makes them an invitation to rapists.

Tucked behind the pathways exist dwellers who have little interest in what is going on beyond their own hard-fought-for four walls. Their houses are well mortared machines for living in - and for unscrupulous landlords, efficient machines for extortion. Families can cocoon themselves from home to shop without the need for discourse. Many like it like that. And during the day, pushchairs and toddlers emerge from within those walls en route to oases of colour and sanctuary - the towns play parks.

Some of the underpasses which make crossing roads safer for those children, during darker hours serve as meeting places for youths claiming temporary refugee status from war-torn families. Their threatening behaviour, often more imagined than real, leaves these places as no-go areas after dusk.

Other underpasses are being colonised by the homeless community - many of whom represent the lost souls drowning in a sea of neurosis, otherwise known as the New Town of Hassledon.

Morning. The sun glows through the young trees of Hassledon and nothing moves, not even a crisp packet. The assorted leaves decked with early morning dew, glisten on each side of one of the town's green routes.

Mitchell Woods is waiting for his boy to deliver his drop. Without it, Mitchell's day is not easy to contemplate. He eagerly anticipates the moment he will leave school to work with his dad. Yet the thought is clouded when he remembers how hard manual labour can be – even for a few hours on a Saturday. His ideal would be to earn enough to satisfy both his addiction and his girlfriend, Maisie. Does such a job exist? He wonders.

For the present he is playing *KillaTeds* on his phone. The dexterity of his thumbs will hopefully propel a teddy bear over a playground assault course of swings, roundabouts and slides. If his thumbs fail and time runs out, the playground turns into a grotesque, outdoor torture chamber. Mitchell advances teddy towards the steps of the slide to the accompaniment of hip hop beats. He hopes to get to the next level of the game where his teddy bear has to battle with the *GrizzaTeds* - a ruthless bunch of gangster-like bears. But time again is getting short and there are only seconds left for teddy to reach the top of the slide.

If Mitchell is not quick enough, when teddy goes down this slide it will turn into a razor-sharp blade slicing the bear in two, leaving it impaled on spikes either side of the blade. Teddy is almost at the top of the steps and the accompanying music has switched from the easy-going hip hop rhythms to the allegro dramatics from Weber's *Oberon Overture.* And then... the phone signal fails and the game freezes. *Shit.* His drop has still not appeared and Maisie will be waiting. He calls his contact number for the drop. There is a connection and he can hear the other side ringing but it just rings and rings. *Answer for eff's sake.*

A few hundred yards down the path from Mitchell, walks a father in a tracksuit labelled *extra extra large* but still not large enough. One hand pushes a pram. The other holds the lead of an ageing Staffordshire terrier. The child in the pushchair - a miniature version of her father.

Further ahead is her elder sister, Freya, on a scooter, who heads towards an underpass where she sees *that* tent. Her excitement for the day dampens as she comes to a halt and scoots back to her father.

A homeless man sits outside a pop-up which still carries a fading yellow tag; the father reads *Fab for Fests* but feels it should be changed to *Suitable for Survival.* Freya thinks the man sitting by the tent has drawn a spot on his forehead with a red felt pen, but her father knows better.

"Don't go on too far Freya, give us a chance to catch up, love."

Despite it being early morning, the sun's intensity causes the father's fringe to stick to his forehead. He wipes the sweat away, while noticing up ahead that his elder daughter has thrown her crisp packet to the ground.

"Freya, I saw that. Pick it up now!" he shouts. She ignores him. "Freya, do you expect me or anyone else to pick it up for you?" Freya is reluctant, having built up a good momentum on her scooter and knows her friend Molly is not far away.

"Freya! You dropped something! Pick it up. Now!" says the father more loudly but he is out of breath from the effort of raising his voice. Freya, who can sense more irritation than threat in her father's voice, turns around and picks the crisp wrapper up. "Good girl, Freya."

Further along the path, Mitchell is still waiting for his drop. Patience is his anti-talent. His last spliff was smoked from the freezing cold of his bedroom window in the early hours. Mitchell toys with the idea of bunking off school but thinks twice. He is unaware the boy he is cursing has no choice but to truant from a school over a hundred miles away. If the boy returns to school and informs officialdom, he could suffer the consequences. Death. He tries the contact number again but this time it is engaged. He tries again. Engaged.

Resigned, Mitchell puts on a favourite track he has down-loaded. His girlfriend who he would normally have met by now, hates it. The track by his favourite artiste, XL, makes a bass-less sound through his phone's speaker. A ticking drum machine and a continuous rap refrain: *Shut the fuck up just shut the fuck up* is interrupted by the orchestral sweep from the first movement of Sibelius's Second. There is also a string pad providing lush bedding for the vocal obscenities.

In the distance another familiar sight, one which annoys Mitchell. The *fat fucker* of a parent with his daughters and dog. The older daughter scoots past him.

Approximately one mile away from Mitchell, are Portia and her mother Vicky. They are about to enter what many of their Hassel on the Hill neighbours consider the *lower altitude* of Hassledon. To help pacify her husband and make Portia's chances as favourable as possible to follow her dream, Vicky has agreed to take Roger's truck to the garage for a respray. "Mum can you drop me off somewhere before the school? I don't want anyone seeing this," says Portia.

"Of course," says Vicky competing with the radio which is broadcasting the last act of Wagner's *The Flying Dutchman* – mortality versus immortality.

Despite the defacement, Vicky finds she enjoys being vertically level with vehicles of a similar height. Usually, she is stuck behind undercarriages she regards as overgrown robot nappies. "Do you reckon the garage will have the respray all done before my singing lesson?" asks Portia, concerned that she will get to see Mrs English in time.

"I should hope so," says Vicky.

They stop at a pedestrian crossing both aware that people are staring at the vehicle, so Vicky winds down the windows and hopes the bombastic power of Wagner will cancel out the more contemporary art on the side of the truck. Portia on the other hand cannot decide if heads are turning for her, the music or the graffiti. She asks herself if being called a *knob* is a suitable put down for a young woman. It could have been worse, she supposes.

Yet on Portia's mind is her singing lesson. She is fully aware that polishing pieces for her upcoming exam will be of paramount importance for her teacher. To convince her teacher otherwise will take some explaining so she rehearses the words which begin: *Mrs English, do you mind...*

Mitchell kicks a large twig into the trees, trying to dispel anger. It's still a no show and no phone reply from his drop. What the hell is going on? Who will Maisie be talking to? He fidgets and in so doing rummages inside his pockets to find a stick of chewing gum. He undoes the wrapper, tosses it to the ground and tries to chew his impatience away.

The obese father, his younger daughter and dog are now only several yards from Mitchell. The father catches Mitchell's attention and points at the silver wrapper Mitchell dropped. The father then points at a bin only a couple of feet away. Mitchell apes him, exaggerating the father's gestures, but concludes his imitation with an upturned finger at the father.

"Excuse me, you dropped that," says the father halting the pram while pointing his finger again at Mitchell's debris. Mitchell just smiles at him and raps out the refrain *shut the fuck up just shut the fuck up*.

"Excuse Me! YOU DROPPED SOMETHING!" says the parent more loudly and now finds it hard to catch his breath again.

"Yeah?" replies Mitchell. He holds the phone speaker so it almost touches the father's ear. *Shut the fuck up just shut the fuck up.* The father cowers.

"Do you mind picking up what you just dropped?" asks the father again. Mitchell pauses the music.

"Pick it up yourself, you fat cunt."

"Excuse me, this is my daughter," says the parent also checking his eldest in the distance. "As I said, do you mind picking it up please? And I'm not impressed with whatever is coming from your phone, especially with youngsters around," Mitchell detects a quiver in the father's voice. He grins but still can't see his drop appear.

"As I said, fatso, pick it up yourself. Besides, it might keep fucking losers like you employed, won't it?"

"I doubt you'd be willing to pay for them."

"Too right, you great gut bucket."

"Look, I've got a good mind to report you to your school," says the father trying to decide from Mitchell's minimal school attire, no tie or blazer badge, which school he might attend.

"Be my guest. That's if a fat fucker like you doesn't suffer a heart attack walking up the hill to get there,"

"When are we going to get a move on?" says the girl in the push chair who has heard similar language at home time aimed at teachers from disgruntled parents.

Traffic can be heard on the nearby road. The father and Mitchell's eyes are locked, but the father makes out through the corner of his eye his older child as she scoots on further. She is far too close to the roadside edge.

"Freya!" he shouts but Freya ignores him. Only yards from the kerb, Freya is scooting on towards her vision of beef in gravy with roast potatoes – better than what her family usually has. Freya's head is also full of *High Five,* her favourite group. *High Five's* music makes Freya and her best friend Molly feel

19

like stars as they copy their idols' dance moves. This new enthusiasm has helped Freya start looking forward to school.

Her friend Molly at the other side of the road, manages to free her hand from her big brother and uses it to beckon Freya. Freya, impatiently looks right but not left. She has the latest *High Five* tune looping through her head and this diverts her concentration. Her friend on the other side of the road sings the *High Five* song. Freya joins in. Her friend dances. Freya imitates. The cry "Freya!" from her distant father is barely noticeable. Holding her scooter impedes her movements. She wants to join in *now* so she shoves the scooter out onto the road, but in her haste it buckles under her legs. She nearly trips over but after regaining her balance finds herself staring, frozen, at what in her eyes are the menacingly bright lights of a vehicle coming straight at her.

"No!" cries Vicky as Portia feels the seat belt cut into her chest.

Freya's father hears a squeal of brakes accompanied by the more deadened sound of rubber on stone and sees vape-like smoke rising from the road. Another sound. Metal on flesh? He can make out his daughter in the middle of the road, eyes wide open. A blonde girl dashes out to grab her. An ominous serenity is broken by cries of "Mummy! Mummy!" The blonde girl puts her arm around Freya. Her father hurries as fast as he can to his daughter, leaving his other daughter and dog with Mitchell who instinctively picks up the dog's lead and walks towards the roadside. The dog seeing Freya in distress, tugs itself free from Mitchell and lollops to Freya.

The father, drops to his knees and embraces his daughter with the biggest hug he has ever given. He cannot kiss her cheeks enough. She is safe. Thank God.

Vicky, with tears in her eyes gets out of the truck and comes to the father. She keeps repeating the word "Sorry." The soaring closing bars of *The Flying Dutchman* can be heard from the car's sound system. Wagner's heroine leaps to eternity – but Freya is still in the here and now. "Turn that off please Portia!" shouts Vicky who cannot decide whether to crouch down towards the father and daughter. The blonde girl, noticing the dog meandering back across the road picks up its lead. The father sees his younger daughter walk towards them. Mitchell stands by the pushchair at the side of the road watching. The blonde girl gives Mitchell a glance. There is something uneasy in his demeanour.

"Are you both okay?" asks the blonde girl bending down towards Freya. As she speaks, she re-buttons the top button of her blouse she recently unbuttoned at a suitable distance from home. There is traffic accumulating on both sides of the road. A driver further down the queue of traffic, cranes his neck out his window and disappointed there is no drama, blasts his horn. The blonde girl shouts "Shut the f...." then "Sorry" reminded by Vicky's glaring eyes she is amongst minors.

Mitchell, from the side of the road, sees the young girl in the arms of her father. She is only crying, therefore breathing and therefore still alive and therefore he is relieved to know he is not part guilty for the death of someone's daughter. He regrets the language he used previously on the young girl's father. His eyes are on the blonde girl who has just yelled at the complaining driver but then remembers his rendezvous and hurries back to the woods. A figure emerges from the trees – his drop.

The youngest daughter sees her sister cry and decides to join in, creating a duet of distress in the middle of the road. At the same time more drivers start blowing their horns turning the whole scene into an ensemble of angst. The father lets go of Freya and ushers his younger daughter to safety on the grass verge while the blonde girl, without asking takes Freya by the hand and walks her over too. She asks what she considers to be the most important question in the world: "When's your birthday?" The girl stops crying briefly as she answers "June." The car that nearly crushed Freya now pulls off the road but it still causes a minor bottleneck. A small audience has gathered there too but they just watch. The blonde girl's schoolfriend, Leah asks "You okay Maisie?"

"Fine thanks," replies Maisie with a smile.

"Look Maisie, sure you're okay? It's just that I've got to see someone before registration."

"I'm sure. It's ok. I'll be coming soon - that's after *he* decides to show."

"Oh *him*. Don't know how you put up with him Maze. Anyways see ya later."

"Yep, see ya."

"Oi, You!" shouts Mitchell running along the path when he sees the familiar figure retreating back into the trees. This figure, much smaller than Mitchell, pauses and finally turns to him.

The young boy stands with his hands in his jacket pockets and stares at nothing in particular. Mitchell can smell the brand new leather of the boy's jacket "Sorry," he says, reaching inside his blazer pocket to bring out cash. The boy takes the money, does not count it but tucks it into his jacket. A sudden breeze picks up and blows a chewing gum wrapper into

Mitchell's vision as he averts his eyes from the boy. "How about some respect?" says the boy.

"Okay..Sorry, again," says Mitchell. He cannot believe he is under the control of someone so much his junior. The silver chewing gum wrapper is blown out of sight by a heavier breeze. The exchange is complete, lesson learned and the boy disappears. Mitchell wishes he could spliff up now but instead heads to where Maisie will be.

Smiling at the child, now safely on the other side of the road, the blonde girl looks up to see Mitchell approaching. The child releases herself to be with her friend Molly, who is also crying from the shock of seeing her friend almost run over. The girls comfort each other with a hug. The father thanks the blonde girl and asks her name. "No probs. Maisie," says the blonde girl, happy to see the man's daughter is safe and no longer in distress. He stares at Maisie for a moment. She is used to this.

"Everything okay? Sorry again but if there's anything..." says Vicky.

"It's fine, thanks," says the father.

"Sure?" says Vicky.

"Sure," says the father as Vicky turns back to the driver's door of her husband's big black wagon. Maisie smiles at Vicky and gives her a brief wave.

Mitchell, seeing the father talking to Maisie wonders if he should wait, but instead takes advantage of the slow traffic. Looking straight ahead, he walks directly towards Maisie who smothers him in an embrace. "You're precious," she says to Mitchell. The dog barks. She is still holding its lead.

"Thanks for all your help," says the father tapping Maisie's arm. His watery eyes are set on her, Mitchell notices. "Thanks..." she says. Her return of gratitude is arrested by Mitchell who pulls her mouth towards his. He kisses her on the lips and then turns to the father with the same smile Maisie has adored for years. The parent looks puzzled.

"You are very lucky my daughter is still alive. *Very* lucky." says the father looking directly at Mitchell who translates his stare as *You are very lucky to have a girl like her. Why is she with a such dickhead like you?* The father turns back to his daughters and with the dog, walks them to school.

"Maisie, you okay?" says Mitchell. Maisie taps Mitchell to remind him that they are standing directly in the path of Vicky's vehicle. Mitchell looks up, sees the girl in the passenger seat and lets go of Maisie. He has never seen the girl before. She has a certain refinement of features almost as if she has been filmed exclusively in high definition. *It's only the daughters of the fucking rich who tend to be good looking*[1] says Mitchell to himself but he can't remember where he heard those words. Mitchell sees her lips - lips that could kiss the world and it would still want more.

The girl in the vehicle turns away, but her facial image will be imprinted on Mitchell's mind for the rest of the day. She has become his *idée fixe.* He wonders if her parents would give him the same cold reception as Maisie's folks nearly always do? Maisie looks at her and wonders if she has an estranged dad like Mitchell's, who lives in a complete shit hole that is too horrible to even think about let alone use for the occasional shag. She also ponders if like Mitchell, this voluptuous girl lives in a home where the walls are paper thin?

Has she got a boyfriend? Mitchell wonders. No. Both Mitchell and Maisie think the girl they see probably has the means, freedom and facility to fuck who she wants and where she wants.

Maisie has been following Mitchell's line of gaze and drags him out of the way of the truck. Vicky leans over her daughter to give Maisie a thumbs up. The traffic is slowly moving again and Mitchell notices the graffiti below where this *posh bit* is sitting. Will he ever see this girl again? "Ha! Big dog small knob!" shouts Mitchell while fisting the side of the girl's door. The truck which only started moving, suddenly stops. Vicky is about to yell abuse but sees Maisie give Mitchell a shove on the shoulder blade, and drives on. The girl whose face is only inches from Mitchell turns back to him, gives him two fingers, winds down the window and shouts "Toss Off!"

"Sod off!" shouts Mitchell while giving her a single finger but the action is in vain as Maisie with the full force a spasm of jealousy provides, tugs him so hard Mitchell falls back straight onto the grass.

Leaving Mitchell there she walks on, assuming she will soon feel Mitchell's fingers thread into hers. But after ten yards or so, nothing. She turns to see Mitchell's body flat out on the grass. He's being silly. She walks back to him.

"Come on Mitchell, get up," says Maisie. Still no movement. "Come on. We'll be late." Maisie kneels down. Mitchell lies motionless with eyes closed. She takes his arm and tries to drag him up. "Mitchell, it wasn't that bad a fall." Maisie starts to feel guilt seep slowly into her chest. She gives his face a brief slap. No reaction. "Mitchell, Mitchell!" Nothing. She puts her head next to his face to check he is breathing. Nothing. Pulse?

"Fooled!" shouts Mitchell. Maisie falls flat on the grass next to Mitchell. This is a position and very familiar situation for the two of them - another outdoor venue for their more intimate moments.

Maisie gets up hoping the people walking by have not recognised her on the ground. Mitchell remains on the grass. Maisie watches him giggle away. It reminds her of the time she first got to know him - a sunny September all those years ago when Maisie, Leah and two others, a year above Mitchell, took him into their care. Back then as a new boy he was smaller than most of the others in his year and Maisie suspected he suffered bullying. On bright warm days, she and her friends would take him out on to the playing fields and the way he was now prone on the grass verge brought back Maisie's first memories of *her cute little pet* lying on the lawn. His spiky fringe has not changed one bit and neither has his cheeky grin.

They would often tease and tickle him and Maisie loved running her fingers through his hair. It was irresistible. However, she began to dislike all the teasing Leah gave the young Mitchell which often erupted in fugues of laughter – especially when Leah broached subjects she thought rather too personal. "Mind your own business Leah," Maisie would intervene on Mitchell's behalf.

He was a compliant student back then and never in trouble with his teachers. He told Maisie his dad said to him *keep your head down and do your time.* He did. When he showed his first report to Maisie and her friends, the girls replied with a fortissimo "Well Done." But after a year of frolicking and fun, Mitchell - now nearly as tall as Maisie - had some news. His mother discovered a note tucked in a sock belonging to his dad from some other woman in his dad's life. His mother tossed the note on to the bed before collapsing into a heap of tears. Mitchell sneaked a glance. The note finished with the words: *ps. You're only after my body.*

Maisie heaves Mitchell from the ground and rewards him with a long kiss after he says the word "Sorry."

"Mitchell!" shouts Ms Smith; Maisie and Mitchell's English teacher's cutting tones sever the couple's embrace. "It might be none of my business but may I say there's a time and place for showing one's affections. I thought that you of all people would have known better Maisie?" While speaking, Ms Smith briefly reveals her full face which, whatever the weather, is usually concealed behind the tight grip of her macintosh collar.

"And Mitchell, I do hope I will not have to be entertaining you again during periods three and four. That's your GCSE music lesson, isn't it?"

"Yes Miss," says Mitchell cowering from Ms Smith who is also Head of Arts.

"And by that Mitchell, I'm asking you to show more respect to Mr Peters," says Ms Smith continuing to walk with her characteristically determined tread. But then she turns to say. "May I make it very clear that I have *far* better things to do than supervise the likes of *you* during my non-teaching time." Some boys in Mitchell's year walk past to see Ms Smith admonishing him and shake their heads, more in pitiful shame.

"I can't help it Miss. Mr Peters hasn't a clue how to deal with the likes of me." Ms Smith clucks her tongue and shakes her head. "Okay, but that does not mean you can act like a prat. I don't want to see you. Is that clear?" says Ms Smith pausing. Mitchell makes no response. "Is that clear Mitchell?"

"Yes it is, isn't it Midge?" says Maisie punching Mitchell's arm. He nods.

"Thank you Maisie," says Ms Smith. Mitchell stops Maisie as they watch Ms Smith march off in her usual huff and rush.

"Ms Smith can just *toss off*," says Mitchell under his breath but loud enough for Maisie to hear him.

"*Toss off*. That's what that girl in the truck said. Are you trying to imitate her?" says Maisie

"No. It's just that Ms Smith sort of reminds me of an older version of that posh girl."

"I don't think so," says Maisie

"If you took that stupid straw hat off she was wearing, she's just *so* Ms Smith. A younger version though. Bet she lives somewhere like Hassel on the Hill."

"You seem very interested in her Midge."

"Just curious, that's all Maze. Mind you, felt sorry for her having to go around with that graffiti on the truck. Ha! Someone doesn't like her!"

"Can you just shut up talking about her Midge?"

"Sorry Maze, just curious. And speaking of curious, what are you doing periods three and four?"

"Thought you would know by now Midge. Period three, history, and four's a study period where I'll be in the library."

"Fuck the library, I've an idea."

"And that is?"

"Come to the music room during your free."

"But you'll be with your stupid friends who just casually invite themselves into the music room. I'm not joining them."

"No they won't. Go on Maze, I've got something special in mind. Just for you Maze."

"Oh, and what's that? I'm intrigued."

"Just come along. You'll see."

"Can't we meet at break?"

"No I have to see the maths teacher about something." Maisie stops walking and so does Mitchell.

"You know what Mitchell?

"What?"

"I seriously thought you were a gonna earlier Midge...you bastard!"

"Well you'd better make the most of me while I'm here then."

"What's that supposed to mean Midge?"

"You'll find out. Come to the music room, period four... please Maze"

"Okay."

"Shit, I can hear the bell. Was hoping to skin up. Bollocks!"

"Good!" Maisie grabs Mitchell and they give each other a peck on the cheek. "By the way Midge, why did that father say you were very lucky?"

"Who are you talking about?"

"You know, the one whose daughter nearly got run over."

"Oh him. He's just a cunt."

"Why?"

"He tried to make me pick something up."

"Mitchell." says Maisie, holding Mitchell straight in front of her with both hands.

"What?"

"Learn to count to ten"

"One, two, three, four, five.." says Mitchell as he dashes off towards his tutor group he can see in the distance. They are queuing up to enter a demountable classroom. "Remember, period four Maze!" he shouts from a distance holding up four fingers.

1 *From The Stranglers song Ugly (Universal Music 1977)*

Chapter 3

I n most music lessons, well after all the other students have arrived, the door bangs against the wall and Mitchell enters. "Hello Mr Peters!" says Mitchell with a certain glee. He struts behind Mr Peters and goes straight to the piano where he flings open the lid with such force it causes the whole instrument to reverberate.

Then by using just his middle fingers, Mitchell thumps out what represents the entire product of two years GCSE practical preparation: a rendition of the *Peppa Pig* theme. Mitchell plays it repeatedly until he decides to acknowledge Mr Peters, who by now has made several appeals for Mitchell to stop. As always, Mitchell replies: "I thought this was a music lesson" - an answer that makes his teacher give up even trying to argue.

At moments like this, Mr Frank Peters wishes he could rip out certain pages of his life story and replace them with new ones. Are schools really that desperate they have to resort to employing the likes of himself? Or is this his punishment for only achieving a *Desmond* degree? He hates the job so much that when he leaves school at the end of the day, he greets the bus stop like a friend.

After Mitchell has finished performing his sole repertoire to zero applause, he slams the piano lid shut. Then ignoring

Mr Peters and the rest of his class, he heads to the back of the room, puts on a pair of headphones connected to a computer and that is the last everyone hears from Mitchell for the rest of the lesson, hopefully.

Depending on his mood, Mitchell also has a whole barrage of other ways to vex the class. His favourite is mimicking a fellow student called Celia. When she answers questions, Mitchell will ape what he considers her *hoity toity* voice. Eventually a student, not Mr Peters, will take it upon themselves to fetch senior management.

Moments later at the door will appear the flint-like face of Ms Smith, Head of Arts. She first glowers at Mr Peters giving the teacher a shiver of guilt and then glares at Mitchell. With her spindly forefinger, she beckons Mitchell to come with her. He will leave the room protesting he hates music lessons and Mr Peters is a *fucking useless teacher anyway.* Ms Smith gives Mr Peters a sharp nod as she shepherds Mitchell through the door.

But today is different.

Mr Peters takes the register. "Mitchell."

"Here Sir!" says Mitchell.

Mr Peters looks up with incredulity to see Mitchell sitting upright with arms folded. Mr Peters ticks Mitchell's name and says "Right."

"Okay everyone, it's not long until your practical exams, so please get on with...what you need...to get on with," says Mr Peters still shocked to see Mitchell's smiling blue eyes. The teacher takes advantage of this apparent thaw in the cold war between them. "I wonder Mitchell if it isn't too late to try some singing for your practical. Are there any songs you like?" says Mr Peters. Mitchell replies with a big loud *Fa la la la la, fa la la laa!* - the opening of the *Largo al Factotum* aria from *The Barber of Seville* - Rossini's human horn signal, which in this case announces Mitchell's readiness to offer his *dis*-service. Mitchell knows the aria as it is featured in the *KillaTeds* video game he plays. Mr Peters smiles but then his face, like so many times with Mitchell, reverts to the default of disappointment. "You've an amazing voice Mitchell. If only you could alter your course from destination self-destruct," says Mr Peters who suddenly realises those words could equally apply to himself ever since he opted for teaching. "No and I don't care," replies Mitchell. He puts his headphones back on his head and waves off Mr Peters. The teacher shrugs and turns to see Celia taking out music with the name *Beethoven* on it. It restores Mr Peters' smile.

Meanwhile, other class members move towards their respective work areas. Waiting for the next level of *KillaTeds* to load, Mitchell observes Mr Peters usher Celia into the corridor of practice rooms. "Hey, Nathan," calls Mitchell "Do you reckon Celia and Peters have done it yet?" Nathan shrugs his shoulders and begins to type while Mitchell continues to try and eject a teddy bear from a playground swing. If teddy launches on a suitable trajectory, it will clear a duck pond. If not, the pond will turn into a pool of piranhas and teddy will be devoured to the accompaniment of the *Dies Irae* from Verdi's *Requiem*. Luckily teddy succeeds, clears the pond and now moves on to the next level to the sound of hip hop beats. Mitchell shouts "Yes!" and imitates the game's drum beats.

He irritates Nathan who wishes he could enjoy the solace of a practice room but every week is the same. Why can't Mr Peters devise a rota?

With the teacher out of the room, and none of Mitchell's associates drifting in after bunking off other classes, Mitchell wonders if he can go to his hideout to spliff but is disappointed to see a staff member standing solidly outside the door. Anyway Maisie, as arranged, should be showing up soon. He sees Nathan pick up a guitar and sing:

How can those eyes so beautiful and blue,
  Make me so sad when I think of you?
  As the wind blows through your golden hair
  I wish you'd know it's me who cares.
  Hope you may see you're the one for me
  Hope you may see it was meant to be
  Instead of what is plain to see
  It's nothing but a TRAVESTY.

Nathan finishes then blushes when he realises Mitchell has taken off his headphones and has been listening. *Travesty,* the song's title, is a word Nathan has recently learned in English.

"Tune okay Nay," says Mitchell to Nathan, who smiles with relief. "But what girl would want someone who writes such wussy words as those?" Yet Mitchell does not realise Nathan's words: *May see* are a play on the name Maisie, Mitchell's Maisie - who Nathan adores and wonders why she has anything to do with such a prat as Mitchell. Hence, *Travesty.*

To Nathan's surprise he sees Maisie at the door. Mitchell gets up to welcome her. As Maisie enters, Nathan's pulse rises and he picks up his guitar. He does not dare to sing but just strums the chords to his song. She smiles at Nathan which lifts his poor spirits to some heavenly place. Yet Nathan's vague hopes are dashed as his strumming becomes background music for Mitchell and Maisie to kiss. He watches Maisie's head move from side to side and seem to feed off Mitchell. It hurts. What Nathan sees would make the perfect video for *Travesty*.

Mitchell can hear the distant sound of Mr Peters and Celia rehearsing. "Ssssh" he says, as Maisie feels the rough contours of his skin brush against her lips. On tiptoes, they enter the corridor to the practice rooms. Through the first door on the left are two boys rehearsing. Their song opens:

Crumbs from the sandwich of a butchered breast
   Fall upon the cleavage of her sunbed chest

"What's that?" says Mitchell.

It's a song by Mr Foster-Pilkington, the supply teacher. We discovered he has a *YouTube* channel" replies one of the boys.

"What?" says Mitchell. "We need to use this room, so would you two mind if..."

"No, we're rehearsing. And anyway, you're banned from using the practice rooms" says one of the boys. Maisie appears from behind Mitchell. "Please guys, he's with me," says Maisie. "I wouldn't ask if it wasn't important, I need this room to help Mitchell with his coursework." One of the boys begins to move, the other remains. Maisie goes over to him "Please, you'd be doing *me* a ginormous favour." The boy stays put. "Come on," says Maisie, touching the boy's shoulder with a smile. "We'll only be about fifteen or so." After a moment he reluctantly leaves.

As the boys head along the corridor back to the main music room, the last one to leave taps the other and says "Bet I know what those two will be up to. I've got an idea. This will be *so* sick."

Mitchell opens a window. He's been dying for a spliff all morning but Maisie tugs him and her action not only pulls him to a wall opposite but conquers the craving too. They start to kiss. Shortly afterwards, Mitchell starts to pull up Maisie's skirt but she forces his hand down. "What's the matter?" he asks.

"Not here, surely?" says Maisie.

"Why not?" However, Maisie remembers the posh girl Mitchell had his eyes on earlier and after a few moments, acquiesces. Mitchell's trousers fall as the room is filled with the strains of Beethoven's Op 23 Violin Sonata penetrating through the wall from next door. Maisie can feel him hard against her hip. The Beethoven drops to a whisper but then starts to slowly and gradually career towards its closing bars. Maisie feels Mitchell enter. The music after a steady pulse becomes more relentless, gathers tempo and crescendos. Mr Peters can be heard: "Yes!..*crescendo a – po - co – a – PO CO*. Yes, keep going! That's it!..Oh yeah. More!..*piu mosso*, that's right! Celia...Yes!" The Beethoven stops. There is silence.

Outside in the corridor, the evicted boys can hardly wait to look at the video footage they have recorded. The sound of a violin retuning allows them to creep slowly back to the main music room.

Nathan is rehearsing his song again but stops as the boys enter the room. "No, carry on. Sounds epic, man!" Nathan encouraged, continues while he sees the boys watching something on a mobile. It seems both captivating and amusing.

Mitchell and Maisie hear the Beethoven start again. "No, don't spliff Mitch – those guys will be back in a mo," says Maisie as she tidies herself. She leads Mitchell out of the practice room and the two of them are in the corridor when the Beethoven comes to a sudden halt.

"Think I left it next door," says the voice of Mr Peters from the adjacent practice room. Maisie darts back into the room as Mr Peters opens a door. Mitchell stands in the corridor, face to face with the teacher. "Didn't I make it clear you are not meant to be anywhere near these practice rooms Mitchell?"

"Sorry Sir, was just coming to ask you something." says Mitchell.

"And what's that?"

"What was the piece you were playing."

"It was a Beethoven violin sonata," says Mr Peters

"Sounded great."

"Thank you. Now excuse me." Mr Peters moves towards the practice room where Mitchell and Maisie were. Through the door's window Mitchell can see an image he has so far beheld as nothing less than beautiful but is now a potential harbinger of much woe – Maisie's leg protruding from under a table. Mitchell stands in front of the door to shield Maisie who must *not* be discovered.

"Mr Peters." says Mitchell.

"Yes," says Mr Peters.

"The practical exam."

"Yes, what about it? Look, can you get out of the way, I need to get something from this room,"

"That one I was singing earlier – Fa la la la la, Fa la la la," sings Mitchell not moving.

"Rossini's factotum aria?"

"Yeah, that. I want to do it for my practical." Mr Peters pauses with astonishment.

"The music might be in here, if you let me through."

"Mr Peters –"

"Yes?"

"Actually... er...we could download it from the internet and print it off using the printer in the main room. Can you show me how to do that, please?" Mr Peters pauses for a moment and is about to request Mitchell to move out of the way but as Mitchell reiterates *Can you?* he decides to capitalise on Mitchell's new found enthusiasm and turns towards the door to the music room.

Maisie is doing her best to conceal herself and wonders how on earth she ended up in this situation. She remembers Mitchell telling her about the note his mother discovered. *You only want me for my body.* His father left the family soon after. In his absence, Mitchell took advantage and became more wayward. He boasted to Maisie of how easily he could get round his mother. She would often use more carrot than stick to try and coerce her son. Eventually his mother started leaving him on his own in the evenings. He used his new found freedom to play video games, and discovered he could sing after inviting Maisie and her friends round to practice karaoke.

At school, his vocal abilities made him more popular and helped him to emerge from his shell. He was becoming the cool kid who could not only sing but also, to the admiration of his classmates, defy teachers. Unfortunately for Maisie the students she used to protect him from were now becoming his friends. At the same time Mitchell was also metamorphosing from her cute little pet to a decidedly handsome young man. His whole being, not just his spiky hair, now became irresistible to Maisie.

The bell rings out a headache in the corridor to signal the end of the lesson. Celia, carrying her violin exits from the practice room. "Keep up the practice Celia, you sounded wonderful today," says Mr Peters. "Yes Celia, I could hear you from the main room. Sounded wicked!" says Mitchell. Celia nods at Mr Peters but puts up a wall of diffidence when she brushes past Mitchell.

"What was I about to get?" says Mr Peters.

"We were about to go and download my song in the main room," says Mitchell.

"Oh yes... Rossini's factotum, but there was something else." Then to Mitchell's surprise, Mr Peters continues "Oh, what was it?" Mitchell wonders if Maisie might have fully concealed herself by now. The teacher clicks his fingers. "Oh... I'll remember later. Let's go and find your aria. It will be easier to find on a copyright-free site I know." Mitchell breathes again – on Maisie's behalf.

"After you Sir," says Mitchell, holding his hand out towards the main music room, inviting Mr Peters to go before him. Impressed by Mitchell's new found civility, Mr Peters reaches the threshold of the main music room but then stops.

"Excuse me people. If you don't mind, I would appreciate all gaming and *YouTube* viewing, or whatever it is, to be conducted elsewhere," says Mr Peters when he sees a number of students huddled around a mobile phone. Mitchell can hear his name being mumbled amongst laughter. "Why are they talking about me?" says Mitchell to himself. He is getting worried. Under different circumstances, he would push past the teacher and crash straight into the room to see what was going on. This time he stays put and waits behind Mr Peters, who stands with his arms folded to watch the room slowly clear. At last, the two of them enter.

The teacher goes to the computer Mitchell was gaming on earlier and, taking a seat, starts to search for Mitchell's aria. Mitchell is looking at the ajar entrance door and through it he sees boys outside in the main corridor. One of them comes to the door and spotting Mitchell, nudges the door further open by shoving his arm through the gap. With one fist over his elbow he jerks his forearm upwards. "Get in there Mitch!" says the boy.

"Out!" shouts Mr Peters. The boy leaves but Mitchell can see boys outside making jerking movements as they thrust their pelvises at each other. *They know* thinks Mitchell, now realising exactly what they are imitating. His growing anxiety and frustration of not being able to go outside while Maisie still risks the very real possibility of being discovered, rekindles his agitation and in turn, his craving for a smoke.

He looks at the other door, the entrance to the practice room corridor and sees Maisie. After glancing quickly at her while Mr Peters continues to search for the Rossini aria. Mitchell nods towards the entrance door and Maisie starts to tiptoe across the floor. "Ah *there* it is," says Mr Peters. He looks up to see Maisie. "Hello Mr Peters," Maisie says. The teacher is confused. He finds something rather gauche about Maisie's comportment. "Hello Maisie, what can I do for you?"

"Just wondered where Mitchell was and now, well, I've found him."

"It's a shame Mitchell isn't more like you Maisie." After which Mitchell darts towards Maisie and dragging her out of the room, says "Forget the song, I've decided I don't want to do it after all. Cheers." Mr Peters calls out to him but Mitchell ignores him and chases down the corridor after the boys he saw aping him earlier.

Even if he finds out exactly why those boys are ridiculing him, he is too late. Though the footage is viewed by very few - in hearsay and rumour it is talked about by many. Mitchell, Maisie and Mr Peters are soon to learn the destructive, and at the least, the wholly embarrassing power of social media.

Chapter 4

With Portia Masters' growing passion for opera, she and her mother loved everything about Margaret English from the very beginning. The teacher's cream-white door flanked by two imperious classical-style pillars made most visitors think they were entering a mini opera house. On the walls of Mrs English's vast entrance hall were smiling pictures of Margaret and her rather older looking husband. Amongst the framed photographs as a centrepiece, was suspended an African hunting spear which Portia soon learned Mr English had brought all the way back from Kenya. Yet what Portia did not know was that the only kill he had made, was in obtaining the hand of his wife Margaret. He was rarely seen - but without his support, The English School of Vocal Studies would not exist.

Across the hall floor that made Vicky and Portia feel like they were stepping on a large black and white chess board, Margaret led Portia and her mother to the hub of her empire, the *studio*. In this room, Portia was impressed by the numerous pictures displaying her teacher-to-be in myriad operatic roles, all suggesting an eminent and glorious past. She had been leading lady in all the most famous roles from poor Mimi to countless countesses. The black solid frames added to the gravity of

Margaret in her varying degrees of dramatic pose. Or else they emphasised the glory and importance of such moments as Mrs English hugging a celebratory bouquet or sharing a post-show toast with fellow players. They represented a theatre of memories Margaret refused to relinquish.

Success oozed from her countenance in nearly every picture. Yet very few of her students realised her unpaid triumphs in the world of am-dram had all been underwritten by her husband's successful career as an actuary.

Not only opera – but posters of choral concerts where her name was printed as no less than SOLOIST, added to Portia's more than favourable impressions of Mrs English.

These wall hangings had served their purpose splendidly over the years by reassuring parents of aspiring young singers that they should have absolutely no need to question the notion that Margaret English was *the* person to transform their child into a singing phenomenon of stage, concert platform and perhaps more recently, *YouTube* channel.

Portia's mother was taken by the precise hand gestures of Margaret English - all made with studied exactitude. Having heard a brief history of the young Portia, the teacher's answer included words purporting no less positivity than 'excellent', 'wonderful' or the classic 'marvellous.'

"Of course, this will take some time - with the correct guid-ance and training," she hastened to add. Then having been acknowledged by little more than a nod from Portia's mother, she opened her voluminous diary with the flick and flourish of a thick scarlet ribbon telling Margaret *precisely* where she needed to be. Margaret entered Portia's details accompanied by the busiest and most business-like sounds from her ever-pin-sharp pencil. She defined the entire situation. Mrs English rose from her chair and tightened the belt of her dress - a habit verging on the compulsive, yet demonstrating complete command of her attire and thus herself. Portia noticed how Margaret lifted the piano lid, polished her glasses and swished open pages of music. Her every gesture was and always would be first and foremost a performance. All her students adored her for this attribute. Vicky liked her outfit too. It looked like a dress she saw another opera singer wearing once when interviewed in her luxurious home.

Dominating the centre of the room was a grand piano, on the top of which were placed several certificates.

"Now, what would you consider to be the key to all great singing?" was the first thing she asked Portia, who had no answer. Margaret broke the silence with the words: "Re-laxation...Relaxation is key. You must learn to relax," said Margaret, startling her new student with a loud grand chord on her grandest of pianos.

"Okay, starting from here, let's try ascending the scale. You know... *Do re mi.* Now while you sing, I want you to think this is the easiest and most *natural* thing in the world. Okay?"

So that was the start of Portia's journey into the vast and mysterious world of vocal production. After Portia demon-strated her abilities, Margaret said, "I think there is a rather fabulous instrument inside your daughter. In fact, there's definitely the makings of a dramatic soprano. *But* this needs careful nurturing and, of course, *work*."

After the illustrious teacher detected the look of pleasant surprise from both Vicky and her daughter, she reached for her diary again. "Can I recommend we book eight lessons in advance? A consideration, of course can be made..." Margaret said with a raised eyebrow. After an affirmative nod, the teacher's pencil was once again made busy, accompanied by the more tentative sound of biro on cheque book.

Five years have passed since that first meeting. Portia is now Mrs English's star pupil.

"I was wondering, er..." says Portia as she stands by the piano at the start of her lesson. She is slightly daunted by the fact that Mrs English has all the exam pieces ready on the piano with *Post-It* notes, allowing her to locate the relevant pages with absolute efficiency.

"Wondering what?" says Mrs English. A buzzing noise accompanied by a flashing red light on a window sill interrupts them. "Oh, Malcolm can get that. Anyway, you were saying?"

"Yes, I was wondering if today we could do something different?"

"Different? But your practical exams are so close and we need to go through your pieces."

"Yes, and I'm hoping success in my exams will secure my conditional offer for The Royal Academy."

"So we'd better start then." There is a knock. "Yes?" Malcolm, Mrs English's husband, puts his head around the door. "There's someone with a delivery for you and they insist you sign for it. Sorry, I did try," says Malcolm. In all the years she has been frequenting the English's house, this is the first time Portia sees Mrs English's husband in person. She can hear a sports match cheering its way through an ajar door. She can also see Mr English's very ruddy complexion, similar to one of her teachers at school. An affinity with whisky comes to mind.

"Oh...okay then. Sorry Portia, I won't be long." Portia does not find Mrs English's aggravations encouraging. In her teacher's absence she gets out her mobile and a small list; two of the necessary accessories she hopes will help towards changing her father's attitude. Her determination renews the confidence she thought she had lost before the lesson.

Mrs English enters the room and deposits a parcel on a desk. "Right! Let's not waste any more time. The Schumann," says Mrs English. She sits down and is about to play the introduction when she notices Portia has her hand raised. "Yes, Portia?"

"Sorry, Mrs English, I need to ask you a favour."

"And what is that?"

"My Dad, he's being funny again."

"Oh dear, what's he saying now?"

"Basically, what he says is that I've got to show that I can make my singing work financially or else he will not support me through college."

"I thought he'd come up with an arrangement and all was agreed."

"No, last night we had a bit of a scene. It was our next-door neighbour's fault actually."

"Oh, I'm intrigued." says Mrs English removing her hands from the keyboard and placing them neatly on her lap. Portia anxiously gazes at the metronome on the top of the piano and thinks how Bizet's *Carmen* extricates herself from prison with Don Jose's help by singing the *Seguidilla.*

"Well, not to waste time..." Portia explains her plan to Mrs English who after listening, heads straight to the vast library of scores she has collected over the years. "Let's first start with *Ri-go-let-to*!" Mrs English says the opera title as if opening the shutters to a fine Venetian vista. "*Caro Nome,* page..." she says walking back to the piano with her head in the score. "Ah

46

yes, what Gilda sings after her first encounter with a certain *chap.*" Portia wonders if Gilda would also have given two fingers after encountering the same *chap* she had, earlier that day.

Mrs English plays the introduction but stops. "Shall we warm up first?" says Mrs English turning the introduction into a loud chord announcing her first scale. "Is there time?" asks Portia.

"There must always be time to warm up."

Portia, sneaking a glance at the clock, begrudgingly agrees.

After scales, they start. Portia's mobile is recording but half way through Verdi's aria, Mrs English stops. "Portia can we do the middle section again?" The section is repeated, a take. Good. Portia is ready to move on when Mrs English now remarks, "You're clipping the upper notes of what some music theorists would call a succession of consonant skips."

Portia wonders if they will get through the half dozen items she was hoping to record within her hour. "Oh, please don't breathe there. Try and sing that phrase all in one breath as I've told you before. It sounds awkward otherwise." Portia corrects her breathing and in turn the phrasing. Finally another take is accomplished. There might just be enough time to get the project recorded.

"You must count like mad during this bit, again!"

Why is it today of all days my teacher has decided to be ultra fussy? Portia asks herself.

Eventually after similar interruptions, at last they reach the final song. Portia looks at the clock. It has gone past the hour. The next student is due any second. Portia has her fingers crossed as they seem to glide through the *Seguidilla.* "Oh shhh...sugar! I'll let Malcolm get that again." says Mrs

English as the buzzer goes and the red light flashes even more frantically.

Moments later they are nearly at the end of the song. A great take as far as Portia is concerned but only seconds from the end there is a rap at the door. "Damn," says Portia under her breath. Malcolm puts his head around the door again.

"The next student wonders if they can start as soon as possible as they've got an urgent dental appointment after the lesson," says Malcolm

"Tell them we'll be no more than a couple of minutes," says Malcolm's wife from the piano. They do another take of the Bizet aria but only a few bars from the end, Mrs English stops playing. "Sorry Portia - that coda. We really could do that a lot better." They recommence. Then at the same spot they hear a different buzzing noise coming from the hall outside. Mrs English gets up and goes to the door. "Look, I'm extremely sorry we're overrunning, but can you save your warm ups for when you come into the studio please?" asks Mrs English. Portia can hear the mumbling of a woman's voice saying words including 'our' and 'hour'. Mrs English asks for a modicum more patience. Portia, on the next take knows she has made mistakes but remembers someone saying *Perfection's one thing, a release date's another.* She has what she wanted: the key that will unlock her dreams - six complete tracks. Job done – hopefully.

Chapter 5

From around a corner in the echoing corridors, Ms Smith, on hometime duty can hear the noise of students. With stealth she treads towards the sound source. She can see a tight circle of boys beguiled by the spectacle of Mitchell *performing well* as one of them put it. "Who can blame him? I'd probably do the same if that's Maisie," said another in the ring as he feels a tap on his shoulder. "Excuse me. You'd better give that to me," says Ms Smith. Turning ghostly white, the owner of the phone and footage hands it over. Earlier that afternoon he nearly deleted the video but had a hunch such material might have some kind of collateral and managed to send a copy to a storage space somewhere in the clouds.

"So you can absolutely reassure me this is the only copy of the video that exists?" asks the head teacher only moments later. "Yes," is the reply from the student.

Mr Peters is summoned to the head's office first thing the next morning. They sit either side of a large oak table. Behind this is a cabinet displaying silver trophies won by the school through various sporting fixtures. There is nothing on the table except an open laptop and a graduation photograph of a girl Frank Peters presumes must be the head's daughter. For some reason this picture makes him realise he has completely failed his responsibility *in loco parentis.*

"Sorry, I'll come straight to the point Mr Peters. Yesterday was a display of gross incompetence. I have no other words. In fact, I've never known the like of it before," says the head teacher leaning over the table towards Mr Peters who sits upright with his arms folded. After a moment, the head slouches back in his chair with his hands clasped behind his head. He pauses to consider the visage of his soon to be ex-music teacher, Frank Peters - dark complexioned with thick, jet black hair (some think he has had it dyed) and deep brown penetrating eyes. Mr Peters stays still and remains silent. He too has no words. What happened yesterday is indefensible.

The head's office for Mr Peters has the same static and sterile atmosphere as a doctor's surgery. Like many of the school's younger miscreants when hauled into this room, he feels his guilt pollute the air, which grows increasingly concentrated as the gravity of the situation sinks in ever deeper. The head teacher sits up to lean towards Mr Peters again.

"It was your responsibility as acting head of music to make sure the school's department was a safe learning environment for *all* our students." Again the head pauses with his thumbs, that had previously moved in sync with his vocal inflections, now raised. He sits back but now strokes the slight growth of developing beard. "All I can say is, thank goodness Maisie was hidden in the video and it is only hearsay that it was actually her. But we all know in this school, she is - heaven knows why, Mitchell's girlfriend. As you can imagine, her parents are furious. However, I've spoken with them and they have decided not to take action against the school on the condition,

I'm afraid, that I dismiss you with immediate effect."

After another pause, the head raises himself from his chair, which Frank Peters also takes as a cue to stand. "It's a great shame this had to happen. I know it was not entirely your fault and we've already decided to permanently exclude Mitchell. The person who took the footage and was stupid enough to parade it around will not be having an easy life for the foreseeable. But nevertheless, it all happened under your watch Mr Peters and I hope you realise just how badly you have let us down."

"Sorry."

"So am I, Mr Peters, so am I. However," the head pauses again as he leans down to tap something into his laptop and finally closes it. "Luckily for you, our old music teacher who only retired last year has agreed to come back for the remainder of this term. We are all aware Mitchell is not the easiest of students and the blame in the end is firmly on him. So, I have decided not to put this incident on record."

"Thank you."

"Oh don't thank me. However, you may appreciate we will not be giving you a reference."

"Oh, okay."

"Well it's not okay is it. But here we are," says the head approaching his door. The two are now opposite each other. There is no handshake. The only courtesy offered is the door being opened by the head with the words "After you Mr Peters."

Mr Peters is led for the last time across the reception area decorated with pictures of students. Those in safety goggles undertaking scientific experiments remind Mr Peters how student safety is of paramount importance. If only I had taken more care, he thinks, on seeing others in a drama production with one dressed as a school caretaker. Then he notices students in an English lesson featuring one with a face radiating both charm and ambition. She is the much younger Maisie with her hand raised. Her parents raised something else – the issue of Mr Peters' gross incompetence.

Finally he passes the receptionist who would normally give him a bright welcoming smile and often a cheery farewell at the end of the school day. But now she ignores him by pretending to study something on her computer screen.

The head, whose tie flaps in the breeze, escorts Frank Peters in silence to the school gate. Mitchell and a woman Mr Peters assumes is his mother, approach them. Mr Peters looks at Mitchell who refuses to acknowledge him, yet Mitchell's mother seems to realise the entire situation.

Mr Peters walks away from the school and feels a strange sense of relief when he returns once more to his friend, the bus stop, for the very last time.

He watches the cars and vehicles going by - many he supposes on job-related journeys. Are any of them on their way towards a cul de sac – a dead end that ends with the sack? Or are some lucky enough to have occupations where their fortunes are not so dependent on the inherent fickleness of human beings?

Frank Peters muses on this and realises his chosen vocation almost exclusively depends on human interaction.

It was all his own fault. He could have left university with a much better degree if he had picked less demanding options with fewer challenges. In a previous life he thought he had a career as a concert pianist - until that fateful night.

It was drink which put an end to Frank Peters the recital pianist, just as he was about to play to the largest audience of his career to date.

At first he was an unknown, giving occasional concerts at local libraries and churches. With no real ambitions other than becoming a professional pianist, he settled for day jobs which required zero sacrifice of his free time – time he would dedicate to practice. One of those jobs was telephone canvassing for companies selling commodities such as home improvements – where Frank believed the biggest improvement made was to the company's bank balance.

After a recital at a church with what he considered to be the most outstanding acoustics, he decided to use the venue to record a disc of late Haydn and early Beethoven piano sonatas. He intended selling these recordings at concerts. However, thanks to a friend of a friend of a friend, the disc found its way to a music critic who reviewed new releases for a major broadsheet. The critic gave high praise: *Peters plays the Haydn with the full sense of anarchy and eccentricity which this work from the supreme musical prankster requires.* The same critic also introduced Frank Peters to the managing director of the *Kos* label. The MD heard the disc. *A must-have asset* was his verdict and agreed to release it on his budget yet prestigious label.

With this success, his audiences and venues grew. No longer was he appearing in places where office workers spent their lunch hours munching to music, his concerts now attracted the serious listener.

It is a well known tip for climbers not to look down when ascending the more precipitous slopes. Unfortunately, Frank Peters had the habit of peeking from the wings at the audience for whom he was about to perform. This became his personal *don't look down* and as he saw the ever-increasing numbers in the full glare of the house lights, his pre-concert nerves began to suffer more and more.

In the loneliness of hotel rooms he preferred to read rather than turn on the TV. On one occasion where his stage nerves were beginning to produce the all too familiar and unwanted pre-performance nausea, he found himself reading about the pianist and composer Benjamin Britten who also suffered before concerts. This became so bad that the legendary composer, it was said, once drank half a pint of brandy before performing. Frank Peters decided this might be a possible remedy – the hotel room mini bar stood replete. Not being a seasoned drinker, at first a small tipple would settle his nerves but then as the dizzying heights of success grew higher, the more dependent he became.

It was during a solo recital at a theatre (which normally hosted plays and pantomimes) that Frank Peters' fate changed overnight. Theatre stages can sometimes become a deadly obstacle course for the unwary.

For a member of the audience, Peters' fateful concert might have proceeded as follows: *You enter the venue. You're relieved to find your internet booking is not bogus. You recheck your seat number. Buy your programme. Find the correct seat. Settle in that seat. Open the programme. Stand to allow gangway for a fellow audience member (now, now, temper, temper – we have all been in this situation, have we not?). Be seated again. Join in with the applause as the performer walks on to the stage. Try reading the last few lines of the programme notes before the lights go down. Too late, the lights go down. The applause continues but then dies. That magical moment of silence and expectation before the first few notes are heard. Nothing. What's the matter? you ask. You hear murmurs coming from the front. You wait. Again, nothing.*

Whispers coming from the stalls by the stage tell you that something has gone wrong. Very wrong. An accident.

Frank Peters' had walked on still trying to decide how to interpret a certain phrase: Forte or just mezzo forte? Allegro vivace or maybe just allegro? More rubato towards the end of the exposition? A slight diminuendo at the end? His mind plagued with decisions was not focused on his motor faculties. Result? A broken thumb after tripping on a plug socket lid left up. Severe physical pain, then eventually the even longer lasting pain of realising it was the end of his career.

Following an operation, Frank Peters could still play the piano well but not to the standard required for a concert pianist. For some while, he could not bear to touch the instrument. A naturally talented singer is said to have a golden larynx. Peters' pianistic larynx went from platinum to some annoyingly cheap and rusty alloy.

Yet his love for music remained. He was married to the art and desperately wondered how to continue the relationship. Unlike many successful pianists, due to poor exam results Frank Peters had not pursued the conventional route of music college or university.

Instead, he had been a child prodigy with the great fortune to be nurtured by an excellent teacher - herself a retired recitalist. Yet his early love for the piano caused his school work to suffer – particularly English which took him several attempts to achieve a suitable grade. Maths was not too bad. At an early age he was already interpreting and executing the most complex sonic fractions by sight-reading music with all its intricate divisions.

As a mature student he enrolled on a music history and theory course at Silversmiths College in South East London. At the time, it was the only course in the country with such a programme open to part-time students. This meant Frank Peters had to commute a considerable distance to attend evening classes at the college. Three train changes were required to complete the eighty-mile journey from home to class. However, despite his solo career coming to an abrupt end, he was still receiving royalties from his one and only release. This gave him the time to be more flexible with his working hours. He therefore returned part-time to telephone canvassing.

His first music essay was returned with the opening comment *Parts of this essay simply do not make sense. Please read through what you have written and ask yourself if this is what you meant to say!* This set the tone for the remaining four years of Frank Peters' degree course. It was most frustrating for all concerned. Peters could interpret scores of music and analyse them much quicker than his fellow students but he could not articulate his findings in written form. He also discovered, being a slow reader, that digesting the content of heavy tomes on music history provided a considerable challenge. Many times, he considered giving up.

In the end, however he managed to graduate with a lower two – a *Desmond*. He was disappointed but then he remembered he had so far not taken out a student loan or grant for his course. Surely a maths-based degree would be a more successful venture, he thought.

Frank applied for a college much closer to home to learn accountancy but to his shock he found he was no longer entitled to any government funding, having already sat the finals of a first degree. The person interviewing him told him maybe his best option would be to take a PGCE with a view to becoming a secondary school music teacher. He did, but realised in horror he had invited himself into purgatory. For his PGCE, to his surprise, he managed to scrape through. However, he soon began to hate noisy classes - a very different sound to the one he could once control to near perfection as a pianist.

Several years later there were very few royalties coming in from his release. Other artists recorded the same programme to even better acclaim. After barely surviving as a teacher, he resigned from his first full-time position and opted for supply teaching on a casual day-to-day basis which suited him better. Then one day, though he knew deep down that spending a whole term at Hassledon High could be a mistake, the honey-voiced consultant at his supply agency cajoled him into ignoring his instincts - hence, his blighted long-term tenure at Mitchell's school.

Back at home, he can still see the vivid image of his now ex-head teacher releasing him from his position for the last time. He considers his options. The type of jobs he did previously don't pay enough to cover his rent and other outgoings, so he forces his reluctant hand once more towards the phone to call the supply agency.

A few weeks later, on a Friday afternoon, Mr Peters sits back listening to nothing but silence. He has learned to live with loneliness. It is another facet of his life he is beginning to accept as failure. He has had relationships but with his zealous obsession with music, he imagines his past partners soon felt they were in some kind of affair where the other woman in his life was music. In all fairness to them, they probably thought they were being used too. Yet he wonders if it was him or the pianist they wanted.

He awakens from his reverie. Somehow he has survived five more days of temporary teaching. It is essentially baby-sitting older kids. He is absolutely sure some of them have shares in the manufacture of paracetamol.

He is about to nod off when he hears a tap at his window. Is that part of a dream? Who is that tapping him? He dozes on and feels the tapping again. He half opens his eyes. There is a familiar figure at the window whose shadow takes away much of the late afternoon light. Is this a nightmare? He slaps himself a few times. The person at the window is singing exactly what he heard in the dream. Frank Peters sits up to see it is Mitchell Woods.

Chapter 6

Weeks before Mitchell knocked on Frank Peters' window, he too was summoned to an audience with his head teacher. Like, Mr Peters just minutes earlier, he had nothing to say for himself. However, as soon as the head mentioned that Maisie's parents did not want to see him with their daughter ever again, Mitchell told him to "Mind his own effing business".

"Mitchell!" intervened his mother. But straight away, the head rose from his seat and terminated the meeting.

"So that is that," said his mother as they left the school. On their way back home, not a single word passed between mother and son.

Mitchell was not looking forward to returning home. At least before the practice room incident he was free to visit Maisie's house and sit with her in apparent innocence on the sofa, while Maisie's mother, Mary Moore, would offer cups of tea.

If only your family were not so prudish the whole incident might not have happened he concluded in his reply to a text from Maisie that evening, when the scandal was spreading like bush fire. *If you weren't so impatient...* was Maisie's reply. The huge embarrassment and monumental shaming of their daughter, convinced Maisie's parents they no longer wanted to see Maisie with Mitchell and would certainly not allow him to set foot in their house again.

Instead, except for the few friends whose friendship did not go much beyond the school gates, Mitchell's only choice now was to exile himself to his room – anything to avoid his mother's *fella* Gavin who, in an alarmingly small number of visits to Mitchell's home, had managed not only to get his feet under the table but also right under Mitchell's skin. Mitchell's appraisal of his mother's new man was confirmed when Maisie deemed him *a creep*. Mitchell felt like a prisoner in his own home, restricting and carefully timing his movements to prevent even the briefest encounter with Gavin.

It was a Saturday night when Gavin first entered Mitchell's life. Mitchell was sitting on his own in the lounge, absorbed in a game of *KillaTeds*. He could feel the house shudder as the door banged against the hall wall. This was followed by the sound of his mother humming a tune she had most probably caught from a pub juke box.

But then came the unfamiliar frequencies of someone else's tones. The living room door opened, ushering in a cold draft from the front door. Mitchell's mother, stepped into the lounge. Gavin appeared in an unzipped fleece. His hair looked like it could do with a comb, and wiry glasses magnified his eyes in such a way they looked disproportionate to the rest of his features. He just said "Hi" with a face which could not decide whether to smile or not. Mitchell returned the gesture with a brief inspection of the person. He seemed okay.

Sandra took Gavin into the kitchen. Mitchell refrained from the video game and sat still, listening and trying to decipher the noises coming from the kitchen. This was the first adult male his mother had brought into the house since his father

Ryan had departed.

There was the familiar sound of the gushing tap, the click of the kettle switch, the water boiling, the snap of a cupboard door being opened followed by a drunken slam. The familiar clink of a teaspoon putting coffee into a cup, but then the unfamiliar words "Milk, sugar?" followed by the even more unfamiliar baritonal: "No milk, just one sugar, thanks."

A minute had passed since the kettle clicked itself off. Mitchell waited for the cups to be stirred but instead – silence.

Mitchell crept out of the living room towards the kitchen's threshold. The door was ajar. He saw the two of them in the land of snog – as his Maisie would call it. By now his mother would have wrapped her hands around a cup of hot coffee and brought it into the lounge to sit down next to her son. Instead he saw Gavin's hand up the inside of Sandra's jumper. It must have been a sixth sense but Sandra pulled herself away to notice her son was staring at them from the door. She quickly adjusted her hair. "Don't you think you ought to be in bed?" was all Sandra could say to her son. Gavin, embarrassed, moved away from Sandra's side, coughing into his offending hand. Mitchell just left them and went up to bed.

Mitchell did not mind Gavin at first but it was only a matter of weeks before Sandra allowed her new *fella,* as she referred to him, almost free run of the house and gave him a key. Mitchell's dislike started with Gavin sitting in his place on the settee and commandeering the TV remote. Then he had a liking for bringing home a favourite takeaway which, to Mitchell's distaste, stank the house out for days. He wondered if Gavin *only wanted her for her body* too as he would lay in bed during the early hours listening to the rhythmic creaking of their rickety rackety bed.

Sandra, probably as a sort of pay back, did not object to Maisie making more frequent visits and spending time in Mitchell's room. All she said was "I hope you know what you're doing." Gavin's presence did not make Maisie feel comfortable at all. She told Mitchell she could always feel Gavin's eyes on her. And why, she wondered, did he nearly always need to come upstairs when she was with Mitchell in his room? Maisie began to shun visiting Mitchell which made Mitchell begin to hate Gavin's very presence. He stood for all the deficit in Mitchell's life.

Therefore, until the practice room incident, he preferred going to Maisie's despite what he considered to be her stuffy household and stuck-up mother. It was, at least, a change of air. Maisie's family seldom indulged in takeaways. Yet he cursed the fact that Maisie had to share a room with her elder sister who always tended to be more in than out. Maisie regretted this too. Her younger brother had a room all to himself – *life's a bitch* were the words Maisie did not need to remind Mitchell of. His dad, Ryan, now lived in a flat - but due to the state of it, this was not an option for Maisie. She envied her friend Leah - an only child with her own room and parents nearly always in their local pub, unlike her own who on the whole had a dim view of such establishments. How ironic Leah had no *fella*. Life was not fair.

Mitchell's escape from his sudden new reality revolved around a cocktail of spliffs, music and *KillaTeds.*

He had attained a level where the KillaTeds had become opponents of a rival gang called The *GrizzaTeds.* Verdi's *La donna è mobile* heralded the arrival of the main Grizza Ted as he attempted to lure the KillaTedettes. But concentration wrestled with curiosity, and curiosity won. Mitchell had no choice but to trawl the latest social media postings about him from his ex-school colleagues. He was just thankful the much talked about video was not on any internet platform - so far. When his mother had first talked to the head prior to their short-lived appointment, he assured her the video had been erased and it was no longer being seen by anybody. Yet it seemed the whole of the school except the amateur porn stars themselves - himself and Masie - had watched it. He dared himself to try and envisage what it looked like. From all the jaunts and piss takes he had so far received, he had no doubt the footage left little to the imagination - except his. Maisie had texted him last night to tell him the boy who filmed them had also been excluded.

Just fuck off. Sandra looked at a worried Gavin as they heard those words coming from Mitchell's room. Gavin thought the words were aimed at him. But neither he nor Sandra realised Mitchell shouted them to try and erase all the shame welling up inside him. Cursing himself loudly was his way of releasing the safety valve against a humiliation past boiling point.

Lying on his bed, he considered where his life was going. He wanted to go out but the jail of embarrassment restrained him from venturing into town. Too many would recognise him and they just *knew.* Then he contemplated a situation he was unable to avoid - working with his dad, and his workmates. Most likely they too would have heard about the video. Knowing some of his Dad's colleagues, he guessed some would probably pay to see the footage of him and Maisie. Was it really consigned to cyber hell? How would they greet him when he turned up on his first full-time day? The thought of the arduous duties awaiting him was bad enough.

Yes it was all there on his formerly favourite social media page. *Mitchell permanently excluded.* His 'performance' received mixed reviews: adversaries provoked his self-humiliation. Some demonstrated total disgust while others gave high praise. But all exhibited a certain underlying sense of envy.

He tried to clear his mind by scrolling to other pages, with more decent but far less exotic content, telling of family gatherings and suchlike. Then he saw an image of a face - which looked familiar. It was a sponsored ad. Mitchell would normally scroll straight past these promotions. But what he saw - the female face made him pause. He was sure he had seen her before but could not think where.

He studied her refined features. Her lustrous eyes seemed to be staring directly at him. She was advertising her album of opera arias. He clicked on the link. A piano began followed by a voice. He listened to the singer called Portia Masters, keenly trying to translate certain nuances of her voice. Did her tone give any clues to the person she might be? For the first time, listening to her made Mitchell forget about his situation. He was in another world. Accompanying the music were more images of Portia. From swimsuit to a fur coat which looked almost alive, nothing seemed to have been spared from her wardrobe. There were no other words for Mitchell. She was beautiful and so was her voice as it sang the sighing strains of Cleopatra's aria from Handel's *Julius Caesar.* He recognised the track too. XL had used the instrumental portion with a back beat on one of his more recent tracks. The violins sighing to Cleopatra's arabesques - if image and music formed a perfect marriage, it was this. The two made Mitchell want more of both her and her music.

Mitchell read the accompanying blurb which revealed she was local. He was sure he had seen her somewhere. Then he saw the girl looking down towards him from above and his reverie was shattered, *it was her.* He was certain, the girl he saw sitting in the truck. *Toss off.* Mitchell wondered if she too had read about what he had done. Would she have used a practice room in the same way as him?

But then a text from Maisie flashed onto his mobile screen - one of the many since the exposure of their tryst. The one he received the night before read: *Mum and dad don't want to c u with me eva again. No way! Can we talk? Really need to c u! Love you far too much. Don't regret ANY time with you! BUT They've grounded me! RRRRRR! XXXXXMmmmm.* Mitchell had no desire to play Romeo outside Maisie's window so texted her back telling her it would probably be best to meet up the following day. Maisie's latest text read: *Just found out you've been thrown out. But u always will b in my life. Can we meet after I've finished? Really, really need to c U! Love U! Yours adoringly XXXXXMmmm.* After reading this, Mitchell felt a pang of guilt about being so captivated by the opera singing girl. There were still a few hours to go before he could go and meet Maisie.

He got up from his bed and turned on the speakers which connected to his phone. XL had a new track out. It featured the sunrise from Haydn's *Creation.* The sampled section was on a loop. With it, XL had a laid a back beat and a rap. The loop kept building to a crescendo and then went to the beginning to start the slow climax again. The track was simply called *Creation* and the rap lyrics were all about how all those so-called upstanding people were destroying the magnificent creation called the world. Already it was receiving thousands of likes.

Mitchell loved it and downloaded the whole EP. This included extra tracks which were remixes of the track itself but XL also wanted his listeners to appreciate the source so he had added untampered material from the original piece.

His thoughts turned again to the contemplation of working every weekday with his dad. The shovelling, the lifting, the sweeping, the bruises and burns – both physical and verbal. So far, he found comfort in not having heard from his dad about the video. This thought, however, was not so good. If his dad remarked in any piss-taking way, he could not throw his hypocrisy straight back at him.

Such thoughts kept revolving around his head. After being up all night checking each ridiculing comment on social media, he now felt *so wasted*, worn out. Sleep took over.

He dreamed he was back with his dad at the local swimming pool aged seven. It was the first time he tried swimming without *water wings.* He lay flat in the water looking at the rivets, bolts and metalwork high above on the swimming pool roof. His father supported him with his hand under his back while telling him to relax and just lie still. Despite the screams and shrieks from children all around him, he managed to let himself lie horizontal in the water. Gradually he felt his father's hand letting go and, to his amazement, he was floating. It was true, you *could* float. The dream continued and the noise of the kids around him was superceded by the voices of a man and woman singing a duet. The female singing reminded him of images of a biblical Eve he had seen in scripture books at primary school. This Eve, with her long black hair looked similar to the girl he saw only yesterday. The voice and the figure singing with her was his. He was listening to an extra track on XL's Creation EP. It was the Adam and Eve duet from Haydn's masterpiece. XL requested his fans to listen to it without the added drums.

Mitchell woke up with idea that he could probably make a living singing. But how? Singing in a rock band? Maisie had friends who were in bands which he had been to see with her, mainly to keep her company and keep admirers at bay. One of these called *The Launderette 3* was a so-called *indie* band which commanded a small following playing in the back rooms of pubs. Often its members would perform their set with their heads down looking at their instruments hardly noticing the handful of people present. Usually these were a few girls with dyed hair shuffling around the floor in unlaced docs, while their *we're not going out together – it's complicated* sort of boyfriends just watched by the side. Would any of those bands have him as a singer anyway? Many of their members were total geeks who considered Mitchell a somewhat lesser individual.

To pass the time he rolled another spliff and smoked it out of his window. It did not last long - at least working full time would give him the cash needed for more smokes and he would not have to ration himself so much. But then he remembered Maisie. She entertained the thought that, with his increased income from the building site he would be able to afford to treat them to a night or two at *Premier Sin,* as she called it.

After finishing his joint he lay back on the bed again and searched for Portia Masters' sponsored ad. He listened and found the combination of her visage and voice at least as addictive as his smokes. Not only did he find himself wanting to listen to certain tracks of hers repeatedly, he also found while playing *KillaTeds he* was humming along to the *GrizzaTed*

67

singing *La donna è mobile* – men could be fickle too.

In the days to come Mitchell's expletive-ridden shoutbursts, were slowly being taken over by his operatic declamations. At one point, his mother asked if it was himself singing or a record. She was surprised when Mitchell said it was him. She also told him his operatic singing annoyed Gavin. "Good" was Mitchell's reply. He knew he most certainly had a voice and he wondered if that voice would maybe, one day, duet with the girl whose album he had now downloaded and listened to nearly all the time. Sometimes, without realising, he found himself singing along to all the opera extracts from *KillaTeds* and what XL had put out. His searched YouTube for more arias. He was addicted.

Chapter 7

O nly a few days after Portia's first roadside encounter with Mitchell, she could not believe how many copies of her album had sold - in such a short time too. Admittedly a lot of the sales were thanks to her fellow sixth formers who bought it more as a favour but also encouraged their friends and relatives to do the same. For online trading, this was important. A surge in early sales would get her product a high ranking on the site which hosted it, and in turn put it at the front of the virtual shop. Even with the commission taken by her online distributor: *SellaSong*, Portia was sure her album had sold enough copies to impress her father. Of course, advertising her product on social media also attracted some unwanted comments including indecent proposals. But these were more than balanced out by comments praising her release which in turn, prompted further sales. The money from downloads was in her account almost as soon as a sale was made and that was what mattered - for now. Thanks to the speed of the internet, she had managed to execute the whole project from plan to profit in only a few days.

Roger thought he had become used to the sound of the printer in his office but the sudden juddering it made as it jolted into action still gave him an unwanted shock. "Got a good mind to throw that thing down the bloody stairs," he said.

Portia entered her father's office. "Dad, have a look at this," she said. She took the document from the printer and put it in front of her dad who was at his desk studying the accounts of a client. "What's this Portia?" said Roger. He looked down to see an immaculately manicured nail pointing at the top of a sheet of paper. Portia brought her father's attention to the heading *Statement of Accounts* and then moved her finger to what was underneath: the name *Portia Masters*. Below her name was the heading *SALES*.

Roger, having spent his entire working life scrutinising such documents knew exactly where to look next. "Mmm, so you made an album. You didn't tell me you were going to do that," said Roger. "As I said, I thought I'd surprise you dad," said Portia. "So I take it you have achieved these sales in just a day."

"Setting up my online account and a modicum of promotion before I recorded the album certainly helped."

"Very well done indeed Portia." Portia had never felt so proud of herself. By the sound of her father's voice it seemed the arrangement with the property she was to manage would be going ahead – and music college, subject to satisfactory A level results, would become a reality. However, there was silence, and knowing her father, silence was ominous.

"But I didn't know you had any recordings. Did you hire a recording studio?"

"No dad, I recorded them at Mrs English's only the other day."

"What – during your lesson?" Portia was not comfortable with the sudden change in tone from her father. "Yes, the one

I had only a couple of days ago."

"So you're telling me you used what should have been your lesson - which I paid good money for - to record an album?"

"Okay. If you feel like that dad, I'll reimburse the lesson fee with my royalties. As you can see I can easily cover that. Anyway I hope you can see now that I *can* make my singing pay."

"Okay, okay, okay. I'll give it to you. I'm impressed Portia."

"Impressed enough to still exchange contracts on the property?"

"Mmm." Roger paused while examining the figures as if trying to find some flaw. "*SellaSong,* like a lot of internet companies, I've never heard of them. Some dot con making money from prospectors like you. But I must say, these companies do make the very wise and shrewd decision to sell the pan rather than the vague promise of gold."

"I hired the pan and found some gold dad. Anyway if I had more time, I would have set up my own website with a merchant account." Roger looked at his watch.

"Okay. Look, it's a bit late now but I'll phone the solicitors first thing tomorrow."

"Yes!" says Portia bending down to give her father a hug.

Portia awoke again in the early hours and could not sleep. The previous night she had woken up every hour, so excited to see the sales of her album grow and grow, and with the sales some very encouraging comments, mainly from her friends. She was so grateful to all those who had bought her album, she almost felt like hugging them all (well nearly all) individually. And now her goal was in sight. She could not wait, and lay awake imagining herself already in London, studying and performing with some of the best. The dream was about to come true. Finally she managed a couple of hours of sleep, but was wide awake again long before her mother knocked on her door.

Normally she hated being woken up, but early this morning on checking her latest sales figures, she was pleasantly surprised that even more copies had been sold whilst she was asleep. As her father once said *You know you have arrived when you can make money - even while you sleep.* She thought about her dad and wondered if he, like herself had ever achieved such a feat.

Nevertheless her mother still banged on the door. "I'm already awake mum," was her reply. "Can I come in Portia?" asked her mother putting her head slowly around the door. "Portia, it's fantastic what you've done. I'm so proud of the initiative you took. But did you really have to pose in that rather skimpy swimsuit for all to see on the internet?"

"It's called marketing mum," replied Portia.

"I'm just a bit concerned that the more serious music world might regard you in a similar vein to the likes of Darius Dallaway."

"Crisis management, I'll delete it as soon as the contract is signed. Don't let dad see it if he hasn't already. I suppose he's told you he's seen the part that matters most for him – the bottom line."

"*Bottom line* hey? My word, you are turning into a right little business woman."

"It's called fighting fire with fire mum!"

Portia was enjoying a victory breakfast, so Vicky decided to put on her album. Her father came down. "Whose are these most wonderful dulcet tones?" said Roger.

"It's the very wonderful voice of your daughter and hit

recording artist, Portia," said Vicky placing Roger's boiled egg and toast before him. He informed her he would phone the solicitors in Lewisham regarding the property's exchange as soon as they opened at nine. Unfortunately for Portia she had to go to school, but wished she could be with her dad as soon as the news was confirmed. "It's okay Portia, I'll text you the moment I have signed."

So Portia and her mother set off again - this time without incident, to Portia's school. She could not focus on her first couple of lessons, her head was so full of highly encouraging comments with sales to match. "Portia, can you tell us the type of chord Haydn uses in bar eighty-three?" said her music teacher. Portia was not following the score at all. The only score she was interested in at that moment was the one her father would tell her. "Sorry, what bar number Sir?"

"Oh Portia, please follow. Just because Haydn uses a... anyone else?"

"A diminished chord Sir," said another student.

"Yes Portia, just because Haydn uses a diminished chord it does not mean you can diminish your concentration. Please follow."

Yet she could not stop looking at her watch. It was mid-morning and she wondered why she had not received her dad's text. He had said he would phone the solicitors first thing.

The break time bell went. It was a sound Portia half-hoped for, but at the same time the butterflies in her stomach half-dreaded. She had to make the call.

"Hi Dad, have you exchanged?"

"Portia, I'll come straight to the point. No. I'm afraid the vendor doesn't want to sell. In other words they've pulled out."

"You're joking dad. Is this legal?"

"No one is under any obligation to sell, unless they've signed a contract – which they obviously haven't. Sorry Portia. That is that I'm afraid."

"Can't you make them a better offer?"

"Again, sorry Portia. As you know, buying that property would have already stretched us to the limit."

"So is the whole thing off? College I mean."

"Can we talk later about this Portia please. I've things to do and so have you, I presume."

"Okay dad." she said and terminated the call without a goodbye.

Portia could not concentrate for the rest of the day. She began to wonder during each lesson what the point would be of achieving exam success if it was not going to help her with her dreams, or at least to have a better life. She imagined her father would not be all that motivated to find an alternative property. It was getting too late. She had a horrible vision of the whole thing falling through. She knew very well her father would not be willing to support her through college and he most certainly would not wish to disclose his income if she applied for a maintenance loan.

Chapter 8

Frank Peters knew teaching agencies were first and foremost competitive businesses with minimal liaison, let alone co-operation between each other. Therefore, he realised if the practice room incident did not appear on any official record, it would not be listed on his DBS certificate either. In the commercial world of education, the dismissal from his last appointment quite easily disappeared under the radar. With no formal action following his misdemeanour, Mr Frank Peters was still a supply teacher. He remained a commodity to be exploited by the other agencies he signed up with, for assignments at different schools. The rumours of Mitchell and Maisie did not travel much beyond Hassledon and were certainly not known at schools in neighbouring towns.

Frank failed in his half-hearted attempts to find other jobs as well paid as day-to-day supply so he had no choice but to settle for further daily bookings with other schools. His only change in routine entailed earlier starts for the necessary journeys to another town.

Today, only two weeks after his dismissal, Frank has a booking at a private school just outside Hassledon. He hates the thought of teaching the children of parents who can buy privilege. But the money he desperately needs puts aside moral debate. After a short bus ride, he walks all the way up the school's long and grand driveway, overtaken by motors some might describe as *flash*. They transport their passengers towards the school building which looks like a stately home. He has been hired to deputise for the music teacher who is away for the week undergoing a minor operation.

It is another world. The food is excellent compared with most state schools. There is even a multiple choice of coffees available in the staff room. The uniform is worn immaculately by the vast majority of students - and likewise their hair and general appearance. He quickly realises the lower year students, who he teaches for most of the morning, are on the whole far more biddable than their state school counterparts – despite pockets of arrogance which can largely be ignored.

After a fantastic *luncheon* (as it is timetabled), he is sched-uled to take the upper sixth form A level music class. He has been looking forward to it all day. Yet it is in this lesson that he first experiences significant student transgression. He takes the register of just six students - though quite large for an A-level music class. He reaches the name Portia Masters. "Portia" says Mr Peters.

"Here...sort off," replies Portia raising her head temporarily from her arms hunched on the table. One or two students start to snigger. Mr Peters does not know what to do. He has always had little interest in the pastoral side of education. While he loves his subject, he is irritated by the inevitable luggage that teaching in schools can bring. He has never really tried to understand the more recalcitrant students with obvious issues – either temporary or otherwise. Mr Peters is a numbers person not a people person. He prefers analysing music scores and recognising recurring patterns and motives. He has little interest in knowing a piece of music was written during the composer's nervous breakdown due to the end of some affair with a nymphomaniac. Why couldn't he have got a favourably-termed loan to study something statistical or anything which would not include Joe Public? Especially now, when he fears he cannot even hack it in what his supply agent deemed an 'easy school'.

He looks at the instructions left by the regular teacher. *Continue with practicals* it says. Mr Peters relays this to the class. They all head off to the luxury of one practice room per student. Portia does not move. She remains sat at her table, face down with her long black hair spilling over her arms. A student notices Mr Peters looking at her. "She's heard some bad news recently and behaves like this – but mainly with supply teachers," says the student. Portia overhears. It prompts her to look up.

"Can you mind your own business," says Portia. Mr Peters, at a loss when challenging abnormal behaviour, knows from experience that performing music, for practice or an audience, is not easy when feeling distressed as Portia obviously is. "Maybe you could revise some of the history element, instead," says Mr Peters.

"There's no point. I won't be able to go to study where I want to anyway, even if I get five 'As' in my exams."

"Why's that?" asks Mr Peters.

"Oh it's called having a dad who's a complete bastard." As soon as he hears the words *dad* and *bastard*, Mr Peters feels his toes no longer touching the bottom of the swimming pool. This problem needs to be tackled by a teacher married to the whole education *thing*, he thinks. He is scared by the intensity with which Portia stares at him when saying these words. The

77

same student who told Mr Peters about Portia earlier beckons him and whispers "Her dad, I think does not want to fund her maintenance through college. It's strange because only two weeks ago she was over the moon."

"Are you talking about me?" shouts out Portia. "Yes, as far as I'm concerned it's not worth working towards A levels any more if you've a dad who tries to make going to college as difficult as possible. Oh, and even if I was able to go, he sees the entire venture as a way of exploiting his own daughter. I was really looking forward to going to *the Academy* where I was so hoping to study with the soprano Catherine Cumberland. Have you heard of her?" Portia pauses, waiting for a reply from Mr Peters. He answers "Yes the name certainly rings a bell."

"Well, she's the best and she's heard me and says she thinks she could take my singing to where I want it to be. But then dad seems to be enjoying the fact that a certain arrangement has gone pear-shaped."

"What arrangement was that?"

"Oh, another earner. I think he only wanted me to go to college so I could look after his property speculating. Now the deal's fallen through, and that's that. No college, no Catherine Cumberland, no singing career." Mr Peters is confused but says:

"Are there any other colleges or teachers you could consider?"

"No, it's Catherine Cumberland or no-one else. She's amazing. I've got her on my phone, do you want to hear her?" says Portia, already scrolling down to find the right track. She plays it - *Dido's Lament* by Purcell. The descending bass sends Portia into tears. She tries to wipe her eyes with her blazer sleeve, murmurs "Sorry" and runs off into an empty practice room. "Mmm" is all Mr Peters can say followed by "Poor girl." The student who told Mr Peters about Portia's predicament has nothing to say either and can only shrug his shoulders.

Mr Peters feels useless again. He has found a disturbing increase in students with a whole plethora of problems, both in state - and as he discovers now - in private schools. If he had as much care for people as he has for music he would probably be much better placed to handle the emotional wiles of teenagers. But teaching in the mainstream for Mr Peters has always been - and he sincerely hopes will always be - nothing more than a stop-gap while he wonders what to with the rest of his life.

The door opens and a small woman, dressed in what Mr Peters cannot decide is either a nurse's outfit or overalls, walks into the classroom. She sees the student who acted as Mr Peters' unofficial advisor earlier and goes straight up to him "Looking forward to crewing across the Atlantic this summer Henry?"

"Yes Madame," says Henry.

"Well, it must be very exciting for you. Stay safe". The woman then addresses herself to Mr Peters "Hello my name is Mrs Potts, student welfare." she gives Mr Peters a warm handshake and even warmer smile. Then with a tone which conveys the strongest concern says "I just thought I'd pop in to see how Portia is getting on."

"She's in the practice room," says Mr Peters. Then Mrs Potts, after reading Frank's face – spelling the word *worried* all over it, heads straight off to find Portia.

About twenty minutes later, Mrs Potts knocks on the door of another practice room where Frank Peters is with a student playing the Canzonetta from Tchaikovsky's Violin Concerto. They stop as soon as Mrs Potts enters. "Tchaikovsky?" says Mrs Potts. The violinist takes his instrument away from his neck and nods, "Sounds great. Look, sorry to disturb you sir, but do you mind if I have a word?" Mr Peters at first wonders if he is in trouble – but walks out into the corridor where he sees Portia. Mrs Potts makes sure the door to the room Mr Peters has just exited is firmly shut. The violin continues. "Portia has something to say to you Sir."

"Sorry Mr Peters for my behaviour," says Portia whose demeanour, compared with earlier, looks as if it has received some kind of nourishment.

"It's okay, er" says Mr Peters who realises he does not know the girl's name.

"Portia," says Mrs Potts as she takes hold of Portia's arm. "Now Portia. Maybe Mr Peters, who I believe is an excellent pianist, might help you with the song you're practising. Yes?" Mrs Potts pauses to look at Portia who nods and smiles at Mr Peters. "Okay. Why don't you go to that spare practice room and prepare while I have a quick word with Mr Peters?" Again, Mr Peters translates *quick word* as potential trouble coming his way.

"Sorry again for interrupting you Mr Peters. You see, it's just that Portia has started behaving, as you saw earlier - in a rather worrying manner. It's something that's happened at home which I won't go into. However, we are very worried about her present state, and hope it doesn't have an effect on her exams. They are only weeks away now, you see. It's a shame really because she's one of our star students; you ought to hear an album she's brought out"

"An album?"

"That's right, it's available online, it's just amazing how talented she is. When she produced it only two weeks ago, we had never known a student to be so ecstatic. But now she's in a state all the staff at this school are very concerned about. You know it would be so bad to see her fall at her last hurdle." Mrs Potts looks to the floor as if she can see the life story of Portia flash by.

"Oh, that's sad. By the way - the album, I must give it a listen. What does it consist of?"

"Oh, opera favourites. Just google the girl's name, Portia Masters and you should find it."

Chapter 9

"**Y**ou're amazing in bed" says Maisie as Mitchell seems to use more energy than ever. Maisie wonders if it is the illicit venue which excites him or is it something else? Drugs? Mitchell stops. "What? Just in bed?

"Oh...shut it...just..." murmurs Maisie who only a few minutes ago was cursing the sound of her rickety bed - the same bed that has carried her sleep, her illnesses, her fantasies and dreams from the age of twelve to the present. But gradually, the noise of the creaking joints of her wooden bed recedes into the background as she goads Mitchell to continue with the proverbial "Yes."

A faint thud from downstairs is more felt than heard. They stop. "Shit," says Mitchell.

"That was the back door," whispers Maisie who has got to know the cause of every single knock, thud and creak the house makes. Silence. Mitchell moves himself within the narrow confines of Maisie's single bed as they lie side by side trying to decide what those murmurs coming from the kitchen may mean. "Mum," whispers Maisie.

They have never dared to *do it* in Maisie's home before, even during the days when Mitchell was welcomed to Maisie's house. Maisie feels she is on the verge of being caught *in flagrante.* It is not so much the sexual act she is afraid of being found out for. She dreads being discovered betraying her mother's trust.

"Damn. She'll twig it all and kill me if she sees me," says Mitchell who knows Maisie's mother carries around her very own micro-climate of fear which can be unleashed without notice.

This is unexpected. Maisie had thought the house would be all hers till late evening. With Mitchell no longer working weekends, Maisie was so looking forward to this. Unbelievably her younger brother and elder sister were both going to be away at the same time. Also, her mother was not due to return from her shift at the care home till after ten and her father went away early that morning on a club outing. This promised to be the very rare occasion where all the stars would align for the couple's perfect idyll, or so she had thought.

Mitchell looks around Maisie's shared bedroom and notices all the loose womenswear poking and drooping out of drawers and cupboards. Flotsams of cosmetics on the dresser, Maisie's sister's posters of male film and pop stars – a very alien environment for the male species and certainly not the place to find a ready excuse for an uninvited boy to be caught in.

"Shit, just stay silent," whispers Maisie again. Then from downstairs they hear music. It is the CD Maisie thinks her mother has become addicted to. *Magnifico! Favourite Arias Sung by Darius Dalloway.* Mitchell recognises – *La Donna è Mobile* from Verdi's *Rigoletto* – the signature tune for a new character recently introduced in *KillaTeds*, the leader of the *GrizzaBears: Il Duca.* "I know this" says Mitchell. He very nearly sings along but then remembers he's not a licentious Duke but a young man, scared stiff of encountering Maisie's mother. Then he

83

recalls the video from the practice room talked about by the whole school. He dreads Mrs Moore facing him – her outrage returning and being converted into something uncontrollable and violent.

Maisie in the meantime sits up and puts a shirt on. She has an idea. Maybe if she can go downstairs, distract her mother in conversation and turn up the music, then maybe, just maybe, Mitchell could sneak out unnoticed.

There is a tread on the stairs. For Mitchell and Maisie it feels like a minor earthquake. Their pulses stop and both freeze. Since the practice room scandal Maisie has been repeatedly told in no uncertain terms that Mitchell is not welcome in their home again. Only a few days ago Mitchell came face to face with Maisie's mother in town and he knows this will not end well.

It was by chance she saw Mitchell outside the pub with his dad, Ryan and some workmates. She walked over the road nearly getting hit by a cyclist "Watch it!" shouted the cyclist "No, *you* watch it," shouted Mrs Moore as she concentrated on the vision of Mitchell sitting with his dad and colleagues half drunk. "You! You're" she was so angry she could hardly get the words out "You're a disgrace and, and I never want to see you with my daughter Maisie again. Look at you, you are nothing but a loser going absolutely nowhere. Just like these drunken losers. I don't want Maisie's future wrecked by the likes of you!" Mitchell's associates burst out laughing. Ryan, Mitchell's dad said "Wrong Mrs, I'm going to the bar."

Mitchell sat blushing. On the building site he had the piss taken out of him and had often been shouted at by his workmates. But this, coming from a person who seemed so alien to their whole culture with a speaking voice they all mimicked as soon as she finished admonishing him, was too much. Teachers he could handle but not Maisie's mother, Mrs Moore. He thought about packing Maisie in, but she had so much that was good which trumped all the baggage that came with her – not least, her distraught mother. They got on, despite disparate backgrounds. Maisie understood Mitchell and he knew it.

If he had been on his own it would not have been anywhere near as bad, but he was with older peers he was still trying to impress. "You keep away from Maisie or, mark my words there will be trouble." She emphasised her last word by slapping the wooden table with a heavy hand, just where Mitchell sat. It made him jump. As Mrs Moore walked away, all his colleagues gave a collective "Ooh!"

Maisie was frequently reminded how her act with Mitchell had disgraced the family. How for days as the rumour began to spread, her mother found it hard to leave the house by the front door, stand in shopping queues or even sit in the dentist's waiting room. She imagined everyone she saw knew she was the mother of a promiscuous daughter called Maisie. She also believed those who knew her blamed her for allowing her daughter to become nothing less than a dirty young slut.

Both indoors and outdoors, Mrs Moore would look at people, certain they were trying to sneak glances at her as if saying "You should be ashamed of yourself." She felt like asking them outright. Come clean (oh the irony). But all Mrs Moore could do was try her best to console herself that maybe they did not know – or if they did, were not thinking of it at the time, or that they did not even remotely link her face with that of her daughter's.

Maisie knows that Mitchell can probably hold his own

against Mrs Moore but the repercussions will be quite dreadful for herself. She promised her mother she would not see Mitchell again. Mitchell wonders, if discovered, could he not request her mother to go easy on her daughter as she is trying to study hard towards her exams and does not need the hassle?

Whatever - here he is in her bedroom. Maisie decides to anticipate her mother who is now nearly at the top of the stairs. She opens the bedroom door. Her mother is standing right in front of her. "You'll catch the death of cold," says Mrs Moore. Maisie realises she has got Mitchell's shirt on but then sees her mother looking at her bare legs.

"Thought you would be dressed by now," says her mother.

"No, er, was about to use the bathroom but if you want to go first." says Maisie.

"Just getting something from the bedroom. Go ahead and use it." says Mrs Moore. Maisie is still standing by the door. "You okay Maisie? You look a bit flushed."

"Oh, just a slight headache Mum."

"Well I've got some aspirin in my bedside drawer. I'll throw the packet on your bed."

"It's okay mum, I'm sure it's only a minor one, it will pass."

"Okay then I'll just make sure I turn down the music when I go back downstairs again."

They are now gazing at each other. "After you Mum." At last her mother moves towards her bedroom. But Maisie remains by her door. No way must her mother have second thoughts and drop the packet of aspirin on her bed or more accurately on a mound of blanket concealing Mitchell. Her mother pauses again before entering the threshold of her bedroom. "It's okay. As I said Maisie, I've no wish to use the upstairs loo, if that's why you are waiting."

At last Maisie makes the bold move before her mother might become suspicious.

Maisie is seated on the toilet when she hears her mother shout "Look I'll put the aspirin on your bed anyway."

"Shit" say Maisie and Mitchell in unison. Both are trapped. Both know any second now there will be the start of one enormous and eruptive quiz.

Maisie waits in the sanctuary and reprieve of the bathroom, knowing an explosion is imminent. She can hear the bedroom door, which she just closed, being opened. There is a pause of several seconds. Maisie has visions of her mother standing by the door, her hand playing on the handle as she stares at Mitchell lying on the bed. Her mother will say nothing, compose herself, shut the door again. And then.

"Maisie!" shouts her mother. Maisie makes no reply. She knows this could well be a vocal fanfare that announces the beginning of a verbal hell. "Maisie!" her mother shouts again more loudly.

"Yes!" replies Maisie. "I'll just be a moment."

Maisie hears the familiar sound of those floor boards on the landing creaking away as they always have done ever since she could ever remember. Usually it's followed by the sound of her mother placing linen in the upstairs airing cupboard.

"Yes Mum?"

"There's a packet of aspirin on the bed for you." Maisie does not know what to say. She is amazed. Where is Mitchell? Did he jump out of the window? "Okay thanks Mum."

"Oh I love this track," her mother says as the music down-stairs comes to a stirring finish. Mrs Moore runs down the stairs. The second track on Darius Dalloway's album starts, but after only a few seconds is interrupted by the Verdi aria restarting. This time Mrs Moore can be heard humming along to it.

Meanwhile Maisie puts her head around the door of her room. Mitchell appears from behind the wardrobe.

"That was close," whispers Mitchell.

"Wow I thought that might be the beginning of World War Three for a moment," whispers Maisie.

"So how am I going to get out of here, without your cow of a mother noticing me?"

"Excuse me Mitchell, just mother will do."

"Okay, okay, but how am I to get out of here without having to face an ear bashing? I'm thinking of you as well, by the way."

"Look, mum's downstairs listening to her favourite album, I'll go down, turn the volume up and encourage her to keep listening while you sneak out."

"Okay." While Maisie puts on some leggings and heads downstairs, Mitchell reaches into his pocket and brings out a small plastic bag. He saved it for round two with Maisie. He sees a mirror on Maisie's dressing table. He hopes, with the help of the line on the mirror, he can get the confidence to front the worst.

"Isn't Darius a wonderful singer Maisie?" says Mrs Moore when Maisie enters the living room.

"He is. Not my sort of thing really but he can certainly sing," says Maisie, reaching for the remote to turn up the sound.

"Would love to hear this man live. Please, not too loud Maisie." says Mrs Moore.

"Maybe we could arrange it for you and Dad to go and see him – a birthday treat? I'll buy the tickets."

"That would cost a fortune Maisie. No way! Excuse me, just need to get something," says Mrs Moore leaving the lounge. To Maisie's horror, peering through the lounge door, she sees her mother mounting the stairs again. She follows her out.

Mitchell, who was about to sneak out, is on the landing and sees a head of hair approaching. It is not Maisie so he dashes back into her room.

"Who's that?" shouts Mrs Moore as she sees a body disappearing.

Mitchell does not know what to do. Why didn't he go sooner? He wants out, *now.* There is no escape. He looks at the window, it is too narrow for him to get through, let alone jump out of. Damage limitation is needed so he lies on the bed. He can still hear the Duke's aria from downstairs, then suddenly gets an idea when the orchestra performs the interlude for the final verse.

Mitchell starts to sing along loudly with the music downstairs. He is amazed how he can reach the notes but realises fear and adrenaline help him. The door starts to open and following the music coming from down the stairs, Mitchell holds the long high note towards the end of the aria. Mrs Moore pauses by the door listening – "I didn't know Maisie had this album," she says, opening the door fully. She stands on the threshold frozen, shocked at what she sees. Mitchell stares back and after a suspended moment, springs off the bed in sync with the music. There is a look of total bemusement on Mrs Moore's face. Aghast, she wonders if she is dreaming. She turns to go to the bathroom to throw water over her face. She sees Maisie. She too has her mouth wide open, mirroring Mitchell but for quite a different reason. Mrs Moore holds the arms of her daughter to confirm she is real and the whole scenario is truly happening. It is.

Mitchell, standing tall, sings along with the orchestral postlude even though Darius Dalloway has finished singing. Mrs Moore remains still and stunned. The sound of Mitchell's voice is immense, especially in the small confines of Maisie's bedroom. Opera for Mrs Moore has so far only existed on television, theatres or large open-air venues, not in such a small space as her daughter's shared room. Her stunned face loosens as Mitchell stops singing. A few seconds of silence follows, Mrs Moore turns and without a word walks past her daughter down the stairs towards the living room where the next track is Darius Dalloway's rendition of Vaughan William's *Vagabond.* Likewise, Maisie is as nonplussed as her mother and shrugs her shoulders at Mitchell wondering if she too is in the middle of a dream.

She is relieved her mother has not made a scene but then she is horrified by what she sees on her bedside table: a small mirror with a razor blade on it. "What the fuck is this?" Maisie whispers, picking it up.

"A confidence booster that seems to have just saved me... and you," says Mitchell.

"Mmm" says Maisie. "So you've moved on from dope to whatever was on this?" Maisie shakes her head. "Is the room completely clean? If my sister found any of this...I won't even say. What is it anyway?"

"Coke. And the rest is in my pocket.

"Coke?" Maisie, in a panic, scans the room.

"Sssh, Yes, can we just go? I need some air."

They go downstairs together. Maisie does not know what to say, but opens the door and holds it for Mitchell to walk out of the house. She dreads to think what her mother might say when she must go back into the living room. "Want to come round mine while the storm settles?" says Mitchell.

"No, I'll have to face this head on." Maisie realises she is in Mitchell's shirt which makes her feel exposed. She starts to close the door.

"Sorry Maze."

"Oh, we'll talk about it another time. Not looking forward to this and you'd better be on your way. Thanks anyway Midge." She would normally have kissed Mitchell but knows her mother might be watching through the net curtains. "Sure? I'll wait outside if you want."

"No, fine." Maisie closes the door and walks to the living room.

Her mother is listening to Darius Dalloway singing *This nearly was mine.* Maisie puts her head around the door. Her mother is in a daze and is looking at nothing in particular. Then she gets up to switch off the music. She turns to Maisie and points to a space on the settee which Maisie takes as an invitation to sit down. Maisie cannot decide if what follows is a good or bad silence. "I suppose I can't really stop you two from seeing each other, can I?" says Mrs Moore eventually. Maisie gets up.

"Can I make you a drink?" asks Maisie, on her way to the kitchen.

"No I'm fine," says her mother. "Why doesn't Mitchell try taking singing seriously? What I witnessed a moment ago was the worst and the best. I don't think I'll ever forgive him for disgracing you – and us, but he can certainly sing."

"Always thought that myself but I don't think Mitchell is prepared to take anything *that* seriously."

"He ought to."

"In cultural studies we watched a video about a world-famous opera singer and he says he always practices and even continues to take coaching lessons. Doubt Mitchell would be serious enough to take singing lessons, especially if he had to pay for them."

"Whatever - I have to say I was impressed. Still hate him though for the dark cloud he brought on this house. But as I said, it's plain to see I can't keep you two separated."

"Look mum, I'll encourage Mitchell to take lessons or something. One day you might be proud of him."

"Mmm. One day. First of all you can get properly dressed by changing that shirt. It's revealing far too much of you."

Chapter 10

Frank Peters, has no energy to do much else except revisit social media, to see if there are any more postings about the practice room incident. Luckily there are none. It is yesterday's news – or rather, ancient history for the online world. Scrolling on, he sees a maths teacher offering *free introductory one to one coaching.* He reads through the ad. The lessons are offered free in order to get recommendations for the teacher.

This gives Frank Peters a thought. It could be his ticket out of being used as a reluctant cash cow for unscrupulous teaching agencies. His hopes dim however as he thinks about the horrible comeback he might get by advertising with his own name, Frank Peters. Maybe he could do the same under a pseudonym? He remembers how much he enjoyed coaching individual students who were willing to practice and therefore teachable beyond mere technicalities. They were fulfilling moments which did not require prison warden mentality, a prerequisite for all classroom teachers, and a facet all but absent from Frank's being.

Piano tuition, first lesson free. Also coaching for singers and instrumentalists. Please leave a comment and I will PM you. He waits for responses. Nothing. But then comes the unwanted call from an agent. He cannot believe the school he was in the other day still wants him to return. Such is the desperate state of education, thinks Francis. It is only Friday late afternoon and his whole weekend is wrecked with the thought of Monday's return to mayhem-ville.

He rechecks his phone to see if he has received any interest. Nothing – early days. But then a ping, what was that? Had someone left a comment? His hopes are dashed when it turns out to be the usual confirmatory email of his dreaded Monday booking.

As the evening progresses, he almost forgets about his half-hearted ad. His end of week headache has cleared enough to listen to a debate on the radio. They are talking about the singer Darius Dalloway and XL who in their own ways are both enabling opera to reach a wider public. Dalloway attracts his audience by performing the lighter side of the repertoire and packages himself to suit the tastes of mainly middle-income households who might enjoy picnic and opera on a summer's evening. XL is a rap artist whose every release includes a parental advisory warning. He uses more obscure pieces from the repertoire and blends them into his mixes to form a backing for him to rap over. However, as extra tracks, he releases untampered versions of the pieces used in his mash ups. The radio contributors consider which of the two is creating more opera fans by their different methods. Have their efforts boosted box office sales at major opera houses? No. Ticket sales still remain high for favourites like Carmen and La Boheme. But despite XL using samples from more obscure Handel operas, there is no evidence of having to turn people away from *Radamisto*. Frank concludes they are both artists using music for their own ends i.e. to increase their own financial power.

As Frank is about to go to sleep and feeling grateful for the knowledge that tomorrow is not a school day, he decides to check his phone one last time. Alas, still nothing.

While sleeping, Frank Peters is not aware that Maisie has shown interest in his offer - not for herself but for Mitchell. She replied to him *please PM me – very keen on this. Thanks.* Mr Peters awakes in the early hours, at first thinking it is another school day awaiting. But then remembering it is not, he gets the added joy of seeing a reply to his ad. He duly answers the enquiry asking if she (Maisie) is a beginner or more advanced?

There is no reply all morning and Frank begins to lose hope. No-one else has responded. Then, after nearly giving up on any further correspondence, Frank receives this: *Asking for a friend who is a very gifted singer but just needs pointing in the right direction. As you said, you do coaching. If my friend was to continue, how much would it be per hour?* Frank looks at the profile picture of the person who sent the message. She looks familiar but cannot quite place where he has seen her before. Frank replies: *Would normally be £20 per hour but the first lesson is free.*

That sounds fine. Can we try the free lesson please? What's your address? Frank supplies the address. Again studying the profile picture, he tries to gauge how old the enquirer is. He wonders if this gifted friend is male or female. "Stop it," Frank says to himself. "Be professional and stop thinking like some desperado." The time and date is arranged. He is pleased

95

that both prefer meeting the following Friday. At last hope
- and something to look forward to after finishing another
soul-destroying week in the dreaded day job.

Chapter 11

A week later - *Rolling in Foaming Billows.* Frank Peters dreams he is in the front row of a concert. The orchestra and chorus seem composed of all the miscreants he has met in his teaching career. Centre stage is a baritone dressed in a hoody bellowing out Haydn's famous aria. Then, what he thinks is the tapping of someone seated to his left, is enough to make Frank open his eyes. He jumps up from his seat as he hears the line: *mountains and rocks now emerge* to see Mitchell's towering figure up against his window. The phone by his side is buzzing too. He ignores it.

Moving towards the window he sees his ex-pupil, or more precisely, his ex-nightmare. He certainly has a voice. The phrasing could be improved - but what on earth is this all about? Is this just another prank so characteristic of the Mitchell he remembers? Then Mitchell stops and knocks on the window again. "Can we chat for a sec?" Behind him is Maisie. The practice room incident all comes crashing back. "Yes, very good. Now will you kindly and finally leave me in peace?" shouts Frank through the window at Mitchell.

"No Mr Peters, I want you to help me Mr Peters," shouts back Mitchell through the window. Frank looks at Mitchell and then Maisie appears. "Can we have a word please Mr Peters?"

shouts Maisie. Frank stands motionless but all it takes is for Maisie to smile and Frank heads towards his front door. Surely he might get to the bottom of what happened if the offending parties are allowed a word? "Yes? Come to apologise, at long last?" says Frank. Before Mitchell can say anything, Maisie says "Yes, we have Mr Peters. Profusely."

"Well, thank you, but that will hardly make up for the embarrassment and all the trouble you've put me through, will it?"

"Look Mr Peters, as Maisie just said we're really, really sorry but..."

"But what? Too late now. Now please leave me alone. Every second of my weekend is precious and I most certainly do not want to share it with the source of past miseries."

"People change Mr Peters," says Maisie.

"Do they now? You could have fooled me."

"Okay we'll go. But just one question."

"Yes?"

"What do you think of Mitchell's voice"

"Impressive, now go."

"Look, I answered your ad. Can't we just have a free lesson as you stated?" says Maisie sweeping a hand through her hair. "Our claim to your free hour is as good as anyone else's." Frank is still hesitant. "Perhaps just a chat. If you really don't want anything more to do with us, then fine. We won't annoy you any more. You have my word."

"Oh... Mm... Oh...okay then," says Frank as he pulls open the door to let the couple in. Maisie, on entry can see immediately it is a lounge furnished with loneliness. Sparse. The hi-fi, the television, the books, the bare white walls, the empty wine bottle by the side of a sofa. It is clear the sofa has only been sat on by one person - one side is deeper than the other. Mitchell realises this is the place where Mr Peters would finally find peace and quiet after the end of a demoralising and humiliating day. A pang of guilt hits him and he almost wants to leave but then Maisie, as if reading his mind says "Mr Peters, before we go any further, Mitchell has something to say to you. Don't you Mitchell?" Mitchell looks away from his old teacher and cannot help but grin. His face has to do something to try and disguise his embarrassment.

"Look, I'm really, really, sorry about all the grief I put you through Mr Peters. At the time I was all bit f...sorry, messed up, but now...you know, I just want to say sorry," says Mitchell.

"And I do too," said Maisie.

"Oh thanks. So you think a simple apology like that can put right all the sleepless nights I had. Right... Okay, and thanks again for the little concert outside my window just now but I'll have a think about whether to accept your apologies or not." says Frank. He looks at Maisie who is wanting to cut in again.

"I completely understand and sympathise with you Mr Peters. There is no question about it, what we did was disgraceful. But yes, there is something else Mr Peters," says Maisie.

"Oh yes, what exactly?"

"Well, you did hear Mitchell sing just then, didn't you Mr Peters?"

"Yes, Haydn. I would never have guessed I would hear Mitchell singing Haydn anywhere – certainly not outside my window.

"Just shows people can change," says Mitchell.

"In some ways I'm not entirely surprised. It's all coming back now. Despite all your appalling behaviour Mitchell, I

99

knew you liked classical music more than you were prepared to let on. You just hated the thought of me having anything to do with it, didn't you?"

"My mum tells me that you were once a famous pianist," says Maisie, trying again to steer the conversation onto a more favourable course.

"Yes I was until…"

"What happened?"

"Oh, a long story. Don't mess with things your body wasn't designed to take – especially in large quantities," says Frank who suddenly thinks he might have said too much. He notices Mitchell take a particular interest and give an ill-concealed smirk. Frank is absolutely sure Mitchell has and probably still is dabbling in certain substances, even when masquerading as a student.

"We all make mistakes it seems." says Maisie turning to Frank and Mitchell.

"Yes we do. Anyway, what do you want?" says Frank.

"What do you think of Mitchell's voice Mr Peters?"

"As I said, it's very good, very good indeed. But what have I got to do with it?"

"Well, we were thinking maybe you could help Mitchell with his singing," says Maisie.

"Well, sorry but I'm not a singing teacher. There are many locally though. Maybe you should get in touch with one of them."

Mitchell coughs to say "I've already contacted a few and they nearly all seem to be trying to train Ed Sheeran wannabes or whoever. Or they think I ought to be in a boy band. No effing chance – sorry Mr Peters. I want to sing opera and stuff." Frank raises his eyebrows at Mitchell. He thinks maybe he has changed, just a bit. When he last talked with Mitchell there would have been zero chance of him apologising in any way.

"I admire your integrity. Seems you don't want to sell yourself out then?"

"No, he doesn't. After what my Mum said, I googled you. It turns out you were a brilliant classical performer. This is what Mitchell needs, a serious musician not a star maker," says Maisie.

"It's a shame, Mitchell that you didn't show this willingness to me all those weeks ago."

"No, but he's willing to pay you and make up for it," says Maisie. Frank thinks about this.

He heard Mitchell from behind his window and was impressed. He has a spectacular instrument and the chance of coaching such a talent certainly makes it tempting. But then he remembers all the humiliation Mitchell brought.

"Mmm."

"Next on our list, if you don't want to do this, is a certain Mrs English. Apparently, she is very well established and specialises in opera. But we thought we'd give you first refusal. See it as Mitchell's way of trying to atone for his crass behaviour those months ago."

Mitchell turns to Frank's record collection. Frank has heard of Mrs English and has a good idea of the type of teacher she might be. He once went to one as a young piano pupil. They have a certain self-righteousness - but he is also envious of them. They are usually attractive women who had designs on a performing career when their then boyfriends would act as porter and chauffeur, taking them to rehearsals and auditions. Eventually the boyfriend (usually an investment banker or similar) becomes a husband who does not want his spouse gallivanting all over. So he provides the funds and means to set up his wife's teaching practice. Despite their performing careers ending, they are still lucky to be able to teach this way. Frank imagines many such women would probably get eaten alive if they were to class teach music at a bog standard secondary school. The more he thinks about Mrs English, the more he does not want to give Mitchell away.

"Okay. Let's not waste any more time. Now I might just have a score of *The Creation*, the piece that bit you were singing comes from."

Frank goes into another room where he has a vast library of scores. Maisie takes Mitchell's hand and takes advantage of Frank's absence to kiss.

The score is found and the sounds Frank gets out of his piano as he plays the introduction to the aria, thrill both Mitchell and Maisie. "Bloody hell, Mr Peters, you're fucking brilliant!" says Mitchell, hearing him make the stormy introduction sound like a whole orchestra. It inspires Mitchell and with all his might he blasts *Rolling in Foaming Billows* to create a storm in a living room. Maisie notices Frank nodding as if in total agreement with the way Mitchell delivers each line. Then as they are about to go on to the cantabile section, Mitchell stops singing.

"Why have you stopped Mitchell?" asks Frank looking bemused.

"That's the only bit I know because that's the bit they use in *KillaTeds* when a teddy bear is flung into a lake full of piranhas."

"Mm, quite." Frank pauses "But you can certainly belt it. You need to work on your phrasing more. However - regarding your voice, you are a complete natural."

"So, what do you reckon Mr Peters?" asks Maisie. Frank thinks about it. Maybe this is his passport out of the nowhere job of supply teaching which he hates, to getting some sort of performing career back on track. He knows his days as a soloist are over but, thanks to accompanying Mitchell's inspiring delivery, he could feel his old talent and flare returning.

Also, despite Mitchell's adolescent antics, does he not, sort of, owe Mitchell the music lessons he failed to give him? Again, this is a singer with the most amazing voice. He could even try out some of the compositions he has been writing recently.

"Okay. I will," says Frank "But if I do this, you must be prepared to take my advice. And do some serious work."

"He will," says Maisie.

"Will you Mitchell?"

"Yes" says Mitchell.

"Okay, let's see how it goes. By the way, just out of interest, what do you do job-wise at the moment?"

"Work on a building site with my dad. Good thing I don't want to be a pianist, look at these," says Mitchell as he holds out his calloused hands.

"Wow, they seem to have taken a battering."

"Too right, the rest of my body has too. That's why I want to do singing. It's an escape route."

"We'll see what we can do Mitchell."

Chapter 12

Portia Masters recently received her exam results and now knows for sure any thought of going to study at her first-choice college is out of the question. "Disappointed is an understatement," she told her mother. She felt like her singing ambitions were all but gone. It really hurt Portia to see all her friends get the grades they needed. Some posted videos on social media of themselves opening their envelopes, reading the letters and then going wild, jumping up and down in ecstasy. She envied the way they could all shout "I'm in, I'm in!" or "Wow! Uni here we come!" Despite feeling quite nauseated by all these celebratory antics and exclamations, a friend sent her what she considered to be a sympathetic email telling her that nothing could stop her achieving success as a singer.

You are amazing! My mum and me are big fans already and we can't stop listening to your wonderful album! Portia's friend then went on to mention the way *the album inspired me to achieve the results I needed!* Well Thanks. Good for you. That hurt.

Unfortunately, her grades were more like slime ridden rocks rather than stepping stones. Even when precariously piled on top of each other they were still just not high enough to look over the wall - a wall with the pathway to her dream teacher,

Catherine Cumberland, on the other side. All Portia could see now were bricks pressing against her nose.

Prior to her results, she began to wonder if the whole episode had been a carefully orchestrated scheme of her father's. The property deal had fallen through at the worst possible time.

As soon as her father heard of his daughter's disappointing results, he gave his initial commiserations and sympathy but all too quickly offered her a job at his firm. Both mother and daughter could not fail to notice an element of glee in Roger's voice as he made the proposal. He mentioned it was possible to buy success – "And some *do*. But for that you'll need a good income, and I'm offering you that very possibility," he said. Portia could not deny her father was providing a very attractive package.

Out of anger, with both her father and herself, Portia turned it down. But her act of defiance was short lived when she tried other options. Her results, despite not enough to get her into her first-choice college, might have been enough for somewhere else.

A university on the west coast of England initially looked attractive, more for its location than the course. But the thought soon dampened when Portia remembered her father's reluctance to fill in any of the required forms or worse, the flat refusal to support her.

Not giving up that easily, Portia found she could be entitled to a minimum maintenance but soon realised living on a bare minimum income so far from home would not be appealing. Abandoning the thought of any kind of college course in the near future, she looked at local jobs. She felt so marooned living where she was. Not being able to drive made it worse with only a few buses a day serving her village. Her mother offered to continue her chauffeuring services but Portia wanted to show she could look after herself, so she hurriedly booked a course of driving lessons. Yet even if she was more mobile, the job opportunities were very limited, not least for their remuneration.

In her interview for waitressing at *Enrico's Bistro*, as soon as the boss heard Portia speak, he glanced at her attire. "Despite being known as a bistro, this place is for working class people to come and enjoy a reasonably priced meal or a cuppa. A greasy silver spoon if you like," said the owner Portia thought was Enrico, but whose real name was Shane Brady. Her hours were from eleven to three. However, from the start she found the environment quite alien. She knew her work colleagues were secretly making fun of her *spiffing* accent, and as soon as she told them she lived in Hassel on the Hill and named the *snooty* school she once attended, a minor cold class war began.

Even Brady joined in once when he saw Portia resetting a table. "Excuse me. I hope I am not being too impertinent, but I sincerely hope it may not be too much trouble to ask if her ladyship would be so kind as to see what the people at the table by the window might require. If you would, we would be so awfully grateful for your graciousness." Portia stopped laying out the cutlery and stared at Brady. "Go on then," said Brady. After clucking her tongue Portia went to the party by the window. Her nickname became Grace, which Portia hated.

A chef spilled something on the floor and Brady detailed (he was once a Leading Cook in the Navy) Portia to come and mop it up. "I suppose you're not used to this. At home you probably have a maid to do this sort of thing," said Brady thinking Portia was making too much hard work out of it.

"No, my mother and I share such chores," said Portia who

felt like lancing Brady with the mop handle.

"Well, you could have fooled me with the speed you're doing that. Come on *faster!*" Portia on hearing those words nearly slammed the mop down and left. But her need for money proved the greater tether. "Faster I said." Portia with full vigour hit the mop against a skirting board. It snapped. "It's okay we have another in the cupboard," said Brady smiling at Portia.

It was not only the abuse, but she also hated the music he played from some local radio station consisting of *the hits* on a continuous loop. Even at low volume, it insidiously became increasingly irritating. The repetitive nature of what Portia considered fatuous songs, made her wonder if they were created by those suffering some sort of obsessive-compulsive disorder.

Yet the last straw did not come from being ridiculed by her boss or colleagues. It happened on an unusually busy lunchtime when a customer requested a beef lasagne but sent it back because it had *vegetables* in it. Without thinking, she put her hands behind her back, untied her apron and tossed it straight on to the table. It landed on the offending lasagne directly in front of the complaining customer. After the words "Toss Off" Portia marched straight out of the door nearly knocking over a young couple as they entered. Brady chased Portia down the road and shouted with all the breath he could muster "You're fired!"

"And you're dire!" she shouted back.

As she walked on, Portia mused on the idea that perhaps her dad's offer was not so bad after all - especially when he had told her *Enrico's Bistro*'s accounts and tax affairs enjoyed the stewardship of his firm. In the same way Brady was so quick to judge her character, Portia made rapid assumptions about Brady too. He had associates who Portia decided were dodgy. She did not recognise the names on some of the supplies Brady received.

She could make alterations to his accounts which might result in the following letter: *Dear Mr Brady, If it might not be too much trouble, you might care to look again at your tax return. It appears there may be some rather pertinent discrepancies which you might care to explain.* Portia already relished the idea of hearing the tax inspector addressing Brady with those words. Of course, Brady would not see the connection between Portia and his accountant. His wife Debbie did all the bistro's bookkeeping and sent her files and records annually to a company called *Account Masters.* This was where Portia went, straight after dismissing herself from *Enrico's Bistro.*

"Is Roger Masters there please?" she enquired through the intercom at the firm's entrance. "Who's that?" said Roger's secretary.

"His daughter Portia." There was a pause.

"Would you like to come straight up." The door buzzed and Portia pushed it open with the realisation that not only the likes of Brady might suffer, but her father could too. Maybe only very slightly, but nevertheless...

Chapter 13

Mitchell's father Ryan, a couple of work colleagues and the barman, Les, are drinking in the public bar of *The Faithful Retainer.*

For years, the four of them have chatted, drunk, argued and sometimes inflicted injuries on each other, but have somehow remained as solid as the mahogany that supports their pints. Since Ryan was kicked out of his family home, his friends have become his new family at *The Faithful Retainer* – now a much more inviting place than his solitary flat.

Ryan's friend Les, an ex-army lance corporal, was employed by Dave the landlord because he knew the moment he saw him that he had the necessary bouncer-like qualities required by the pub on occasions. Yet the way Les shoves tables and chairs into place, often demonstrates a certain contempt for his role – and not least its boss. Nevertheless, he has to remind himself where his wages and accommodation come from and count his blessings. All too often he has seen former colleagues residing on the wrong side of the doorway he slams shut every night.

Before the smoking ban, the walls of the public bar were described by Les as 'prison protest brown'. With some help from Ryan he was detailed to scrub them clean. Information about sporting fixtures and dated drink adverts have recently been replaced by posters advertising a singing competition. This event is another attempt to attract more punters and thwart, or at least delay, the pub's execution and subsequent reincarnation into luxury flats. Ryan hopes his son has not heard about the contest – especially with what he sang. Why couldn't he sing *proper* music – not hoity toity opera? *The Faithful Retainer* is the last bastion where Ryan and his friends can retain their identity. He does not want to see another family broken up.

The singing contest has generated much local media coverage and excitement, especially due to the rumour that it will be attended by a scout from the popular TV talent show *Top Vox*. Dave the landlord has his contacts.

It is the evening of the contest. Ryan and his colleagues are picking at takeaways. Next door in the lounge, Dave - through a microphone - keeps repeating the words "Testing, testing, one, two, one, two."

"I think you've tested us enough," says Les, prompting a snigger from his small audience around the bar.

"Aren't you compering tonight?" says one of them.

"No, his royal ponceness has decided *he* is going to do it," replies Les trying to scrub away a stain with his anger, but looks up to see someone entering the bar. "Hello Madam." A woman and a young girl stand by the door. Two of the men turn and focus on the woman's chest bulging out of her leopard spot coat. Both imagine she would not have looked out of place on another recently removed fixture: the calendar, *Mamms of the Month*.

"Is the singing con-" says the blonde woman who suddenly freezes. Ryan recognises the voice. It is Cathy, the self-appointed principal of *The Academy of Stars-to-Be.* The one who thought Ryan only wanted her for her body – the information which destroyed his marriage. "Why the hell did I keep that note?" thinks Ryan, turning to look at her.

Ryan's colleagues' eyes dart between himself and the woman. He offers her some of his takeaway. "No thanks. You know I hate that muck," says Cathy while holding her coat more tightly around her. Ryan smirks.

"You need to be next door love, through that passageway over there," says Les swerving his legs over the bar to usher Cathy and the girl into the lounge bar.

Ryan reminisces on his brief dalliance with the woman. Her attempts to cultivate performers remind him of his son's new found ambition to become a *poncy opera singer* of all things. His only parental advisory to Mitchell would be to keep up with the fucking rap. The general consensus Ryan and his friends have on opera is *total shite.* "Is your son going to be singing tonight?"

"Blimey, I hope not. On the site he's becoming an embarrassment. You know what - he suddenly launches into fucking Mozart or whatever. And the lads laugh at him. They look at me as if it's my fault. But he's seems serious about it. He's taking lessons. For tonight he's got the keys to my flat. If he knows what's good for him, he'll be round mine with that girl of his."

Later, Ryan, Les and colleagues decamp to the lounge bar which, despite being early evening, is already busy. Les and Ryan are getting peeved because:

1. They are not able to have their usual laugh and joke with-

out the danger it might offend the occasional youngster standing at the bar with their mum. Ryan suggests they should return to the other bar but his friends want to stay and watch. Ryan thinks of returning home with some more take-outs but remembers his son might be there with company.

2. Les has no time for chat as he is fully occupied. He finds himself having to mix endless combinations of non-alcoholic refreshments including the rigmarole of preparing cups of tea. Les is more used to putting a glass under a tap, flicking it, and that is that.

"The cavalry has arrived" says his boss Dave, presenting two young barmaids. "I'll leave these girls in your capable..." Upon which Les immediately promotes one of them to Teas Maid-in-Chief.

Ryan has ventured into the lounge bar only once before by accident. During his first visit to *The Faithful Retainer,* he got lost returning from the gents and found himself in a room with unblemished furniture and unscathed upholstery, a room ancient and modern, everything untouched. The ill-fated wedding room in *Great Expectations* came to mind, the only part of the book he could remember from school. Now the room is invaded by a crowd of strange faces and wannabes. Teas, coffees and other light drinks being ordered. Wines instead of beer.

Not far from Ryan is a table with a clean white cloth, a silver bubbly bucket and three upturned wine glasses - the judges' table, Ryan presumes. It looks so *terribly* organised. He cannot decide if this is the new direction for *The Faithful Retainer.* Ryan hates pubs becoming more like restaurants or wine bars.

And now, standing next to him is a woman in a violet frock, speaking in a posh voice. "Is the coffee decaffeinated, fair trade and freshly ground? - Oh vegan milk please. Thanks." *Bleedin' heck where does she think she is?*

The lounge is becoming replete with mixed tribes. Ryan is dreading the possibility of his son Mitchell appearing. He looks over at his ex who has an entourage of young females gathered round her. Her arm is around a girl with a demeanour similar to a nervous flight passenger. Yet his ex, Cathy, also looks worried as she continually scans the room. Who or what is she looking for?

She keeps scrutinising the judges.

"Ladies and Gentleman. May I welcome you all to *The Faithful Retainer's Search for a Star Talent Contest*," says Dave as he both accelerates and crescendos his delivery. There is applause. Dave revolves his portly figure - "And on the table over there we have the judges," said in the same way Les mimics from behind the bar. This receives less applause because no one recognises any of them except the woman in the middle who is Dave's wife, Mel. "May I say it's great to see a lot of new faces here. And I hope, after this evening to see you here again - but enough of my yapping...Let's greet our first contestant," A young girl in a skimpy frock mounts the stage. "It says here she is a student of *The Academy of Stars-to-Be* and is going to sing the Tina Turner classic *Simply the Best*. So, as she's brave enough to be the first on tonight let's give her a big, massive, *Faithful Retainer* welcome for Trish." There is moderate applause at first but then Ryan can hear his ex, Cathy, encouraging her students by saying "Come on girls, support her." The applause greatly increases as the song's intro begins.

Dave leaves the stage and heads to the bar. He lays a sheet of paper on the bar next to where Ryan is sitting. Ryan glances at what he presumes is the running order. Fifth down on the list is a name that makes him want to leave straight away, Mitchell. But then Les places another pint in front of him.

The girl finishes her song and Ryan can see the singer's mentor, Cathy with her arms in the air leading the applause from her table. She looks delighted and even smiles at Ryan.

Sitting immediately to the side of the stage Ryan notices a girl in her twenties. She looks like she has nothing to do with his ex's academy. She wears a cowboy hat slung behind her head and clutches a guitar. Her form reminds Ryan of a favourite punk number: *I love my baby 'cos she does good sculptures, yeah!* As the first contestant leaves the stage, the girl with the guitar cuts through the applause with the words "You're awesome!"

Next comes a young boy, who Ryan thinks looks like an escapee from the *Bugsy Malone* production his son Mitchell was in at junior school. On a chair in front of him sits the boy's mother who directs his entire performance while he sings and dances to Michael Jackson's *Beat It.* At the end, she springs up to remind him to take off his hat and bow. He finishes to tremendous applause. His mother looks pleased and the girl with the guitar cups her hands around her mouth to exclaim: "You're awesome!"

A more elderly gentleman in a tea cosy hat is third up, and plays a Dylan song. He gives up before embarking on the fifth verse. But as he comes off the stage to a dribble of sympathetic applause Ryan can hear the girl with the guitar say "You're awesome!"

Ryan looks around to see if his son is in the room. According to the schedule he should be on soon. He says goodbye to his friend Les who struggles behind the bar with what he calls *The quenching of the five bloomin' thousand.* Just before turning to leave, Ryan feels a nudge from behind. "Sorry, just coming in." says a woman who, despite the heat, wears a black plastic mac buttoned right to her chin. She has scarlet lipstick and finely mascaraed eyes. Her voice presents a challenge Ryan has never quite met before.

"Don't mind at all," says Ryan as he stands aside to let the woman through. She makes no reply but just uses her hand to fan away Ryan's beer breath. "Never seen you in 'ere before," says Ryan.

"Never been in here before," says the woman without looking at Ryan. "Two white wines please," she asks Les, which makes Ryan suppose she is with another woman. Therefore, perhaps, available.

"When are we going to hear you then?" asks Ryan. The woman just turns to give him a quizzical look causing her eye brows to crease her skin back into middle age. "I mean, when are going to hear you sing?"

"Sing? Wouldn't recommend it Mister." says the woman.

"Why not, I thought someone as attractive as you would be on stage"

"Well, you're wrong," says the woman,

"Sorry Madam, cash only" says Les. The woman looks more annoyed as she heaves her bag on to the bar.

"So wha' brings you 'ere then? says Ryan who now regrets drinking so much. The woman ignores him and busies herself trawling in her bag for cash. She finds a twenty pound note.

"Thank *You* Madam," says Les taking the money from

115

the woman. Ryan finds Les's sudden change in demeanour unsettling. He hates the way Les served the stuck-up woman earlier and now this one, as if both were royalty. Seeing the woman smile at Les as he hands her his change deflates Ryan. He is beginning to hate her and sees her as a potential temptress who, like Cathy, is probably a virtuoso marriage slayer.

"Oh, keep the change," says the woman waving her hand. She cannot get hold of her drinks fast enough. *What?* thinks Ryan.

She turns to find she is trapped by Ryan standing in front of her and Ryan's colleagues sitting to her left and right. "Excuse me," she says while giving Ryan a blank stare.

"Who's the other drink for?" asks Ryan.

"None of your...look...excuse me. I need to get through."

"Okay, okay - just askin'," says Ryan as he raises his arms in surrender and allows the woman gangway.

He watches the woman head towards a table where another woman is sitting "Are they lesbians?" Ryan wonders. Whatever - he dislikes the woman. It was the way she spoke with a curt, probably *I've been to university* sort of accent, similar to the last woman who ordered coffee. But this woman is a different kind of posh – with an abrasive air, strictly business, and who wants absolutely no business with Ryan.

Put your hands together ladies and gentlemen for...Mitchell." says Dave. Ryan turns towards the stage. No-one goes to the microphone. There are murmurs in the audience. "Calling Mitchell, are you there?" says Dave in an American military-style voice. Ryan stands on tiptoe to look over the heads in the direction of the stage. "Ah, here he is. Ladies and Gentlemen – Mitchell!" Ryan cannot decide whether to bury himself amongst the huddle of people or leave. A person finally comes on stage. To Ryan's relief it is not his Mitchell, but someone different. He hears a guitar being strummed. It is the introduction to *SuperGlu's Soil.* Throughout the song Ryan still scans the room to make sure there is no sign of his son, Mitchell.

Soil finishes again to polite applause. This other Mitchell says, "Maybe I should have done something you all know – you know, the same old crap." The room goes quiet, quiet enough to hear the girl with the guitar say to the disgruntled singer "You're awesome."

Dave announces an interval, and on the jukebox comes the song *If I didn't love you, I'd hate you.* Ryan comes away from the crowds around the bar. He glances over towards his ex, the self-appointed academy principal. She is looking at the woman in the black plastic mac and seems to want to get up from her seat, but people Ryan supposes are mothers of her protégés keep approaching her and she is constrained to talk with them. A thought comes to Ryan. Is Mitchell taking lessons from Cathy? *Oh, the irony!*

"Ladies and Gentlemen," says Dave through the microphone as the next contestant stands by the stage in a Tuxedo, arms folded looking like a crooner's answer to *James Bond.*

"A big hand for Ricky Good!" As Ricky steps towards the microphone, applause erupts, together with whistles from female members of the audience.

Ricky goes straight to the centre of the stage, ignoring Dave. He grabs the microphone and whipping its lead behind him, launches straight into a *Rat Pack* medley.

"I suppose smooth and smart can be a tonic for those living

rough and rugged lives," says someone standing near to Ryan.

"Oh, and nostalgia can provide an odd kind of hope in reverse, I suppose," says another.

"What the fuck?" says Ryan to himself.

Finally holding a last note to loud cheers, Ricky Good finishes. Basking in adoration, he bows to all corners of the room. The girl at the front shouts out "You're awesome!" louder than she has done so far.

"Very rarely do we get Ricky for free. Maybe the presence of a certain scout from a certain TV show might have something to do with it. Eh, Ricky?" says Dave down the microphone. Ricky does not reply. He is too busy fending off female admirers. Ryan looks at the girl with scarlet lipstick again. She is chatting to her friend and seems unimpressed with the crooner. She keeps looking at her watch.

After a generous succession of singers from *The Academy of Stars-to-Be,* the last contestant is finally announced. It is the girl who has been sitting at the front. She takes her time tuning her guitar. People begin gossiping. Guitar tuned, she sits and waits for silence. Tantalising arpeggios accompany her delicate voice. It is her own song heavily featuring the words 'me' and 'I'. Seldom do her eyes open throughout the performance and her demeanour suggests that all the hurt in her life is concentrated in the four minutes and thirty-three seconds on stage. She finishes and waits. Ryan notices his ex, Cathy, responding by just sitting mute with her arms folded. Therefore he cheers the young girl wildly. The girl smiles at him, mouthing the words which a lip reader might translate as "You're awesome."

After a long wait and many more drinks sold, Ryan just about manages to sit upright on a vacant bar stool. He strains his eyes to watch the crooner approach the woman in the mac who snubbed him earlier. His advances on the woman soon turn to retreat which makes Ryan feel better. Even he, Mr Smooth Crooner is rejected. The woman and her colleague get up and leave. All chances to get off with her, no matter how remote, are now gone for Ryan. But then he consoles himself with the fact his son had not taken part in the contest. The last time he told Les about Mitchell's opera singing he spat and said "Bloody opera. Lottery subsidised crap – should have given the money to homeless veterans."

"So, ladies and gentlemen. It's the moment you've all been waiting for - the announcement of the winner!" says Dave. Ryan's ex sits fully alert and tries to decipher Dave's every nuance and expression. The crooner leans on a wall, trying to look as casual as he can about the proceedings. The girl at the front clutches her guitar tightly with her eyes fixed on Dave. The mother of the Michael Jackson impersonator is standing to attention with her hand to her mouth. Her son is nodding off, almost falling off the chair in front of her.

"So the winner is…" says Dave making hard work of opening a gold envelope.

"If it's not Ricky Good I'm going to kill the judges one by one!" shouts a woman in a guttural tone. Dave drops the envelope but before picking it up says "You don't want my Mrs haunting you for the rest of your life, believe me."

"You can say that again," says Les as he notices Dave's wife give her husband daggers.

"The winner…of…*The Faithful Retainer Singing Contest*…is, drum roll please" Les taps his hands on the bar. The winner is...Skye Con..." The academy principal, Cathy, knows who it is before the rest of her name can be announced and starts clapping. But before her applause gains any momentum, the main entrance door to the lounge is flung open and bangs against the wall. Everyone turns, thinking perhaps a fight has begun.

"*La la la le la. Tra La La La!* comes a voice through the door. No accompaniment, no microphone - just an explosion of sound. A core of energy – the like of which no-one has witnessed all evening. All turn, expecting to see a smartly dressed Italian opera singer but it isn't. It is Ryan's son Mitchell in a fleece and jeans singing the Factotum aria from *The Barber of Seville.* "Bloody Nora, what is he on? What did we do to deserve this?" says Les which makes Ryan wish he could vanish through a hole in the floor. But then he notices the woman who snubbed him earlier, re-enter the pub. She is smiling – and at last, begins to unbutton her coat. Ryan's son seems to have her and her friend transfixed. Ryan feels the tiniest pang of pride. "Well, that's me out," says Les taking the end of his old regiment tie and pretending to hang himself as he marches himself into the other bar. Ryan does not care anymore. He is the father of a son who attracts every woman's eye in the pub.

Turning to his ex, the academy principal looks appalled. Ryan shrugs his shoulders at her when she looks back at him.

But then the woman in the mac starts to clap a pulse to Mitchell's singing. Her friend joins, followed by a few more. Ryan's son looks even more confident and with a certain swagger, ventures around the tables creating more smiles. He strokes some of the females as he passes them and lights up their faces. It is magical. Soon, nearly everyone in the room is clapping along. They are happy. Ryan's pride grows and grows as his son accelerates towards the end of the aria. After a long high note Mitchell ends to a storm of applause and immediately heads for the door. Ryan follows and so does the woman in the black mac. There are cries for more – the first requests for an encore all evening. But eventually the ovation dies down and Dave takes to the stage again.

"Well, what a...er... an...interlude. Well, if everyone has recovered, as I said the winner is...Skye Connor!" says Dave. The applause sounds much more muted in comparison with what Mitchell has just received.

Outside Ryan sees his son Mitchell standing against the wall of the pub catching his breath. "Can we talk? I'm from Channel Productions," says the woman in the black mac, giving Mitchell her card.

"I'm his manager," says Ryan.

"Oh...it's you," says the woman.

"Dad, you couldn't manage a fucking chip shop," says Mitchell.

"Look, just make sure you give me a ring on that number first thing Monday, You are fucking talented. Never heard a voice like yours before and it's about time we had you on TV."

The woman is about to leave when Ryan's ex rushes up and grabs her arm.

"Are you the person from the TV? If so, my name is Cathy. I run *The Academy for Stars-to-Be.* And one of my students has just won. Surely there's room on the show for her?" says Ryan's ex.

"Look, take this card. I'll see what I can do."

"Actually, this woman is more like a Madame who trains young girls to go out singing glorified karaoke in pubs for leering old gits," says Ryan.

"What - like you? Actually, I take that as an insult!" says Cathy, taking a swing at Ryan but Les comes from behind her and grabs her arm in mid arc.

"Ryan, apologise to the lady now!" says Les. Ryan is beginning to hate Les's over-protective stance towards women. He wants to hit him, but realises he is no match for Les and does not want to develop a scene in front of the woman in the mac. With reluctance he says "Sorry."

"And I'm sorry about my dad. He's pissed," says Mitchell to the TV woman.

"Look you, just make sure you get in touch." she says, pointing at Mitchell as she begins to walk away with her friend.

"Shall I give you a ring too?" asks Ryan's ex. The TV woman makes no reply and just continues walking on.

Chapter 14

Sunday afternoons are becoming less depressing for Frank Peters. He has been coaching Mitchell for a few weeks and has found in him a new and vivacious talent to foster. Therefore, the anticipation of another week's supply is not so bad any more. He has relegated teaching to where it belongs – the ranks of a mere dreaded day job, a source of income, no more no less. His real vocation is that of musician. Thanks to Mitchell this may soon become a reality again.

He feels deeply jealous of teachers who, through the love of their job, excel. Frank considers them lucky to have a career choice with numerous vacancies and openings. Trying to make a living as a professional musician means being up against ferocious competition with opportunities that are relatively rare.

Frank has considered playing keyboards in a function band. But despite it being easy money - he can instantly sight read most sheet music - he knows he would find the job annoyingly so close yet so far from where he really wants to be. The venues he would have to play with their guaranteed noise. The weddings, parties, clubs and pubs, together with the drunks. It would not be totally dissimilar to teaching. At least in teaching he does not have to wear a plastic smile and talk with people he would not normally choose to – for example, corporate bores.

It is only a couple of weeks into the autumn term and his supply teaching bookings are already alarmingly busy. He is surprised when a member of the senior teaching staff tells him how much he is preferred to others. If *those* supply teachers are useless - as Frank often considered himself to be - he dreads to think how bad the *really* useless must be.

Although there are bills pending, Frank would still have preferred to enjoy the extra time this slow period for supply teachers usually allows. He would continue to develop his piano technique to keep up with a voice growing larger by the week.

It is three o'clock on Sunday afternoon. At this time in the past, Frank would be sensing dark clouds of trepidation beginning to shroud over his countenance. But Sunday afternoons have changed thanks to Mitchell. An individual he once considered nothing more than a wretch, has become the perfect student and the very person to give Frank Peters hope for a life, perhaps worth living to the full.

He finds his thumb is now more able to cope with the heavier works of late Beethoven and beyond. But today he is to go through an aria sung by Figaro's adversary, Doctor Bartolo. He notes it requires a very firm accompaniment, particularly at the beginning where the jealous doctor makes his declaration to ruin Figaro. Frank is also looking forward to the middle sections where Mitchell's fantastic sense of rhythm (a legacy he assumes Mitchell has gained from listening to incisive rap rhythms) would be something to relish. It is Mozartian rap in triple time.

However, despite the spectacular and natural talent Mitchell obviously has, Frank can never predict his pupil's mood.

Sometimes he will come to lessons ecstatic, at other times seem half dead, but seldom in between. Frank suspects drugs, but there again, his behaviour might be attributable to a tiring day on the site. Therefore Frank chooses not to challenge him at least. Whatever his state, Mitchell can manage to focus, eventually. The bottom line is that he is improving rapidly.

There is a bang on the door even louder than what Frank has become accustomed to. Mitchell has arrived. "Okay, coming."

"Frank! My main man, you'll never guess what!" says Mitchell.

"What" says Frank, pleased to be called by his first name.

"I'm going to be a star!"

"What?" says Frank wishing he could close the front door against a breeze which suggests summer is surrendering to autumn. "Come in. Tell me all." Mitchell enters and paces around Frank's living room, seeming more hyper than ever.

"Last night right, I wasn't going to but Maisie reminded me. This singing competition at my old man's pub. Maisie saw the notice while she was working, you know...waitressing. *Enrico's*. She says everyone there told her she's replaced a right stuck-up cow. So, thought about it. Was getting late. Wondered if I ought to enter.

"Enter what?"

"Listen. Was probably too late. But Maisie says *just go for it*. She couldn't say anything. Her boss, Enrico, not his real name, can't remember his real name. Twat will do. Hates me being there so guess what?"

"You decided to go?" says Frank wondering when Mitchell will stand still.

"Yeah, I did. I could hear like, outside, like this bloke about to announce the winner. So guess what."

"No idea Mitchell. You can sit down, if you want." Mitchell ignores Frank and carries on, one foot to the other.

"I just go straight in. *The Faithful Retainer.* You know. Singing Figaro, full on right."

"Wow! Bet that made an impression."

"It effing well did. I won!"

"Won?"

"Yeah, well not in the sense of winning. Not the contest won. Some young tart won that, I think. But won a slot.

"A slot? What slot?"

"Yeah a slot - on national TV. That slot. This is gonna be mega!"

"So what's this? A TV show?"

"*Top Totty* Maisie calls it but it's a show called *Top Vox.* Heard of it?"

"Er, no."

"It's on Saturdays. Evenings and guess what."

"What?"

"This woman comes up to me, real looker. Dad, silly arsehole, tries to get off with her, doesn't he. Pretended to be my fucking manager. Silly sod. No effing chance. But the woman. Sent me this. Here, look." Mitchell gives Frank his mobile. Frank takes it and reads the screen.

"Well done...hang on, the phone's gone off."

"Give it here. There – just keep scrolling, like that. Then it won't die." Frank reads the email. The more Frank reads the more he wonders *is this the end of his chance to make something of Mitchell and, maybe, himself?*

"So reading this, it seems you won't need me – *accompaniment will be provided either by our resident band or, if necessary, pre-recorded backing tracks.*

"Of course I'll need you Frank. I want you to help me with the songs they want."

"Oh they're telling you what you can sing are they?"

"Hang on Frank. Later it says *we thought this would be better than yet another,* what's this say, *Nissan Dora.* What's Nissan Dora a song about a car?"

"You mean *Nessun Dorma* It's an aria by Puccini made famous when Italy hosted the world cup. So what *do* they want?"

"A Mozart medley, see." Mitchell shows Frank his mobile again. "We were about to do some Mozart this aft so seems like they've read our minds."

"Hmm, Catalogue, Champagne and the one from Figaro. Hope Mozart won't mind being all mashed up."

"And do you know what the best thing is Frank?" Frank is pleased to see Mitchell, at last, has stopped pacing around the floor and is managing to stay still while they share his phone.

"I'll be performing in front of XL. You know, my idol and he might become my coach."

"So if he takes you on as a so-called coach, you won't need me any more?"

"Oh, come on Frank."

"Okay. Without wanting to sound a spoilsport, is there music for all this or have they sent you some pre-recorded backing tracks – you know DIY karaoke?"

"The woman says they will sort it soon." Frank does not like the word *soon.* It means his hopes for re-establishing himself as the artist he once was, will *soon* be gone. *Soon* he will be back to full time supply teaching with no hope of redemption. *Soon* he will be back to the usual depressing Sunday afternoons as Mitchell will also be gone *soon.*

"So, do you want to cancel today and spend your time preparing for this TV thing?" Mitchell finds the way Frank stresses the word cancel has something all too final about it. He sits down and Frank looks at him. Since he arrived he has acted like a wind-up toy which now looks like it could do with winding up again.

Mitchell looks around Frank's living room. Bare fading white walls. The upright piano, the shelves of CDs and books, mainly music scores. A portrait of Beethoven balancing between the wall and the top of his piano. This is Frank's whole world. Music. What else does he have in his life besides his obvious love for music? During the time Mitchell has got to know Frank, he has never mentioned anything to do with a relationship let alone been seen with anyone. If he took this away, what would Frank have left? Probably nothing to look forward to except having to negotiate with prats all day - like he himself used to be, thinks Mitchell.

"Have you never seen the show *Top Vox* Frank?"

"Can't say I have."

"Well before the contestants sing they show a video of the person taking part. You know, what they do during the day when they're not singing. You could be in that video Frank as my dedicated coach – and mentor."

"Oh thanks. Being on television which is fundamentally trying to entertain folk on a Saturday night. They will try and make me look silly I suppose. I'll become their corporate stooge. This is all too reality TV-ish for my liking."

"I'm sure the guys will show you in a good light Frank. In fact we could make a thing of it. Me as the student from hell being turned into a great singer – all thanks to you."

"Doubt they'd let you do what *you* want to do."

"Who knows, they might."

"Look, Mitchell. First things first. Shall we start with the Mozart *we* planned to do? Or shall we postpone it until you get the music *they* want you to do?"

"You don't sound happy Frank."

"I think you'll agree, things have changed. But as you're here, let's make a start."

After the lesson, Frank thinks about Mitchell's erratic behaviour. He is sure he is taking substances to make him act with such gusto to begin with and then slow down. After considerable effort and hard slog, he did manage to get Mitchell to knock his chosen arias into shape. But then he thinks maybe he should have asked Mitchell outright if he was taking drugs. Surely Mitchell could trust him not to go straight to the police if he admitted to such activity. He still performs and manages to achieve nothing short of excellence in his singing. But Frank feels guilty if all that matters is Mitchell's ability to be a great singer. If he has embarked on some sort of addiction - and evidence from previous occasions suggests he has, will this affect his future singing and the possible career which is his for the taking? Why can't teaching just be purely about the subject or the skill? Frank asks himself. Has he taken on too much? Maybe Mitchell is the wrong student? Perhaps it might be better if, after this TV show, someone else does take him on.

The following week, Frank continues his role as supply teacher. His hopes are all dashed, making the days seem longer and the job even more tedious. He foresees Mitchell's idol, XL, taking charge of a phenomenal voice and turning it into something he can purely exploit. But he also tries his best to see it from Mitchell's point of view. It cannot be denied, this is a good opportunity. At least the masses will hear Mitchell and who knows, Frank Peters, might be on telly himself? Now that would surprise the noisy and recalcitrant bunch he covers regularly.

But then something very much more down to earth dawns on Frank. His attempts to advertise himself on social media as a private piano teacher have led to him being lambasted by some anonymous parents reminding everyone of the practice room incident and how irresponsible Peters was.

Chapter 15

"They don't have hod carriers any more," says Mitchell's dad, Ryan, enjoying his co-star status while Top Vox camera crews film Mitchell on location at a building site; "Certainly not carrying them up a ladder like that. It's against health and safety rules."

"No, but this is television and the vast majority of the guys at home won't know that will they? They want drama. Come on Mitchell, one more shot of you struggling, and I mean *really* struggling up that ladder. We've got a great shot. It makes the drop look so precipitous and deadly...if you were to fall," says the director, Fraser. "Oh, and Ryan, can you get stroppy, you know, *come on, put your back into it,* that sort of thing. Let's make this as realistic as possible."

"Come on Mitchell you lazy fucker, put..."

"Cut. Ryan, less of the language, remember this will be going out pre-watershed."

"I thought you said you wanted it to be as realistic as possible?"

"Yeah, this might be reality TV but maybe a little less reality. Okay Mitchell, once again. Bottom of the ladder please." Mitchell lowers himself.

"I hope this will be the last take. The reality is I'm doing my fucking back in…big time," says Mitchell starting to ascend the ladder.

"You're doing great Mitchell. Okay… and…*action*," says Fraser.

With a good mind to drop the hod of bricks on Fraser standing by the cameraman at the bottom of the ladder, Mitchell is fast realising what a downright lie so-called reality TV really is.

"Good, the more pain you show, the more sympathy you'll garner from the guys at home," says Fraser.

Meanwhile, sitting in the catering bus is Esther Ree. She is on site to introduce and occasionally comment on the proceedings, with a smile that suggests she might have been an air hostess - which in fact she was. "Here's Mitchell. Poor Mitchell, during the day works like a slave for his merciless dad," said Esther earlier, smiling at the camera. She only comes onto the set when strictly necessary as she is not comfortable being in the same proximity as Fraser. The two of them have a brief history.

After travelling the world as an air hostess, Esther was talent spotted and entered the world of modelling. She worked her way up through all the parties until she managed to get the hottest ticket in town – The *Le Gen'd Magazine Big Night Bout.* It was at this party that she met Fraser. Esther allowed him to bed her after signing an agreement Fraser always kept on his person. The following morning - Bingo! Fraser offered her the job as presenter for a new show he was to direct called *Top Vox.* However as soon as she'd signed his contract, she left Fraser and it was revealed she had covertly been seeing a star from a popular TV soap. After being dumped for the soap star, Fraser tried all legal means to get Esther dropped from the show, but her solicitor had quietly negotiated a separate contract for her with *Channel Productions*. Failing to oust his former lover, Fraser also tried to part company with the production company himself. But his contract was equally escape proof. *Just try and get on you two* were the last words from the chairman of *Channel Productions.*

Ryan wishes he could go and chat to Esther. In fact he would love to be able to tell his mates back at *The Faithful Retainer* he has done more than just chat with her. But, as far as Ryan can see, the catering bus seems out of bounds for the show's guests who have to make do with a horse-box-cum-kiosk. So far when on set, Esther has given Mitchell's dad nothing more than her smile and an initial "Lovely to meet you." - which is what she says to everyone she first meets.

"Okay guys, I think we have a take. You can come down now Mitchell," says Fraser.

"Thank effing goodness for that," says Mitchell, still very tempted to drop his hod of bricks.

"Right, we'll take a break. Thirty everyone. Mitchell, maybe you and your dad might like to go and have a quick coffee on the catering bus. If anyone says anything, whoever they are, tell them you have my permission," says Fraser smiling and looking towards the bus. Ryan has never moved so fast in all his working life, on seeing Esther sitting by a window in her hard yellow hat.

Yet as he boards the bus he is disappointed to find Esther talking on her phone. When she sees him, she gives a look of incredulity but then transforms it quickly back into her characteristic smile, and gives him a thumbs up. Ryan's hopes are raised until she stands up and brushes past him to get off. He watches her going to carry on the conversation in her car –

a type of car he would love to own, but so out of his reach, just like Esther.

Mitchell's phone pings. It's a message from Frank "Hope all is going well. Look forward to seeing what you've done today on TV!" This makes Mitchell feel guilty. All through the morning while trying to feign the hard-done-by worker, he has forgotten about his old teacher. Mitchell wonders what is worse. Carrying a hod which – despite being relieved of the burden - he still feels painfully digging into his shoulder, or working as a supply teacher like Frank Peters?

After half an hour, as planned, they are back on site shooting Mitchell pushing an overloaded, dirt-splattered wheelbarrow. "Mitchell has not just got to carry heavy loads all day long but he has to use all his might to push them too," says Esther Ree. She stands left foreground while the camera pans to Mitchell pushing the barrow over muddy mounds. "Cut! Say that again. Try and sound a little more pitiful for him Est. You sound like you enjoy watching him suffer. Lose that smile for fucks sake. We've gotta get full on pity from the guys at home," says Fraser. "Take two!" Esther stands in the same place looking directly at the camera and manages to convey sorrow for Mitchell. "Hey, Est say that again and when you say the word 'push', point your finger at Mitchell. Okay? Good. Take three." Esther perturbed, nevertheless does it again. "Cut! Hey we're on a building site not announcing *We'll be shortly landing in Ibiza*. Old habits as they say. Take four." Fraser says to the cameraman under his breath "This is what happens when you get models in rather than proper pros."

"Hey Fraser if you've got something to say, you can tell us all. Otherwise just get on with it shall we?" says Esther. For the final take, make up replenished on her face for the twentieth time today, she concentrates hard on her delivery. While doing so, she does not realise there is a dumper truck coming towards her. As she delivers her last word, the truck splashes black mud all over her white designer mac and bright yellow hat. A speck hits her under the eye. Fraser laughs and shouts "Hey guys, I think we have a take."

"No way are you keeping that," says Esther.

"Hey, who's the director Est? Check your contract if you don't believe me" replies Fraser.

The first footage shown on national TV is from the building site. Then from an entirely different location, Esther announces "After his spirits are rock bottom following a hard day on site, he lifts much more than bricks. When he sings, he lifts spirits." Then comes footage of Mitchell performing to an admiring crowd at *The Faithful Retainer* pub. Before this was filmed, Mitchell's step dad Gavin was not pleased to see his name absent from the guest list. However, the list did include Mitchell's mother and the whole of Maisie's family together with an audience full of extras paid to cheer. Loudly.

In the green room of the TV studio are Ryan and his drinking buddies: Les, the barman and two others. Mitchell invited his mother Sandra, but she declined to come because Mitchell told her *she* was welcome but again, not Gavin. Sandra, having watched the show, knew it included backstage footage of friends and families cheering on their singers and did not like the idea of being confined and huddled together in what looked like such a small space. Especially as it would mean literally rubbing shoulders with her ex-husband.

Maisie is also present. She'd reminded Mitchell to ask the film crew earlier if they could film him being coached by Frank Peters or at least an interview with him. Unfortunately, Fraser the director said such a sequence would deflect and undermine the importance of the celebrity coaches. Instead, Frank Peters had to make do with a cameo appearance, sitting next to Mitchell's mum while watching his protégé performing in the pub sequence recorded earlier. (She was at a safe enough distance from where her ex was sitting, but hoped viewers would not think Frank was her husband as she deemed Frank a bit of a weirdo).

Mitchell is being prepared for the dress rehearsal. He is shown *exactly* his route to walk on to the stage, *exactly* where he should stand while performing, and *exactly* when to speak and when not to, while the judges/coaches give their verdicts on his performance. This reminds Mitchell of the instruction *speak only when you are spoken to.* Was he still at school? Was he still only a child?

As Mitchell walks onto the stage he sees the large chairs where the celebrities will sit. These look like the thrones of extra-terrestrial monarchs. On the show itself, the celebrity judges sit with their backs to the contestants for a blind audition. If a judge likes what they hear they will push down a dome-like button on the arm of their vast seat. This causes them to spin around and face the contestant. The sign fixed to a table in front of each judge (a table arrangement similar to a baby's high chair) then illuminates with the words TAKE ME. This indicates the judge wants to coach the contestant and become their mentor.

The only seat which interests Mitchell is the one his idol XL will be sitting on. XL is the only judge he wants to impress. He has seen the others and for Mitchell they simply do not count. He is eagerly anticipating performing to, and impressing XL. He knows if XL takes him on, his life will be transformed beyond his wildest dreams. Maisie thinks the same, but told Mitchell whichever judge chooses him, all they will want is to make as much money as they can out of him and, at best, turn him into another Darius Dalloway. Mitchell senses a potential element of jealousy in her words.

Maisie's boss was delighted to let her have time off. The thought of someone he knew – even if only for a few seconds, being on national TV was irresistible. Maisie is also very pleased to be there with Mitchell – *but* she is glad her parents have not come. They would not be at all comfortable sharing the small backstage area with Mitchell's dad and his friends who have already cracked open the lager. It is still only afternoon.

As the show is to be broadcast live, the floor manager is not too keen to see Mitchell's associates knocking back *booze* in the green room. She wonders if some intervention may be necessary and is surprised alcohol was allowed into the studios in the first place.

Security is called. A burly man who would probably be feared by even the most hardened rugby player, accompanies the floor manager. She delivers an ultimatum demanding they either abstain or leave. Ryan's friend Les, almost immediately walks out, protesting *This is like being back at bloody school.* Yet Ryan takes him by the arm and stops him with the words "It's okay Les, it's okay. Let's not spoil it for my son Mitchell." Ryan then to show his willingness to comply, in front of the floor manager, Maisie and security, starts loading the unopened cans back into his rucksack. Putting the last one in, he zips it up and says "For afterwards." Maisie smiles at the floor manager who seems satisfied with the gesture, and departs with the security man, forced to slant himself at a certain angle to get back through the green room door.

As soon as they leave, Les is still about to leave too, protesting that he *doesn't want to listen to his son's bloody opera anyway* when Ryan says "Watch." Then he takes the coffee flask off the table, empties it down the sink, gives it a good rinsing and, from the solitude of a toilet cubicle, fills it with a few cans worth of lager. "There we are, I'm sure we can tolerate drinking out of cups." Les is content again. However, Maisie is not pleased coffee is so rudely unavailable and has to resort to tea from the urn.

Show time is getting nearer. Mitchell makes the excuse of saying he has left his mobile phone at home. Despite offers from the others to take photographs of his memorable time, he says he has a far better camera on his own phone than the ones all his associates have. So he borrows Maisie's to pretend he is arranging to meet a friend to collect his phone. But really it is a rendezvous of a rather different purpose. Like his dad, it will involve an exchange in a toilet, this time in a nearby pub.

Mission accomplished and show time is due any moment. The director only recently decided to broadcast it live to create more *spur of the moment* excitement. Mitchell finds himself standing next to the floor manager as he is about to strut onto the stage. Thanks to his rendezvous of convenience, he is exploding with confidence and is looking forward to knocking his hero XL dead. The floor manager has her headphones on and is conversing with the director. "Contestant ready to go," she says through her VHF radio. Mitchell can't wait and the floor manager has to keep holding him back, as if she is reigning in a racehorse raring to go. "Okay, go for it Mitchell and the best of luck," said the floor manager, patting Mitchell on the shoulder.

Mitchell walks out and stands on the designated spot. The music starts with the busy opening to Mozart's catalogue aria from his opera *Don Giovanni*. Usually after the first few bars of a song the studio audience applauds when recognising the chosen song. For Mitchell, no such appreciation is shown as he sings the opening words *Madamina, il catalogo è questo.* He, along with Frank his coach, insists on singing the words in Italian. He knows XL always presents opera in his mixes using the original language, thus helping to maintain the integrity of the composition to the full.

Mitchell performs and watches the chairs from where he stands. To him they look more like furniture which might have escaped from an amusement arcade. As he sings, he imagines he is the Don described in the aria, getting his way with all the numerous women mentioned. He gives hand gestures to the camera below him in an effort to try and show the audience at home the numbers he is singing. Surely he would score as well with women as the Don *if* XL took him under his wing. But so far XL has not turned his chair.

His confidence is, however, given a slight boost when Go Go Gaye, the pop diva turns. He sees the illuminated sign displaying the words *TAKE ME* and moves on to singing the steadier but catchier *Marriage of Figaro* aria. Go Go Gaye smiles at him with her beguiling radiance. It makes him want to take Go Go Gaye too – but not as a coach. The camera now cuts to the green room showing Maisie, Ryan and his friends raising a toast with their china cups to Mitchell's first *TAKE ME*. Most viewers at home observe an odd incongruence in what they see. It looks like workmen toasting the start of a tea break with a glamorous daughter present. A lip reader would be able to translate Ryan's silenced voice as *get in there son.* However, all Mitchell wants is to see XL turn his chair.

Some of the audience seem to recognise the second Mozart aria and Mitchell can hear a ripple of applause as Ben Taylor, the legendary diva swings round. He gives Mitchell a quick nod and more of a grin rather than a smile. Ben is at the very top of his game. Dominating the charts since the sixties, he has a massive voice which simply commands all to listen to him. With mighty material to match, Ben and his songs are an unstoppable combination. Thanks to his literally awesome vocal instrument he successfully manages to reinvent himself through the decades with an ease many performers, including opera singers, still envy. But for Mitchell, Ben Taylor, despite his status is not XL. Meanwhile, Maisie knows if her mother is watching she would probably hope Mitchell would choose Ben as his coach. That as far her parents are concerned would confirm that Mitchell has arrived.

The tempo quickens when Mitchell dives straight into the Champagne aria. At this point Mitchell's machine gun like vocals manage to get the audience gripped. The camera focuses in on individual members of the audience who sit with their mouths open as he fires out the words. This is the biggest display of virtuosity the show has ever had. Jimmy Lang the front man rock star swings round sticking both thumbs up at Mitchell. He also mouths his latest hit single - a cover of the Squeeze song *Take me I'm Yours.* Again, footage of Ryan and his friends can be seen mouthing the number as well. Maisie smiles directly at the camera, blushing as she knows her mother will see her with the type of company she is certain she will not approve of. Esther Ree, the compere, can now be seen hugging her as if she can read Maisie's entire situation.

Mitchell accelerates towards the closing bars and the audience begins cheering more and more loudly. Mitchell desperate to see, XL's chair turn, gives it all he has got. He sings as if his entire life depends on it. He has zero interest in the others. It has to be XL or no-one. Finally, he stops singing to massive applause and the pre-recorded orchestra brings the intoxicating strains to their conclusion. Finally the fourth chair turns. Mitchell can hardly believe what he sees in front of him.

The chair seems to revolve in slow motion as if in the grip of a terrible accident. The more it turns, the more he realises how unbelievably everything is materialising. Mitchell has to wipe his eyes. The audience applause thunders on. He bows but has to keep checking who he sees in the final chair. He can hardly stomach the sight. It is not XL sitting in that fourth chair but Darius Dalloway. Backstage, all of Mitchell's entourage are hugging each other. The camera shows a close up of Mitchell's face. Instead of the characteristic look of elation when four chairs swing round. Mitchell looks as if some tragic news has just been relayed to him. And it has.

"Uugh!" say Portia and Roger in unison as the two of them see the visage of Darius Dalloway appear on their TV screen. *Top Vox* would not normally be their chosen viewing but as they heard Mitchell break into Mozart they had to keep watching. Roger loved the Mozart medley and was highly impressed with

Mitchell's voice but seeing Darius Dalloway appear utterly spoiled it.

Ever since their next-door neighbour, Elaine, made her impromptu visitation and saw Roger's humiliation, he has hated the sight and sound of the name Darius Dalloway. In fact, ever since the Darius Dalloway TV ad campaign started, Roger has always kept the remote near him for emergency channel change. Portia hates him too for being the fake opportunist her singing teacher has warned her about. "But that singer, I'm sure I've seen him before. Why don't you go on this show Portia?" says Vicky.

"Yes mum, he does look familiar but this kind of show would ruin all my credibility as a serious classical singer – sorry, sh, I want to hear what this phoney Darius has to say," says Portia, raising a hand to stop all conversation. "Mitchell Woods, Hassledon's new operatic sensation. You are brilliant and I could take you from the dirt and grime of the building site all the way to, well, where people like me are – if only you would take me," says Darius Dalloway to enormous applause from the studio audience. "Ha," says Portia "Darius certainly knows all about dirt and..."

"Shush," says her father Roger now raising his arm, and listening intently after hearing Hassledon mentioned. Go Go Gaye says how much the girls would appreciate such a young and fresh new opera Diva which is answered by Darius with the words "Go Go, I'm not *that* old, *please.*" The studio audience laughs. Portia's mother Vicky, like many other viewers at home, notices a rather sullen looking demeanour on Mitchell's face while he stands with Esther Ree's arm around him. Vicky has seen the show before round at Elaine's and she knows Mitchell does not look anywhere near as happy as previous contestants – especially those who have just swung four chairs and achieved four *TAKE MEs.* "Portia, I have an idea, potentially, at least," says Roger.

Mitchell still wants to see XL sitting where the over-pompous Darius sits. He is almost tempted to say yes to Go Go Gaye. He is sure she fancies him, detecting the very slightest lick of her tongue as she said the words *young and fresh.* But then he remembers what Maisie said. *They are only out to make as much money as they can from you and turn you into another Darius Dalloway at best.*

Esther Ree asks Mitchell which of the four judges he will choose to coach him. There is a pause as shouts come from the audience. It is a cacophony obscuring all of the names. Thumbs from the audience rise and descend. Some even stab fingers in the direction of their recommendations. But all are pointing at different judges.

Mitchell looks at Darius Dalloway. Maisie is right and he certainly does not want to be turned into the perfect ponce. Mitchell notices the fake opera diva is dressed in a tuxedo with flickering lapels. He considers Go Go Gaye but then thinks of Maisie. If he ended up hurting Maisie in any way again that would be that. Ben Taylor is a legend with integrity – but he still is not XL and neither is the rock singer, Jimmy Lang.

"Mitchell, we are waiting. Who will you choose to take as your coach?" says Esther Ree. The audience goes silent, waiting for Mitchell's decision. "None," says Mitchell. The audience make a huge sigh. The judges look at each other. Esther Ree feigns amusement from Mitchell's reply "No Mitchell, seriously. Who will you take as your coach?"

"None of them. I came on this show hoping to be taken on by

XL who would normally be sitting where he is," says Mitchell pointing at Darius. The camera also pans to Darius who looks dumfounded. He raises both hands in the air as if to say *not my fault.* "Are you absolutely sure of your decision Mitchell?" says Esther.

"Absolutely, I don't want to be coached by any of them." There is another sigh from the audience as Mitchell lifts Esther Ree's arm from his shoulder and walks off the stage. Mitchell's dad and his friends are shown shaking their heads with quizzical looks on their faces.

"So there we are," says Esther Ree, told through her ear piece the footage for the next contestant is ready. So, not knowing the name of the next singer, she announces "Ladies and Gentlemen, I would now like to you all to watch this." A video of a girl sitting in her living room strumming a guitar then begins.

Meanwhile, Mitchell is walking along the corridor leading from the stage. He passes the floor manager who says nothing, but just glowers at him. Another member of the production staff gives Mitchell a grin and a discreet thumbs up. Eventually he gets back to the dressing room. There is anger in his father Ryan's eyes but Maisie goes to hug him immediately.

"Do you realise what you have just thrown away? There's singers who would die to be in the position you were in a moment ago," says Ryan. Maisie lets go of Mitchell to shut the door. She does not want others to hear this. As she tries to close the door, Esther Ree puts her head around and stares at Mitchell. Her eyes are no longer those of the welcoming air hostess. They are the eyes of alarm, as if an airliner has dropped a few thousand feet in an instant. Finally, Mitchell's dad says "Can I apologise on behalf of my son for embarrassing you."

"It would be good if Mitchell would do so," says Esther. Mitchell makes no reply. He knows XL will still see the programme replayed on a streaming channel. "To be honest, I give up. Son, I'm ashamed of you. You've thrown away a golden opportunity which many would kill for. I'm totally ashamed. Even more ashamed than that time word got around about you and Maisie in the video." Ryan leaves with his friends. Esther is about to leave too but says: "Mitchell, some advice. I suggest you get out of here before Fraser comes down. He is livid."

"Don't worry Mitchell. What you have done will probably get more press attention than those who usually win and go with one of the judges. You used these guys and they hate it for it. Do you realise, by tomorrow, you will be a household name. Even XL will know your name *and* your wonderful voice," says Maisie.

The potential magnitude of this information has not yet clicked with Mitchell. He is still euphoric. Yet Esther's last words tell him they must get out of the building immediately. Maisie sees a high visibility jacket hanging in one of the corridors. She guesses there may be press already at the studio door. She tells Mitchell to put it on and raise the hood. He does. Members of the press outside ask them what they think of Mitchell snubbing all the judges. Maisie just says "A shock, never known anything like it. But if you could excuse us, we have a bus to catch. Thanks." They then walk on without further hassle. The high vis works.

To celebrate, Mitchell treats Maisie to dinner. As soon as they sit down, Maisie tells Mitchell the press will probably be outside his house either now or very soon. They will also be trawling the internet to find what they can about him. They will certainly find the gossip on social media about the pair of them in the practice room. But this might help Mitchell's image. If he refuses to say anything to the press – or anyone at all who he doesn't know - for a couple of weeks, he may come out the better for it. Mitchell agrees.

Maisie offers him her family's sofa for the night. Mitchell wonders if being accosted by the press is worse than Maisie's mother discovering him on the sofa in the morning. He decides to chance it at Maisie's. Besides she looks stunning tonight and maybe...

At the end of their meal, he is presented with the bill and realises it will cost him his next supply of coke. He can't explain this to Maisie. She will realise where all his money has been going recently. But hey, by tomorrow he will have all the papers talking about him. His supplier, nicknamed *The Raza Man* will think he's famous and maybe let Mitchell have his supplies on tick.

The Masters are sat on their L - shaped sofa. Roger on one part of the L, Vicky and Portia on the other. They have left the TV on but turned the sound down. "I liked Mitchell - a superb voice and I think what he did shows he's got integrity too," says Portia.

"Earlier you said you had an idea. What was it Roger?" says Vicky who has noticed her husband being unusually busy on his mobile.

"Ah yes, I heard Mitchell is from Hassledon. What do you think of doing a concert with him Portia?" says Roger looking at his daughter.

"Mmm, with his voice and now the scandal of turning down the judges, I think he'll have every agent in the land after him," says Portia while her mother nods in agreement.

"Really? After turning those judges down? Agents will not see him as the most reliable of performers. Imagine this: an agent books him to do a concert at the Festival Hall and he doesn't bother turning up? Or maybe walks on to the stage only to head off again because he doesn't like the look of the audience," says Roger.

"No but he knows, like me, that Darius Dalloway is a phoney and the other judges would not really be on his wavelength."

"Hey Portia, not Ben Taylor? He's wonderful and a legend," says Vicky.

"In the end though, what I'm saying is he doesn't want to sell himself out. He wanted to go with XL, who's very good actually. Some of his stuff is quite ingenious," says Portia.

"I think, if X whatshisname offered to be his coach he would have gone with him. That's what I think made him walk off. He was disappointed not to see his hero there to snap him up," says Vicky.

While Vicky and Portia are talking, Roger has been looking at a local social media site called *Around Hassledon.*

"Going back to my original idea," says Roger. "Portia."

"Yes dad"

"Would you like to do a concert with him? I think you ought to."

"Yes, of course, but you don't know him. And why are you suddenly taking an interest in my singing career dad?"

"Me reckons it is something to do with money Portia, money," says Vicky.

"Ah, of course. I was planning on doing a concert as a follow up to the album I made but most of my friends who might've come to it have all scarpered off to university." Portia looks at Roger who is grinning while looking down at his mobile. "I hope you're not laughing at me dad."

"Not at all," says Roger looking up again, "Here's the perfect opportunity for you Portia. Two of the greatest singers in town united in one concert. Should be a sell-out."

"You're right mum. Money strikes again...but how are you going to get in contact with this guy we've just seen on *Top Vox*? Mind you, I'm sure I've seen him around. His face defo rings a bell. Probably the fact he's local."

"Easy. We find out where he lives using this site, 321 which can tell you where anyone lives. My firm uses it a lot. I've noticed on *Around Hassledon* people are already talking about him." Portia reaches for her phone. It does not take long for her to say "Mmm, despite all the congratulatory comments he's got, not a lot of people seem to like him. In fact there seems to be a lot of dirt being thrown at him already."

"What sort of dirt? Show me Portia," says Vicky.

"Yes you've noticed," says Roger. "It's the sort of dirt the tabloids would love to know more about. All I can say is if this singer is not given guidance over the next few days, his life could turn awful, and very soon too."

"Yes I see what you mean," says Vicky "Do you think Portia, our daughter really ought to get involved with this Mitchell person?" Roger pauses, looks up at the ceiling, then looks down again to continue checking the comments on the *Around Hassledon* site. Portia carries on doing the same. "Oh no. They say he's a sex maniac, and another's called him a rapist. I certainly don't fancy doing a concert with him. No way." says Portia.

"I wouldn't believe everything people say on social media Portia," says Roger who is now finding out exactly where Mitchell lives.

Chapter 16

Sunday morning and Frank Peters wakes up feeling only very slightly better today. Lately he has been particularly down. Another hard week at the dreaded day job has led him to conclude finally that any hope of escaping has vanished. He hates his job so much it's making him hate other things too. He gets paid to be humiliated. When training, he was told never to take what kids say personally - but with his sensitive nature, Frank does.

He has hardly touched the piano since Mitchell last saw him over a week ago, and is beginning to feel life is rather over-rated. This is a belief he holds so strongly that he ignores the recent pains in his chest which he knows he should probably get checked out. But the pains, sometimes sharp, only last for a short while and Frank now prefers the idea of letting nature take its course – especially when he considers life's course to be - crap.

When he watched Mitchell's performance on Top Vox and saw the chairs swing round, he thought it was definitely the end of his protégé for good. Yet he was surprised, like everyone else, when Mitchell turned down all four judges.

Frank always rises earlier on Sundays to make the most of being free from his usual weekday obligations. He is listening to Shostakovich's Eighth Symphony. The brooding qualities of the first movement do not help lift his mood. This unfortunate choice of music is the fault of a strict system he has developed. He possesses a few thousand CDs and, having decided that every CD was once bought for a reason, he insists he must listen to them all and has adopted a certain sequence which dictates which disc is next. Now is the turn of the Shostakovich symphony...

Despite its dark qualities and moments of the utmost turmoil, Frank still finds this a suitable piece upon which to muse. Something tells him he will see Mitchell again. The first movement of the symphony ends and gives way to the bombast of the second movement; at the same time there is a knock on his door which hammers well with the music. Through his window, Frank can see two people at the door - an older man and a younger girl. He wonders if they might be Jehovah's Witnesses or similar. "Hello, how can I help you?" shouts Frank from behind the window. The music does not help to lessen Frank's sudden surge of anxiety. "Hold on." He turns the music down.

"Hello. You must be Frank Peters, Mitchell's old music teacher," says Roger Masters holding out his hand, but Frank does not take it. Frank does not want to reply to the question either. The couple he has never met before seem to know enough about him already. More than enough. He wonders if this has anything to do with Mitchell's sudden rise to prominence. Are they from the press using some kind of elaborate disguise? Usually they will send a solitary reporter. Or, if the story is really big, he would most likely have a whole barrage of reporters on his doorstep by now. "And who are you - if you don't mind me asking?" He notices the young girl – dressed in a sun hat and wearing shades – keeps looking through his window. She seems drawn to his upright piano. He knows the press use attractive people, and she certainly possesses the demeanour and confidence of such types, Frank thinks. She also has a vague familiarity about her.

He has read about devious media ways, and likens the opening assumption *You must be* – to bailiffs jamming their feet in the door you try in vain to close. He believes the press and the bailiffs have a great deal in common. Before you know it, instead of taking goods and furniture, the press will start by helping themselves to parts of your private life (some you forgot existed), make them no longer private but expose you naked to the entire world. Then, if that is not enough, they'll continue to work towards the sure but steady removal of your soul, little by little or sometimes whole.

"Sorry, let me introduce us more fully. My name's Roger Masters and this is my daughter Portia. Frank looks at the girl more carefully as he hears her name. We live locally and we would like to put on a concert," says Roger. Frank finds this very odd at first but then his spirits and hopes are raised as hears the word *concert.* Do they want him to play? Is this the father of an instrumentalist or singer?

"So why are you telling me all about this? Where do I fit in?"

"We believe you know Mitchell Woods quite well," says Roger. Frank finds Roger's tone a little interrogatory but his daughter's smiling mouth seems to soften her father's delivery.

"Er – How do you know?"

"Social media, we noticed your name was associated with Mitchell. Something about a practice room at a school you taught at."

"Oh no, I thought that would have been dead and buried by now."

"Social media's very good at sifting through the dirty laundry only the press could get at, once upon a time. Oh, sorry to sound as if we were being intrusive but we found that some of your neighbours have also been complaining about the noise you and Mitchell make when you rehearse. Although one said last night they're pleased all the noise seems to have benefited the person they have seen around here – before and after the noise. That's Mitchell."

"Of course, they go on social media first rather than approach me directly." Franks pauses. He realises it will only be a matter of time for the whole world to know all about him too. He wants to get rid of this couple at his door, though not too abruptly. "But now it seems he's hit the big time. Did you see him on the TV last night?"

"Yes, we did and many others too."

"Well he's not here. And I haven't a clue where he is. Now he's famous he will probably have no need of me. So maybe you might want to try his parents or others as it seems you've done some quite thorough research on Mitchell *and* me"

"We've already contacted his parents, both of them. He's not at either. We'll try both parties again, of course. But please, just as a favour if you see him, would you be so kind to give him this card and ask him to contact me."

Roger presents the card. It has his firm's logo: *Account Masters* at the top. Before handing it over, Roger takes out a biro and circles one of the phone numbers. Frank is still not convinced. "Hold on. Forgive me but it seems very suspicious that you are trying to contact Mitchell straight after he's appeared on TV. I imagine the papers would want a story from

153

him especially when he turned all the judges down. Apparently no-one's done that. I mean, are you really anything to do with music at all? To me this could all be an undercover press entrapment. Is there any way you can prove who you say you are?" Roger turns to Portia.

"You can check that my company, Account Masters really does exist if you like. Look here's my website," says Roger who holds up his phone, almost the size of a small tablet. Frank looks at it but says nothing. "Portia, fancy letting this gentleman hear you sing something? You know, to show you are indeed a musician. How about, one of those warm up things you do?" says Roger. Portia looks around at her surroundings. They are quite foreign to her. Her whole life has been given so much space: a large house, a school with vast classrooms and playing fields. Frank Peters lives in a small block of flats. The whole complex is the size of a mansion yet the windows and doorways to every dwelling seem remarkably close to each other. She knows at only 10am on a Sunday morning there may well be people sleeping only a few arms lengths away. Portia moves nearer to Frank and sings a quick ascending scale. "Mmm very good," says Frank "But, call me cynical. I still think this is part of an elaborate set up."

"Fair enough. Maybe it's up to Mitchell to decide?" says Roger as Frank finally takes the card. "By the way, how did you get to know about me?" asks Frank.

A woman appears behind Roger and Portia. They turn to look at her. She smiles as Roger says *It's started.*

Meanwhile at Maisie's house, Mitchell wakes up. The sleeping bag's zip is halfway undone exposing half his body. The odour from the carpet and furniture, fresh and floral, immediately reminds him he is on the sofa of Maisie's living room. Through a slit in the thick curtains he sees a clock ticking on the mantelpiece. He is slightly shocked when it chimes ten times. He remembers now. Last night they headed to his home but could already see what looked like press people outside. Before bringing him to hers, Maisie received a text from her mother telling how thrilled she was to see Mitchell on the TV and thought he sounded excellent but wondered *Why oh why did he turn down the golden opportunity of being coached by Darius Dalloway or even Ben Taylor?* Maisie knew her mother had come round to liking Mitchell for being a *marvellous* singer and also always liked the way he addressed her as Mrs Moore. He was no longer the rogue of some months ago who had brought shame on the Moore household.

Mitchell wonders if he ought to sneak out, but then he hears a voice coming through the kitchen hatchway. A kettle is starting to boil. Took him ages to get to sleep after all the euphoria, but he is surprised to find he does not feel tired – just indescribably down. Why should this be, after all the praise heaped on him from the judges the night before? He realises he needs to see the dealer, the Raza Man, but suddenly remembers how much he spent last night treating Maisie to a celebratory dinner. Then he wonders how Maisie's parents will react when they discover he has been on their sofa. Yes, he is more accepted now, but has he put his feet too far under their table or, more precisely too far into their sleeping bag?

He feels trapped again, but stays put, hoping he will hear the sound of Maisie's voice soon – though she must be knackered too. His phone needs charging. The battery only shows a few per cent. It is times like this when he wishes he could play *KillaTeds* to pass the time until Maisie might show and soften the shock of her parents seeing him in their house. The game helps kill his craving too. Yet now he needs the phone for its original purpose – communication, not as a portable amusement arcade.

The knowledge that his state can be easily fixed by the Raza Man lures Mitchell to heave himself fully out of the sleeping bag and off the sofa. He gets dressed and feels better with his trousers and shirt on, rather than, what Maisie's mother would consider the mild porn of them being draped over the sofa arm and on the floor. She could enter any moment, he thinks.

He sits up now and from behind the kitchen hatchway hears the first word of the Mozart aria he sung last night: *Madamina.* It is a baritone voice but the rest of the tune is whistled by Maisie's dad. He seems to be whistling in a way to tell Mitchell he knows he is camping in their living room. Mitchell gets up, considering this whistling to sound cheerful, even friendly. He stands by the living room door. Like the moment he paused before gatecrashing the pub competition to sing Figaro's aria, he once again says to himself *just go for it* and finds himself in the Moore's hallway. In front of him is a selection of neatly hung coats. Looking to his left, the kitchen door is open and he sees Maisie's dad smiling at him. "Being Sunday, her royal highness will probably not be ready to receive an audience for at least another hour or so. Want a coffee? Toast? Well done last night by the way." It's the first time Mitchell has had a proper look at Maisie's dad. He looks so normal, so mild, so nothing to do with Maisie at all.

"Er, thanks Mr Moore but I've got to see someone."

"Okay, if you're absolutely sure."

"Yeah. Tell Maisie I'll see her later. Thanks. Bye," As Mitchell goes to let himself out there is a knock on the door. It is not Mitchell's door to answer, so he waits for Maisie's dad to come and see who it is.

Mr Moore opens the door. "Hello are you the father of Maisie?" says a smartly dressed woman. "Ignore her, she's from the press," whispers Mitchell. Mr Moore holds the door for a moment. "Would you mind leaving this property immediately. No comment," says Mr Moore as he shuts the door. "Mitchell you'd better go out by the back door."

"Who was that?" says Mrs Moore from the top of the stairs.

"The press," says Mr Moore as he goes towards the back door to let Mitchell out.

Outside, the morning is crisp and bright which fully awakens Mitchell. Walking out along a path at the side of the house he sees another person standing in his way. "Why did you snub the judges? Are you too frightened to become famous because of your past? You know, the past which incudes being a sex pest - even at school?" says a man with a phone out ready to video Mitchell's response. Mitchell stops, then barges past him, turns and gives him a V sign. The man follows him – as does the woman who knocked on the Moores' door. She hears the words *sex pest*. "Is this true Mitchell?" says the woman.

"It's total bollocks," says Mitchell, increasing his pace when realising he is being followed by both of them. "A bit on the abusive side aren't we Mitchell?" says the male reporter.

"What do you expect when I hear accusations like that? Leave me alone." says Mitchell who is wondering where he can go to get rid of these intruders. He considers the possibilities. Parents? He knows from last night there will be press outside both their places. Looking behind him, he sees Maisie standing at her front door in a dressing gown. She gives Mitchell a wave while beckoning the two reporters to return. They do.

Mitchell feels he should too but as he walks towards Maisie, she wags her finger at him and holds up her other hand to tell him to stop. Then, with the same hand she starts making a shooing motion at Mitchell. He obeys and notices Maisie making a gesture at the reporters as if she is wearing a watch. Is she arranging some kind of press conference? Mitchell supposes Maisie's parents' pride in their daughter seeing a star, has diminished the shame of the gossip which could hit the national papers. Will she admit she was the other party – and gave full consent? The possible consequences of the allegation just made at Mitchell begin to worry him. Last night in the television studio he was in total control. This morning he suddenly feels threatened with the potential of the whole world against him. Sex offenders are hated. Even if these offences are only rumoured or alleged, his life could still become very uncomfortable.

Relieved to find that at least he is no longer being followed, Mitchell reaches for his phone to call the Raza Man. He wonders if this is a good idea but needs something to bring his confidence back, and feels more down than he did when he first awoke.

They arrange to meet later outside *The Faithful Retainer*. First though, he goes into a newsagents and is surprised, after the hounding he's received from the press so far that he is not on any of the front pages. Flicking through one of the papers, he sees a bold headline half way down page three: *DARIUS - GO AWAY!* There is a picture of Mitchell performing on the show and another one of the snubbed Darius Dalloway. The feature opens with the line: *Viewers last night were shocked when...* He reads the rest of the piece. It is already comparing Mitchell with the promiscuous Don he sang about on the show. Luckily this article has not mentioned Maisie by name. Mitchell searches his pockets to find he has enough to buy the paper. Just enough. Which reminds him: will the Raza Man allow him credit?

Coming out of the newsagents, his head is buried in the newspaper and he bumps into the great bulk of a work colleague. "Hey mate, great to see you on the box last night. Brilliant! Shall I get your autograph now before it's too late?" Mitchell smiles at him but says nothing. He remembers this big framed man is the person who, during coffee breaks, has often commented on newspaper articles about sex offenders and how he would like to spend just ten minutes alone with them. "Will we see you tomorrow or are you too famous now?" says his colleague.

"You'll see me tomorrow," says Mitchell.

"Wow, this will be a first, working with someone famous."

"Maybe." Mitchell realises the papers tomorrow could be full of false reports and gross elaborations about himself. How will his colleague react when he reads those? He wonders if he should just lie low. But where?

From across the road Mitchell can see his dad Ryan and two others being let out of the back door of *The Faithful Retainer* by Les, the barman - another person Mitchell knows is very vocal about what he would like to do to sex offenders. Will he turn his words into action against Mitchell?

It seems his dad and friends had an all-night lock in after returning from the TV studio. Mitchell crosses over the road.

"Hey dad, if anyone you've never met before asks you about me and last night, don't say a thing alright? Do not say a thing. In fact if anyone you've never seen before approaches you, just ignore them. Even if they're the most attractive woman you've ever seen."

"What ya doin' here?" says Ryan who stumbles with his friends towards a waiting taxi.

"Waiting for a friend. As I said dad, don't talk to anyone. Please."

"So if someone even more beautiful than your mum comes and talks to me, I'm to ignore them, am I?" says Ryan whose reply receives sniggers from his friends.

"Yes, especially if you're approached by someone like that dad."

"Don't worry I'm going straight to bed when I get home son." The three are all in the taxi and after Ryan heaves the cab door shut, Les acknowledges Mitchell with a nod. He waves at the departing taxi, returns to the pub and slams the door behind him.

Mitchell resigns himself to the fact that his dad will talk to anyone with a skirt on and wonders what they will think when they are invited into his flat. They will probably immediately suggest they go for a coffee somewhere. Maybe even *Enrico's* where Maisie is meant to be doing a shift later in the day.

The Raza Man arrives. He does a full circle of the car park before he stops. Mitchell, looking around, sees only an elderly woman pushing her shopping along on wheels. After scrutinising the windows above shops across the road, he is confident there are no curtain twitchers and runs to get into his dealer's car. "Hi, I've got a favour to ask you," says Mitchell.

"You want gear on tick, don't you?" says the Raza Man, who

during the week normally wears a suit and tie. He has Radio 4 on. The look on Raza's face is not encouraging, so Mitchell asks "Did you see me on telly last night?"

"What was that?"

"I won on *Top Vox.*"

"Sorry don't watch that sort of shite."

"Well look at this." Mitchell opens the paper to the column his picture is on.

"Fine. Do you want this or not?" The Raza Man has no interest in Mitchell's fifteen column inches of tabloid fame. Instead he opens the long redundant ashtray to reveal a small bag; Mitchell is about to take it but before he can touch it, The Raza Man shoves the ashtray closed. "Credit terms apply," says Raza Man.

"Okay, and what are they?" says Mitchell

"No foliage this week, means a quarter on top the next and so on and so on. Hopefully there won't be too many and so ons. Agreed?" Mitchell cannot work out what he means but he considers the Raza man a reasonable and easygoing sort of guy, so he presumes his terms might be okay or at least standard amongst dealers. So, to the closing music of *The Archers* blaring out from the radio, he takes the bag, opens the door and gets out of the Raza Man's old Merc. Mitchell knows where to head next. It should be a reporter-free zone – that's if no-one is following him.

Then the allegation made by the reporter outside Maisie's house hits him again. But now he has a way of fighting back, at least for the time being, by hitting the coke.

The Raza man reverses loudly. The noise shocks Mitchell. "You forgot something," he says, poking the rolled up news-paper through his window. Mitchell takes it...

161

Chapter 17

"The return of the prodigal son hey? Don't know what you want with me. I'd have thought the very best singing teachers and coaches would be clamouring for you by now." says Frank standing at his door in front of Mitchell. But Mitchell has no words. He is surprised by the tone of Frank's voice. In the distance he sees a girl approaching, with a similar demeanour to the one who came to Maisie's door. "Mitchell Woods, is it true you sexually assaulted a girl at your school? she says. Mitchell makes no reply and just wants the safe harbour of Frank's flat. Now. "Frank," says Mitchell as he puts his hand on the wall and leans into it only to push himself back again. He does this repeatedly.

"Are you the music teacher?" says the girl to Frank.

"Look, you'd better come in." Mitchell enters and Frank closes the door. "That person outside has been meandering here all day. She went a while ago but just returned."

"Another one accused me of rape earlier."

"Try to forget she's there if you can. Blood suckers the lot of them."

"I'll try. Look, I came to say sorry. Maisie and I tried to get you on the show but the director wouldn't have it," says Mitchell.

"Probably because I'm too boring," says Frank.

"No, it's..." The girl outside has her face by the window. She cups her eyes against the glass and says "Mitchell..."

"As I said, ignore her. If she was in here, she'd get into your mind next."

"What, like Hannibal Lecter?"

"Yes." Frank shoos the person but she just smiles at him. He has never been smiled at like that before. Not from a girl as attractive as the one outside. "They're so false, I can see right through you madam. You probably worship the false gods of career progression, expensive trash and all the money and cheap kudos that go with it all," Frank murmurs to himself. "Bye." He closes the curtains then continues "I have to say you sang brilliantly on the show last night but why did they have to embarrass you with the footage of you on the building site."

"It's TV Frank, trying to gain me some sympathy from the viewers. By the way," Mitchell takes out his mobile. "Do you mind if I plug this in?"

"Sure, over there. Oh, and you can sit down if you want. Your constant fidgeting does not put me at ease. I imagine if they'd featured me, I suppose they would've wanted me to look like some sort of stiff prude of a music teacher or something."

"Frank, I just wanted to get on the show. As far as I knew, XL was meant to be one of the judges but as you saw, he wasn't on the panel last night was he? Instead they had that ponce Darius Dick Head instead."

"I'm sure if your hero XL has seen the show, he'll be very keen to get in touch with you. Depends what he wants though. Would his approval of yourself guarantee he'd want to work with you? Have you heard anything from him yet? Mitchell notices his phone flashing. He almost leaps at it and checks it. "Er...No, not yet. Cunt."

"You know what Mitchell"

"What?"

"From the very little I know about press and publicity in the days I was signed to the *Kos* label, I guess XL's press officer will log every single mention of him, big or small. I would be very surprised if you are not on XL's radar right now. Especially having been on national TV and already causing a bit of a stir. Who do you think's outside? I rest my case." Mitchell twitches the curtains. Through the gap he can see the glamorous woman still lurking.

"Bet she went away and spoke to me dad. Ha, bet the smell from his flat spoke even louder. But what can he say? Nothing except how they take the piss out of me at work for singing opera. Big fucking deal."

"They may have also asked him about the practice room incident too. That woman outside would like to know my side too, I bet."

"This morning I was accused of sexual..."

"You already said. Regarding other news. Earlier today, a couple knocked on my door and asked me to give you this. I think they said they want to put on a concert featuring yourself." Mitchell looks at the card *Account Masters*. The name Masters rings a faint bell for Mitchell. "I tried to be vague with them. For all I knew they could have been from the press too, in some undercover disguise. It seemed odd that they came looking for you via myself – especially after your TV appearance. But they said I was the only contact they could get hold of. Apparently they tried your mother and father but had no luck."

"What did they look like?"

"To me they looked like father and daughter – they claimed they were. The father said his daughter was a singer. I didn't believe them, so guess what."

"What?"

"He got her to sing."

"What?"

"Yes on the doorstep, like you did all those weeks ago. She was very good actually. Oh, and for your information, a looker too." Mitchell looks at the card again. "Could tell she had good control with the way she didn't belt her scale out. She's obviously had lessons I guessed. Why not try them now? There might be a gig in it for you and who knows, me as well." Frank lies back in his seat dreaming how a gig could mean enough cash to allow himself a few days off to do a few day's serious piano practice.

"I'm phoning them now." Mitchell looks at the number Roger had circled in black biro and taking his phone from the socket starts pacing about the room with it. He taps in a number which only gives him an engaged tone. "Fuck."

"Mitchell if you just sit down and dial it carefully." Mitchell tries again. It rings.

"Hello, is that Roger Masters?"

"Yes, is that Mitchell? Great. So pleased you called back," says Roger. Frank can hear Roger's voice quite clearly even though he is sitting some distance from the phone. "By the way. Before I say anything, very well done for last night"

"Cheers."

"You did the right thing. You're getting more column inches than what a winner taking on one of the judges would normally get. I admire your shrewdness.

"Er – thanks."

"Look, I'll come straight to the point. I would like to promote you in the form of a concert. Interested?" Mitchell pauses and relays the information to Frank by whispering. Frank replies by raising a thumb at Mitchell. "Er Yeah," says Mitchell.

"The concert would feature yourself, of course and, if you don't mind, my daughter as well. She goes under the name of Portia Masters." There is a pause as if Roger expects Mitchell to recognise his daughter's name. He does, vaguely. "I'm hoping we can capitalise as much as possible on your sudden success, so the sooner we do this the better. Maybe we could meet up with a view to getting things in motion asap?"

"Er yeah, definitely," Mitchell now raises a thumb at Frank, who sits further back in his chair and stares at the bare ceiling. "How about, now?" says Roger. The conversation finishes after arrangements are made.

"He's meeting me in an hour outside the rail station. Wanna come Frank?" Frank gets up from his chair despite his earlier reservations. The likelihood of a concert and getting paid for what he actually enjoys, begins to feel like a reality.

While on the phone with Roger, Mitchell finds he has received three text messages. One from Maisie who has a shift at Enrico's later. He still has very little battery life in his phone, in fact it is almost dead. The effect of the coke he took earlier is also beginning to wear off and he does not want to go to Maisie's house without her being present.

There is another message that reads: *Congratulations on your performance last night on Top Vox. Just to let you know we can make excellent considerations for celebrity singers. And due to their high profile we can always ascertain their whereabouts. May we suggest you get in touch NOW for our unbeatable deals.*

Our special delivery service has many benefits which, if taken up, can outweigh the all too real disappointment and upset of the alternatives. Mitchell has to read the message again. He wonders what on earth someone is trying to sell him. He then ponders what the *alternatives* might be. Are these dealers already on to him and are they too, like the press, following him? However, he realises national television and sell-out shows at large venues are one thing, a local concert is another. Or is it? Mitchell wonders if they will even get to know about this. He tries to dismiss the message as being from someone who is probably just plain mad.

There is, however also a text which cancels all the fears contained in the previous one. It reads: *Hi Mitchell, Sorry I was not able to be on the panel last night. Just watched your performance on YouTube. I have to say you have a most remarkable talent and hopefully, one day we may work together. Have you any concerts coming up? I would love to see you. XL.*

After he reads the text the phone begins to perform its own death rattle. "Shit, you'll never guess what Frank," says Mitchell who chucks his phone onto the seat he has no use for. "What is it Mitchell?"

"Only just had a message from my biggest fucking hero, XL."

"Oh," says Frank with a faint voice. "What, does he want? To sign you up or something and have you on his label?"

"Don't know but he says he was really impressed with me last night and wants to see me perform live."

"Well we'd better hope this concert will do the trick, hey Mitchell?" says Frank in a more hopeful tone as he heads towards his front door.

Mitchell reads another text from Maisie. *Anyone you might bump into from the press tell them to come to Enrico's at five pm.*

167

XxxxxM

"Enrico's Bistro" says Mitchell to the girl still standing outside. She says nothing, only reaches for her phone and, at last, departs.

Chapter 18

Frank stops proceeding any further into the Masters' porch as soon as he sees Portia - this time without sun hat or shades - playing host by holding the door open for himself and Mitchell. In this suspended moment, a quick glance between Frank and Portia seals a tacit agreement. This time they both know how they have met before. They both know it is best not to mention it. Mitchell, as soon as he receives Portia's smile also pauses. He knows full well that if Maisie was with him she would be following every movement of his eyes. They continue into the house and Portia closes the door firmly behind them.

"Hello Mitchell" says Vicky, ushering them into the lounge. Roger is standing. He offers Mitchell and Frank his hand but says no more except "You can both sit down, seats are free." Light refreshments are agreed and Portia becomes housekeeper. "The moment you appeared on the box last night I said I'm sure I've seen him before," says Vicky Masters pointing towards a TV screen large enough to suit the purposes of a small cinema. "Yes, I'm sure I've seen you somewhere else. Your face, seeing you now in the flesh, rings quite a loud bell," says Vicky. Mitchell wonders if the memory card in her brain still stores the incident with the girl she nearly knocked over. "Really?" he says, taking advantage of the vastness of the living room There appears to be so much to see, allowing him to avoid Vicky's inquisitive gaze. "Well, I've certainly seen your daughter before – on her online album, Mrs Masters." Mitchell sits on their enormous sofa. Though there is so much space, he realises there is not so much to look at.

Frank takes considerable interest in the grand piano behind the sofa. In the background he can hear the radio in the kitchen playing Mozart's catalogue aria. "Anyway, whatever Mitchell, we thought you were fantastic last night," says Vicky.

"And put that dreadful Darius in his place. You're going places," says Portia carrying in a tray of china. "Thanks. Soz - what's your name?" says Mitchell pretending not to know.

"Excuse me, I think I heard Mitchell being mentioned," says Frank who has been listening to the radio rendition of the Mozart blaring from the kitchen. It finishes and the radio announcer says: *The look on Darius's face. He was certainly not a happy bunny. Anyway today is the birthday of a certain Miles Smith in Tunbridge Wells who's nine today and he wants us to play the end of the William Tell Overture...*

"There we are, as you can see, they're talking about you on national radio. And here's some refreshments, thanks Portia." says Roger as Portia now brings in a pot of tea and another of coffee. "We must move fast before everyone forgets about you," says Roger.

"Yes, we definitely must," says Portia with a smile Mitchell does not fail to notice.

Mitchell has almost forgotten the accusations levelled at him earlier by a member of the press. He is still elated by the email from XL. His head keeps replaying the words from his idol: *Remarkable talent and we must see if we can work together.*

"What do you think then Mitchell?" says Roger.

"Yeah, okay, of course. So, when are we going to do this?" says Mitchell.

"I think if we move fast, two weeks is not out of the question," says Roger. Frank looks at Roger and wonders why he wants to promote Mitchell. "Can I ask how much you might be paying him?"

"Ah, I take it you're his manager then as well as accompanist?"

"Not at all, just interested to know."

"Okay, we thought maybe a percentage of the door takings, obviously split between Mitchell, yourself and my daughter. Mitchell and yourself will get the bigger slice of course," says Roger.

"I think, unless you could give Mitchell some kind of financial interest in advance, maybe he would be better advised to arrange his own concert," says Frank who surprises his protégé. Mitchell has never seen his ex-music teacher being so assertive. Vicky coughs. "Maybe, though you ought to remember there is a lot to organise in such a short space of time: venue, publicity, front of house, refreshments at the interval, maybe even a licence will be required."

"Yes I appreciate all that. I used to organise my own concerts once upon a time. But how much are you going to give Mitchell?"

"As my wife Vicky said, we will be dealing with all the logistics and publicity and all you and Mitchell have to do is turn up and sing...oh and play the piano of course. So maybe a sixty-forty door split after expenses have been deducted?" says Roger. Frank was hoping he could secure an advance so that he and Mitchell could take days off (yes days off from the DDJ – the dreaded day job) to rehearse. "Well if you can't provide any interest up front, maybe an eighty-twenty split might be more appropriate?"

"Well perhaps you might want to organise it yourself and take the lot. But as we know, TV fame these days, unless it is sustained quickly, soon vanishes. At least our daughter has a local following having sung concerts in the area over the years. As my wife said, we are not inexperienced." says Roger lifting up his mobile to add. "I know exactly who to call as soon as you agree to this."

"So how many did she draw at her last concert?" says Frank.

"It was a *respectable* audience," say Vicky stressing the word respectable as if Frank might have been slightly too personal.

Mitchell, throughout the meeting has been giving Portia surreptitious glances. He notices her composure - in only a moment - has gone from a face of confidence to one of uncertainty. Mitchell wants the concert to go ahead whatever the deal, as he is more than eager to inform XL he can come and see him. It is obvious that Portia, with her hands clasped as if in prayer, wants it too. Frank does not notice this.

"Look I'd be quite happy to do this," says Mitchell. "If you'd asked me only a few months ago, I'd have thought you were fucking mad." Portia laughs at Mitchell's sudden expletive. "But," says Mitchell turning to Portia "I'm well up for doing it for whatever."

Frank looks at Mitchell. Not the first time, disappointment overlays across his face. Being in the luxurious Masters' residence, he has temporarily forgotten about having to return to the far less comfortable world of the classroom tomorrow. He feels Mitchell is allowing a good bargaining position to slip through his hands. Does he not equally dread the thought of going back to the building site? Maybe the work he does is hard but at least it probably only leaves him knackered not demoralised. Frank turns to Roger. He is a person Frank imagines gets what he wants, exactly how he wants it – as proved just now. Do they all know Frank needs Mitchell more than Mitchell needs him? Who will accompany Portia?

"Can I ask who will be accompanying Portia at this concert?" says Frank.

"It will be her singing teacher Mrs English," says Roger who seems to be able to read Frank's mind and might as well have gone on to say *No you will not be able to get any extra by charging a fee as our daughter's accompanist.* "So, if everyone is happy, shall we exchange phone numbers? I'm still old school when it comes to certain matters." Whilst uttering these words, Roger reaches for a writing pad and a pen and waves them in the air to prove just how old school he is, as the others get out their mobiles. Mitchell sees his mobile is nearly out of charge again, so waits for the pad while he watches Portia, protecting her exquisitely manicured nails by using her knuckles to put his and Frank's numbers into her mobile.

"Would anyone like another drink? Tea, coffee, something stronger perhaps?" says Vicky. Mitchell wishes he could say *yes* but remembers he promised he would pop into *Enrico's* before Maisie ended her shift.

As Roger escorts them back into Hassledon, Mitchell thinks what Maisie might be saying or has already said to the press. The cavernous cocoon of the Masters' house took his mind off the very real dangers of the publication of false allegations about him. He begins to wonder if *Top Vox* is involved in some kind of mutual vendetta against him for not playing the game their way. But then he remembers how paranoid coke can sometimes make him. Will Maisie have said enough to get him out of danger? He nearly told the Masters about this but did not want to make them think they were about to be involved with the promotion of an alleged sex offender.

At Enrico's they are having an unusually busy Sunday afternoon. On her way there earlier, Maisie made a detour to both Mitchell's parents' homes and everywhere else she guessed the press might be trying to hound Mitchell - including Frank's, where she was surprised to find neither Frank nor Mitchell. She presumed the press may have beaten her to it and decided to disappear somewhere. But where?

Maisie then asked her boss, Brady, if she could spend the first fifteen minutes of her shift doing kitchen work so the press would have the chance to congregate first. As his employee promised an extra boost in the sales of teas, coffees and snacks, Brady was happy enough to swap roles with Maisie and do some waiting instead.

Maisie is true to her word and her boss watches more and more people come into his bistro. He has never seen his tables so adorned with tools of prime entry gossip such as tablets, laptops, notepads, cameras and mobiles. Many of this sudden deluge of customers seem to know each other as they shout across tables. In fact the noise becomes so great that Brady has difficulty hearing their orders. Then the whole of his bistro goes quieter as Maisie appears from the kitchen. One of the press says *It's her*. Someone taps a glass as if a best man is about to make a speech. In this case it is their best woman who soon gets flashed by a couple of cameras.

Maisie says "Welcome everyone. Thanks everyone for

coming. Hope you are enjoying the wonderful hospitality of *Enrico's*. As promised, I will read my statement." There is coughing from the audience as if some are clearing the air for the young girl standing at the front.

"Yes, I have heard horrendous and quite frankly ridiculous claims of my boyfriend being a guilty party to something as serious as rape. But the big mystery which started on social media in the town is now, it seems, about to go national. So, before you all turn into complete melts. I suppose you are all asking the question: gossip aside, about a video which I have not even seen - what actually did happen?" People are holding up cameras and phones in anticipation of the answer. "Well, I'm sorry to disappoint you all but it was, a big drum roll please...it was me. The only thing I regret is the fact we did it in such an inappropriate place – a music practice room in a school. That is as bad as the whole episode gets and believe me the humiliation that me and my family received as a result is enough. So, if you would be decent enough to put a full stop on the whole thing, it would be most appreciated." There are murmurs of *Thought so* or *What a waste of time* or *He's not that famous yet.*

"Excuse me, I didn't quite catch your name." Brady is now standing by Maisie's side feeling he ought to take on the role as Maisie's press manager. "Iris from Le Gen'd Magazine."

"Maisie Moore," says Brady.

"Why did you not admit to it in the first place?"

"Because when it first happened it was a massive embarrassment for my family."

"So Mitchell's fifteen minutes of fame makes it fine does it?"

"In a word, yes," says Maisie who hears the odd mumble.

She watches the press sip the last of their drinks and start putting the tools of their trade away. "Any more questions?" There is one more from the woman who had been standing outside Frank's flat. "Yes. Was there no teacher present nearby when you two, you know, did it?"

"Yes there was, but it was our fault for taking advantage of him. He was busy coaching a student at the time."

"But your safety was his responsibility. What else could have been going on? A terrorist might have walked in under his nose." Maisie clucks her tongue while other reporters continue to pack away their things.

"Why don't you ask the same question at those schools with mass shootings in the US? There were plenty of staff around at those places. Surely they could have intervened? No, this was under Hassledon School rules. We contravened those rules. Mitchell and myself were the wrong ones. Remember it takes two to tango in this case – not three which would include the teacher. Is that all then?"

"Just one more. Any idea what Mitchell is going to do next, now he has turned down his coaching opportunities?"

"I can't tell you right now, but I'm sure you'll be hearing in due course. Watch this space as they say. Any other questions?" There is silence. "Good, thanks for coming. Anyone staying, I'll take your orders shortly as plain Maisie the waitress." Maisie immediately takes her apron from her boss.

Chapter 19

The Norman tower of St Augustine's Church rises above the red rooftops of the estate surrounding it. Next to the church are former farm workers' cottages and a pub dating back to the times of Charles I. Next to this pub is the rectory from which Bunny Lawford and her parents witnessed - to their great disdain - what they called the *bulldozerisation* of their world. After campaigning vigorously to preserve their village, Bunny's parents lost their battle. They died in the late sixties, only a few years after the first stone for the new town of Hassledon was laid.

Bunny, the sole beneficiary of the rectory, is in the church making final touches to her flower arrangement. It is one of the many duties which she does for the church, and like all the others, she takes it *very* seriously. Her mood brightens when she realises there will be a concert tonight. Then, choosing not to bother walking to the vestry for a towel, she dries her hands instead on her inevitable tartan skirt.

In a corner by the main entrance is the small stack of cardboard boxes Vicky Masters delivered the night before. They contain a few hundred copies of tonight's concert programme. Bunny decides she has enough authority to tear open one of the boxes and allow herself a *mischievous* peep at one of programmes. The name Margaret English brings a smile to her face – she is such a *lovely* pianist and does so much to help all those wanting to sing what Bunny deems *proper* music. For Bunny, modern music goes as far as Vaughan Williams. But she can tolerate certain pieces by Benjamin Britten because decades ago her mother once provided hospitality for Britten and his partner Peter Pears. The name Britten also gives her yet another opportunity to roll her rrrs – the most characteristic sound of her speaking voice.

It is nearly two in the afternoon and Bunny goes to unlock the door opening into the vestry towards the back of the church. This is to give the evening's performers somewhere to lodge all their paraphernalia and access to the basic kitchen facilities. The unlocking of the grand piano is another duty she undertakes with the utmost seriousness.

First in, as always, is Margaret English. "Oh Mrs English, how lovely to see you," says Bunny as the two embrace. "Hello Bunny," says Margaret going straight to the clothes rail in the white-walled vestry, to hang up her evening attire. "Can't wait to see what you have zipped up in there. Is it another of your own fabulous creations?"

"If you really must know, it's the one I wore last concert and the concert before that," says Margaret.

"Oh. Well, the piano was tuned only a couple of days ago Margaret. Maybe you might want to see how it sounds," says Bunny. Margaret ignores Bunny and goes out again to her car. She returns with music under one arm and a carrier with the logo emblazoned in cartoon fonts *A Bag for the World*. "Ah, your famous survival bag," says Bunny.

"Yes, my bag," says Margaret with a sigh, depositing her pile of music and bag on the vestry table. Her survival bag contains nothing more than her own personal china cup wrapped in tissue, a flask of tea, a small Tupperware box and her mobile phone.

Margaret goes to the piano, perched on a carpeted platform in the nave, only a few inches higher than where the congregation sits. She starts to play her favourite warm up piece: JS Bach's Prelude No 1. "Oh Margaret, I love that piece but when I hear it, do you know what?" Margaret ignores Bunny. "I always yearn for someone to sing that wonderful melody Gounod wrote for it." Bunny tries to hum Gounod's tune which prompts Margaret to stop playing.

"The piano's fine," says Margaret heading back to the vestry. Walking towards the main entrance of the church, Bunny repositions a table which she considered perfectly positioned only half an hour ago. She takes out a few programmes and places them in a neat pile, square on the table. Outside, she hears chatting very close to the main door - in a parlance which sounds quite foreign to Bunny Lawford. It belongs to the street or to the workmen who fixed her rectory roof recently. The large metal door knob squeaks when someone on the other side tries to open the heavy church door. A loud hammering follows. Bunny is alarmed. "Go to the door round the back," she calls.

Mrs English is placing music on the piano whilst checking its order with a list she wrote out some days ago. She starts to play the introduction to Cherubino's aria from Mozart's *The Marriage of Figaro*.

"There's some people outside. They seem rather impatient, I'll see what they want...Oh. Hello, can I help you?" says Bunny as she sees Mitchell and Frank walk into the main church. "If you're wanting the jumble sale it's in the hall next door but not this Saturday, the Saturday next." Mitchell has his hood up with his hands in his pockets.

"Sorry Madam but we're performing here this evening, unless we have the wrong venue," says Frank. Margaret English turns.

"So you, I presume are Mitchell," she says, pausing from arranging her music. "Yeah," says Mitchell. Bunny Lawford is confused by Mrs English appearing to know who they are. "My pupil Portia has told me all about you. Now don't worry, it's all good."

"I'm not worried," says Mitchell with a smirk. Bunny raises her eyebrows at Mitchell's general attitude. "Sorry, and you must be here to accompany... actually I know you. You're Frank Perry the pianist, aren't you?" says Margaret.

"Peters, yes," says Frank.

"Sorry yes, Peters of course. Wow. I feel quite honoured. Saw you play, must be some years ago now, a great concert. I'd have thought you would be playing somewhere rather larger than here."

"You'd be surprised - and you are?" says Frank.

"Margaret English, I'm a local singing teacher." Frank holds out his hand but his wet fish handshake surprises Margaret. Inside, he is seething with jealousy. She, with her precise diction and commanding demeanour probably keeps her invariably well brought up private pupils on their toes. He heard her play the Mozart earlier. Frank's verdict? To be born with mediocre talent but an attractive face can provide a person with a more than tolerable existence. He imagines she is part of a couple like those who made up the core of his audience when he was a full-time recitalist.

Franks sits down in a pew and curses his wretched soul. Why

did he have to be born with the sensitivities obligatory for the true artist? The sort of sensitivities which at the same time made him terrified of his own audience – the people who put him there, but made him so paranoid he ended up resorting to dangerous substances such as alcohol to deal with them. As a result, he forfeited other faculties and damaged the vital body parts which allowed it all to happen in the first place. Frank hears Margaret go through the Mozart again. Her interpretation is annoyingly close to sounding amazing, but mediocrity won't allow its true wonders to fully flow from the page. At present it is not as if there are too many notes, just too many plain ones.

Mitchell parks himself in a front row pew. He has been checking his phone all week to see if XL has answered his message about tonight's concert. Disgruntled, he returns to his *KillaTeds* game. Both Mrs English and Ms Lawford turn towards him with alarm as the noise of teddies being killed sounds like babies crying. Then after some ominous laughter, the start of Wagner's Prelude to Act Three of *Lohengrin* turns the heads of both Margaret and Bunny again. "What is that you've got?" says Bunny. Mitchell doesn't answer, he is busy trying to get a teddy bear over another assault course, this time in a hell-like setting. The red of the screen gives his face a gruesome glow. But the teddies begin to build up their defence by winning as much honey from the enemy as possible. The honey oozes love on all their adversaries and weakens them. The glow on Mitchell's face now turns a radiant yellow.

"Would you like to try the piano Frank?" says Margaret. "Sorry, I'll remove my music so you have space for yours?"

"It's okay. Hopefully I'll remember what I'm performing this evening." Margaret lifts an eyebrow to Bunny Lawford who replies with a brief nod. Frank plays the opening theme to Schumann's *Papillons*. The music accompanies Maisie as she glides into the church and goes straight to Mitchell, the couple embrace and begin to snog. Bunny Lawford and Margaret English look at each other. Their brows now crease into disapproval. Frank watches the couple too. He reacts by changing the music to a more sombre piece later in the Schumann cycle. He hammers out its bare octaves - reflecting his frustration for an emotionally austere existence. Silence.

"I've been here before, years ago," says Maisie "Mum used to be in the Hassledon Choral Society. I was only young and fell asleep during a concert but I do remember waking up to this marvellous buffet at the end. It was laid out on tables all along this aisle," says Maisie waving her arm outside the pew.

"Indeed, it was a veritable feast," says Bunny. "Shame the choir finished. Lack of tenors. Much prefer Handel and Mendelssohn to what those awful pop choirs sing at what they call *gigs*. The only gig I knew was a horse drawn one my uncle kept on his farm. Nowadays those forty- voiced pop choirs only manage to make the sound of four. Mind you they have nothing much to sing in the first place - baby this and baby that," says Bunny.

The mention of food makes Masie hungry. She would often have a snack after finishing her shift at *Enrico's* but today she wanted to be with Mitchell before *she* arrives. She gets out her phone to order a takeaway.

"Ready Mitchell?" says Frank.

"Hold on," says Mitchell nearly managing to get another Ted to safety. To hurry Mitchell, Frank starts the introduction to *Sylvia*. "Yes please Maisie, prawn curry, chips with plenty of vinegar." Having relinquished himself from *KillaTeds*,

Mitchell checks his messages again. Nothing. He starts to sing. Maisie loves what she hears. It is the voice which won him her mother's approval, the left hand of Schubert's flowing piano accompaniment under Mitchell's gliding vocals is answered by the right hand echoing in agreement with the voice with the words:

Holy fair and wise is she
  The heavens such grace did lend her
  That she might admired be.

The whole song creates a heavenly communion between Maisie and Mitchell. They finish. "That was incredible. In all my years..." says Bunny but her words are interrupted by kerfuffle coming from the vestry. "Actually, I worked out last night, for Portia's last concert, she was singing at a rate and return of 0.03 pence per note..." says Roger as his voice is heard booming from the walls of the vestry. "I sincerely hope tonight..."

"Roger, there's people in the church who can hear you," says Vicky. Roger stops talking as he sees people have already arrived and are rehearsing. "Sorry," says Roger proceeding into the church. He parades himself in front of Mitchell and Frank, a metal cash box tucked under his arm and a carrier bag in each hand. He pauses in his tracks to give the performers a nod then continues to the back of the church. Vicky follows behind carrying a white cardboard box with *Wines of Chile* stamped on it. Portia carries nothing, but stops. She sits down in a pew the other side of the aisle from where Maisie is sitting, smiles and nods at Maisie, and then Mitchell.

"Hello," says Frank. The greetings are returned.

"Don't mind us says Vicky, heading out with her husband to

get more wine boxes.

"Maisie, this is Portia," says Mitchell, gesturing towards both girls. Maisie smiles at Portia who returns the gesture with a brisk wave. She cannot decide whether to move over and sit with Maisie or stay put. She solves the dilemma by getting up to help her mother and father lift more wine boxes from the back of her father's truck.

"Mitchell – we really must go through my piece if you don't mind. I've altered it slightly since we last looked at it," says Frank, reaching into his bag for the only music he needs for the evening. The opening is discordant but resolves itself as the vocals enter. The piece has boundless energy and pushes the capabilities and sonorities of the piano to the limit. The music unsettles Maisie, who notices how Portia seems to keep holding Mitchell's attention a little too long each time she looks at him. The music stops and Portia applauds Mitchell. Maisie joins Portia, ensuring the needle on her clapometer reads higher than Portia's. She also adds cheers for good measure. "Okay, Mitchell. If you're happy, I am," says Frank. Rather than going straight back to Maisie, Mitchell surrenders himself to the praises of Portia who walks onto the stage in preparation for her rehearsal with Margaret. Maisie folds her arms. She is not impressed with Mitchell who seems to be endlessly checking his phone.

Margaret gets up and heads towards the piano. "Portia, I don't know if we ought to do *Sylvia*, unless the audience wouldn't mind hearing it twice in one evening," says Margaret.

"We could replace it with *Gute Nacht*," suggests Frank.

"Shall we ask Mitchell what he thinks?" says Portia looking at Mitchell who is back in Maisie's arms.

"Yeah definitely," says Mitchell who hears Maisie cluck

her tongue which he knows is a sure sign of his girl getting annoyed. She takes her arms off Mitchell and, shaking her knee says "Excuse me Mitchell, but who's gig is this?" Portia turns away from Maisie's glare by turning the erection of a music stand into a puzzle. "*Gute Nacht*, Maisie, is loads better. *Sylvia* is just lovey dovey pap piece. Well that's what Frank thinks. Right Frank?" says Mitchell.

"What?" says Frank.

"But I love those words, Midge, they're from Shakespeare's *Two Gentlemen of Verona*. We did it in English and it's on my mum's Darius Dalloway album."

"Darius Dalloway?" Margaret turns in horror "Even more reason not to do it, bloody cheapskate.

"No Maisie. As you said, whose gig is it?"

"I wonder Portia, if you ought to do a song associated with that awful Dalloway. So many think the performers actually compose their material," says Margaret.

"Oh...alright then. You win; do it," says Maisie.

Mitchell returns to his phone and absorbs himself in his *KillaTeds* game. The takeaway Maisie ordered earlier has still not arrived. She decides to go and see if the delivery person is lost, they may never have delivered to the church before. Maisie considers it safe to go outside when the piano starts its staccato bass once again and she sees Portia fully engaged in her rehearsal - therefore not able to cavort with Mitchell – for the time being.

Despite the rehearsing going on, the tranquillity of the church's interior contrasts with the noise of the traffic outside and the busy pavement carrying the afternoon crowd. Maisie spots some of Mitchell's old associates passing. She knows one of them, Elton by name. He is with two others passing a spliff between them. They recognise her. "Maisie, saw your Mitchell on the box a couple of weeks ago. Has he had a brain transplant or summat? Can't believe it, watching him singing opera on TV but then he turns down all them judges. Effing hilarious! Now that was more like the geezer Mitchell I used to know," says Elton. The other two nod in agreement.

"Well, do you know what?" says Maisie.

"What?" say all three at once.

"He's in this church," says Maisie raising her thumb behind her. "Getting ready for a concert tonight. I'm sure he won't mind if you three pop in and say hi," she adds pointing to the vestry door which she'd left ajar. "Think we might do that." The boys head towards the door. They stop at the threshold as they hear the voice of Portia coming from inside the church. They begin to mimic her in cod operatic tones. Elton turns to Maisie and she waves her hand at them as if to say *Go on in* but they remain by the door. Maisie meanwhile spots a moped. The takeaways have arrived. She pays the courier and goes to meet the youths still by the vestry door.

The sound of Portia from inside the church stops and shortly Bunny Lawford appears at the vestry door looking every bit the headmistress. "Excuse me," she says as she pulls on the panic bar. "Er Mitchell's bird Maisie said we could come and say hello to him," says Elton.

"Well, I'm sorry, whatever his *bird* says, you can't just barge your way in here. What did you say your name was?" says Bunny pulling the panic bar again. Maisie appears. Bunny looks at the white plastic bag she is carrying and is pondering what it might contain. The only takeaway Bunny has had is fish and chips wrapped in white paper. "*She* can enter but may I ask the rest of you to respectfully *wait*." Elton stands aside but as soon as Maisie enters he darts in through the door before Bunny slams it on the foot of one of Elton's colleagues. "You fucking cow" he says.

"Well Moooove then," says Bunny tugging on the door. The foot is released and Bunny closes the door.

"Mitchell me ol' mucker, how are you?" says Elton, entering the church with Maisie. Margaret stops playing and stands. Portia has never encountered the likes of Elton face to face. She watches him from behind her music-stand and waits.

"Put it there Elton," says Mitchell as he holds out his hand to give Elton a high five. "Hey, you coming tonight?"

"Nah, not my thing Midge," says Elton as he puts his feet up on the shelf where hymn and prayers books are put. "Put those feet down *now* you and show some respect, please," says Bunny. Elton puts his leg down and leans over to address Frank who is sitting the other side of Mitchell. "Hey, it's Peters. How ya doing?" says Elton waving his hand at him. Frank ignores him. "After you left, do you know what we called you?"

"Dread to think," says Frank under his breath.

"Pimpy Peters because everyone thought you were running a knocking shop in your music department." Elton makes a guttural laugh. Mitchell says nothing, just raises his hands as if to say *not guilty*.

"Excuse me, if you're going to stay here, may I ask you to be quiet, and get rid of that," says Bunny pointing at Elton's spliff.

"Alright love, keep your knickers on." Maisie, who now sits herself next to Elton, tries her best to stop sniggering and notices Portia is suitably horrified. "Sorry. Any more words like that and I won't mess around - I'll get the police to remove you."

"No, but I'm Mitchell's mate, aren't I Mitchell?" There is silence. Mitchell looks at Portia scowling at Elton. "Aren't I? Come on you cunt, admit it," says Elton.

"Right that's it. Such foul language in a place of worship – I'm going to have to ask you to leave, *now*," says Bunny getting out her mobile phone and dialling. Elton looks at Bunny, then Portia and finally Margaret whose reaction is to look away and turn over the page of music she pretends to be looking at. He gives one final glance at Mitchell who makes no reaction.

"Okay, I'll fuck off then. Mitchell you're mixing with some right stuck-up fuckers these days. I feel sorry for you man." Elton makes his way along the pew and blows a kiss at Portia causing her recoil, then leaves. Mitchell says nothing while Maisie cannot resist smiling to herself. "By the way, you'll be pleased to know, we've already sold eighty tickets in advance," says Roger to break the silence and justify Mitchell's presence.

Margaret begins the introduction to the Schubert again. They are interrupted by the sound of the door to the vestry being kicked shut with such force it makes a candle in the corner of the church flicker itself out.

At last Portia and Margaret proceed with the Schubert. Maisie moves herself closer to Mitchell. She takes out the takeaway from a very crisp plastic bag and makes no effort to lessen the noise this makes. She opens up the sealed carton and sniffs at the contents as if it is the most wonderful aroma ever. Portia's expression is not good as she experiences the potent odour of prawn. Maisie smiles to see Portia wince as she tries to waft the smell away while singing. Margaret stops playing and waves her hand in front of her mouth and nose "Excuse me, do you mind eating that in the vestry you two.

I'm sorry but it really is quite off-putting," says Margaret. Maisie is pleased with the way Portia agrees with her teacher, grimacing at the sight of Mitchell's takeaway.

"I've never known anyone to eat such...food in church."

"Ah, but as I said earlier there used to be a buffet down that aisle after concerts," says Maisie with her mouth full which she knows very well is not the best etiquette but is keen to get her point over.

"Actually, it was consumed *after* concerts," says Bunny.

Margaret and Portia decide they have rehearsed enough. Bunny Lawford sees Frank about to leave. "Oh Frank, well this rehearsal was not without its moments but I didn't get the chance earlier to I say I found your piano playing marvellous, absolutely marvellous and I really look forward to tonight. Which hopefully should go okay."

"Yes, hopefully it will and thank you" says Frank. Margaret leaves the stage looking at Bunny who quickly goes over to her too. "Oh, and Margaret, you sounded the usual very good too."

Mitchell goes out and makes a call. Having taken time off from work over the last few days to learn Frank's music, he hopes The Raza Man can extend his generosity – at least on his terms.

He ends the call. He can.

Chapter 20

Checking his phone for around the thirtieth time in the last two hours, Mitchell finally receives the text he has been waiting for: *Hi Mitchell, hope 2 C U 2nt. Can u put XL + 1 on the door pls? Hope 2 get down bt if cant will send sum1. Have a gd1.* Mitchell hands Maisie the phone and can only hear a faint *Wow* while he walks towards the back of the church.

"Roger, have we a guest list tonight?" says Mitchell. Silence. Roger pauses and looks at Mitchell. "Guest list? says Roger "Where's the party?"

"The guest list for people I want to let in free."

"Er, I thought we were out to make as much on the door as we can tonight. So, are you suggesting we give tickets away free?" says Roger knocking a bunch of tickets into a neat pile and placing them far away from Mitchell's reach. "No, I've just had a text from XL and he's asked about a guest list."

"Who on earth's XL?

"Who's XL? Are you telling me you've not heard of XL? He's only one of the best fucking producers alive."

"Er language, if you don't mind Mitchell. Look I don't doubt what you say about this person XS.

"XL"

"Sorry XL, but it's up to you." Roger unlocks his briefcase, takes out a clean sheet of A4 paper and places it firmly on the table. He writes *Guest List* at the top, underlines it, and swerves the sheet round "Here." Mitchell takes the pen from him. Mitchell writes XL plus 1. "Thank you," says Roger. He then folds the sheet and puts it in the cash box as if it was an IOU.

"Everyone ready? says Bunny Lawford turning from Vicky and Portia who have already poured out several glasses of wine on a table opposite Roger. He gives Bunny the nod to pull across the great bolt of the large entrance door to the church. "Right, here goes." She wears keys and chains on her person, like emblems of honour. They tell all who see her that she is the trustworthy one – a model of honesty. She opens the doors to a waiting queue. They do not look like the people Bunny usually welcomes to concerts at the church. These are generally younger and lack a certain decorum. A loud voice down the queue shouts "And about bloody time too." Bunny stands by the door with her arms folded and waits until she can detect an element of remorse. After a faint *sorry* she then steps aside to allow gangway.

Roger has never really dealt with physical cash. All his transactions have been strictly on paper. Notes and coins are alien. Having been cashless for so long they feel like accessories to a relearning curve. After only the first few ticket sales, he wonders if he will have enough change in the float for the rest of the evening. Now he wishes he had made the price on the door a nice easy round number. He wishes Vicky or someone could go and get him some more change.

Mitchell returns to the vestry where he sees Maisie sitting on a dowdy armchair in the corner by the sink. An old gas water heater hisses away above it. Margaret English is retrieving the plastic lunch box she put in the fridge earlier. This is another reason she arrives at all concert rehearsals early – to bag fridge space, even before a single note is contemplated.

"Mitchell your phone's buzzing," says Maisie, handing the mobile back to Mitchell. The message says: *Hi Mitchell Seems like you've got a show in a church tonight. Good place to do some praying, I suppose. See you later.* Mitchell thinks maybe the message is a hoax from someone who has nothing to do with supplying anything except pranks. Jealous friends maybe? But the coke he has taken to lift his confidence now begins to raise paranoia. He wonders if maybe he could cancel the show and just let Portia have the whole night to herself. But then he would be letting himself and Frank down. He also remembers XL will be coming along. He decides to just keep himself within the company of others until he performs.

"Have you seen outside?" says Frank standing at the vestry door "There's quite a crowd. I imagine there'll be a good door tonight."

"They've come to see you," says Maisie as she gets up to hug Mitchell.

"That will make a change. At Portia's last concert we were performing only to a couple of dozen," says Margaret draining the last of her tea. "Sorry Frank, can you close the door please," says Mitchell – but he goes over to shut it himself. He returns to Maisie, flicking though a magazine she has picked up. She pauses to look at holiday ads. "Greece looks nice, don't you think so Midge?" says Maisie.

"Yeah great," says Mitchell.

"Don't sound too enthusiastic."

"Sorry, just thinking about tonight. Trying to remember my words."

"You'll be fine," says Frank suddenly realising this is his first concert since the night his performing career ended. So far this evening he has managed to abstain from alcohol and is pleased not to be the main focus of attention, yet he can still feel a certain buzz.

"Mitchell, I've got your dad and a couple of his friends at the door saying you'd let them in for free. Is this correct?" says Roger. Mitchell cannot decide if he should let them in. They are probably half drunk already. "Come on Mitchell, tell me. I've had to leave my wife and Portia to mind the door." Margaret looks up at Roger astonished.

"Oh, alright then, I suppose so," says Mitchell.

Roger leaves the vestry. Mitchell later follows him to see what the audience looks like. He takes a peep and sees the worst. His dad and his friends are sitting themselves down the front row. They are already taking cans of lager out of a bag and already nearby audience members are looking at them. *Where's security when you need it?* thinks Mitchell but then he looks at Les who he imagines could become a useful bouncer, if needed.

Portia and her mother head towards the vestry. On their way they are greeted by people they seem to know. One takes Portia by the arm, an elderly lady who looks into Portia's eyes as if she is seeing something very dear – is it her grandmother? At the front sitting near his dad and friends, Mitchell sees a rather large woman sitting with a younger girl, possibly her daughter. They are scoffing a family sized bag of crisps, knocking them back like solidified liquid. The woman stops in her feeding frenzy to point at Mitchell and nudge the younger girl. Mitchell retreats to the vestry.

As soon as Portia enters the vestry Maisie gets up from her

chair. She does not want to watch Portia reveal the no doubt fabulous frock concealed under her coat, but the force of vanity, like gravity anchors her by the chair. She can already see the eager eyes of Portia's teacher, Margaret, transfixed, even by the way her student removes her scarf, followed by the shaking of her hair - introducing tease. Maisie and Margaret are now equally captivated as Portia undoes her top coat button - slowly. Her teacher's eyes open wider, amplified by the reading glasses she dare not remove lest she misses the very first glimpse. Her pupil now turns to open her coat and puts it on a recalcitrant hanger. *It is a performance, make no mistake about that* thinks Maisie. At last, after a tantalizing pause, suspense is relieved for all watching. Portia turns to reveal a frock, a frock so stunning Margaret finds it hard to swallow. A frock Maisie wonders how many hours serving the tables at Enrico's it would take to afford. Vicky is proud to see on both Margaret and Maisie, the faces of envy.

✳✳✳✳✳✳✳✳✳✳✳✳✳✳✳✳

Portia lifts the skirt of her frock as she ascends to the stage. There is applause started by Vicky, standing behind seldom-used choir stalls. The clapping diminishes and then all goes quiet. Almost quiet. The mother and daughter at the front have finished their crisps and are moving straight on to dessert – popcorn. Portia turns to Margaret. Rising from the piano stool, Margaret stares in the direction of the sound of confection being scraped from buckets followed by a certain slurping noise. "Excuse me, may I ask those two at the front to refrain from whatever it is you are eating, it is most off-putting," she says, sitting down again to the accompaniment of mumbles from the audience. Margaret plays the swaggering introduction to the first song, Verdi's *Sicilia* then repeats it *piano* making it quiet enough for her to distinguish a burp coming directly from her side of the audience. Initially she chooses to ignore it. Her husband also makes such noises.

Portia starts singing, not wanting to halt the performance any further; Margaret then glowers in the direction of the burp. Then a nearby foot starts tapping. This annoys her even more. She is trying to follow Portia but the tapping is so pronounced it becomes her metronome. She turns, this time to give daggers towards the source but then hears the words *More like school this. Shall we come back when Mitchell is on?* A few people shuffle to the end of the pew saying *Sorry* and *Excuse me* as they go. A phone goes off playing the chorus to *YMCA*. Margaret finds the whole situation ridiculous and stops playing. She has had enough. At last, silence. *Is this audience the product of fame on social tedia or whatever they call it?* she thinks, about to get up again. But deliberate and business-like steps can be heard coming down the aisle. Bunny Lawford appears and with a halting gesture towards Margaret, takes to the stage. "Ladies and Gentlemen, boys and girls, please may you take into consideration this concert is not supported by any amplification..."

"I wonder what support she has – I guess 44 double G," says Ryan's friend. Bunny stops to see Ryan sniggering at the remark while others sitting nearby also start to laugh. "Maybe I should address myself to *very* young boys as well," says Bunny, now headmistress. "Anyway, as I was saying, please bear in mind this is a concert *not* a pop concert and maybe a few of you might owe a tacit apology to the *majority* of you here..." Bunny pauses again. She looks down at Ryan and his friend who are now in a fit of giggles. Ryan manages to regain his composure but his friend stomps out of the church. Bunny watches his every move. "I apologise that I didn't make announcements regarding house rules and etiquette before we started. Just please bear in mind these performers and others have been working hard to bring you this concert tonight. So, show your appreciation in the way I'm sure you know how. Thank You." There is a ripple of applause and *Hear Hear* mainly from the more senior voices in the audience. The Verdi starts again. Margaret and Portia make it to the end. The audience have, by now, become quite familiar with the tune which ends to great applause – and a ring pull from Ryan's friend Les.

After half an hour, despite performing in front of an audience she could hardly deem perfect, Portia finishes her set. She returns to the vestry into the arms of her mother who tells her a certain person thought she was amazing and is going to buy ten of her CDs as Christmas presents for all her friends and family. "She asked if you could sign them." This cheers up Portia. Margaret receives a hug too from Vicky as she enters the vestry. "You look like you've just got through a skirmish," says Vicky to Margaret.

"It was more like doing battle than a concert," says Margaret, fishing in her survival bag for her flask of tea, surprised to have forgotten she finished it earlier.

Bunny enters with "Many bravos to you two. You managed in the end to tame the wild beasts of an audience. Consider it a triumph," she says, walking straight to a cupboard which she unlocks with one of the keys on her chain. She takes out a small bottle of whisky. "Would you like some in there?" she asks, pointing at Margaret's tea cup. "No thanks. I'll be driving home after this because my husband is probably getting as drunk as some of the audience right now. The odour coming from those *blokes* at the front is a reminder of what emanates from my husband most evenings. I guess he'll be singing along to Wotan right now," says Margaret. Her smile is restored as Vicky gives her a roll of notes which she slips into her survival bag. "Thank you, Vicky. I feel I certainly earned this evening." Frank looks at her. "Try being a supply teacher in a secondary school. What you experienced tonight was like the height of civility compared to the average classroom," he says, watching Margaret get up. "Oh dear, it must be absolutely unbearable," she says, struggling with her coat.

"Oh no, Poor Roger. He'll hate having to do the bar all on his own," says Vicky rushing out.

Bunny turns to Mitchell snuggling in the armchair with Maisie's arm around him. Maisie knows he cannot stop looking at Portia whose performing attire takes the notion of power dressing to a new level. She kisses Mitchell as if her mouth will douse the flames of desire she can detect in his eyes. "Sorry Mitchell, maybe you would prefer it if we women vacate this room so you can change." Mitchell gives no answer except for a slight look of confusion on his face.

"What? No, I'm fine thanks, all set," says Mitchell to Bunny. The question of attire is the least of his concerns. Will XL or his associates be in the audience or, thinking of the recent texts he has received, might a very different bunch be present?

"So you're telling me you're going to perform looking like *that*?" says Bunny in a raised voice.

"Yeah." Bunny Lawford's face is incredulous at the sight of Mitchell's outfit. He looks more like he might be involved in some sort of sporting event rather than a concert. She turns to Frank and her face straightens. At least he is dressed in jacket and trousers, not tracksuit bottoms like Mitchell. "Would you like me to go out and remind everyone of our housekeeping procedures again and perhaps a basic reminder on how to behave at a concert?"

"If you like," says Frank.

Chapter 21

"**I**t's going to be fine," says Frank again, watching Mitchell embedded in the armchair, cuddling into Maisie. It is Mitchell's first proper concert performance ever. He has never headlined before and thinks of Portia who just sang for half an hour yet has had lessons for several years. Mitchell has had only a handful. *Am I really ready?* Mitchell wonders. But XL is still on his mind and to Maisie's annoyance he cannot stop checking his mobile. There are no more messages from XL. The last one came ages ago. Nevertheless, Mitchell is pestered by the occasional buzzing of his phone with notifications from social media sites he wishes he had never chosen to follow. At the same time, he still keeps on looking. Will an alert confirm XL or one of his crew are coming to the concert? He dreads a very different alert from a source he hopes will be no more than a bad taste hoax. The words *a good place for praying* continue to plague him. Despite the company in the vestry, he is alone in knowing the troubling information.

Bunny, Vicky, Portia and her teacher Margaret all leave the vestry, but before Vicky departs, she urges Mitchell to *break a leg. What the fuck is that meant to mean?* he ponders. Not being a seasoned performer, those words are unsettling. Do they mean she wishes he will have difficulty walking?

In some ways he feels his attire is perfect – nondescript. He could be anyone. He consoles himself by thinking dressed like that he might be able to go out into the audience and stay discreet – at least for a while. No one will know he is the performer until he starts singing.

Bunny returns, putting her head around the door and without a word splays out her five fingers. "Five minutes," says Frank who has seen Bunny's symbol countless times in his past life. He hopes this will be the start of a new performing career and realises immersing himself back into performing has banished all thoughts of the dreaded day job for the last couple of hours.

"Right. Here goes," says Maisie. "Time to go and knock 'em dead." Again, her choice of words is not what Mitchell wants to hear, especially as his mobile seems to vibrate with added aggression. Will he soon be the one knocked dead? "Look - we're all with you Midge," says Maisie, kissing his forehead. Bunny once again puts her head around the door and looks Mitchell up and down. Maisie sees her critical face change to one of resignation.

Mitchell and Frank are waiting behind the choir stalls while Bunny makes her announcements. There is applause again but Mitchell can see his dad and Les in the front pew. The books for the orders of service have been replaced by a small row of lager cans. They receive the attention of Bunny who points her words at them: "And at the end of the evening, if you can take all your debris (stressing the 'r') with you as you leave the church that would be very much appreciated." Mitchell walks past his dad to hear him say the words *stuck up cow* as the applause dies down.

Franks heads towards the piano to occasional jeers from younger voices murmuring the words *He's our supply teacher.* Frank plays a broken chord on the piano in an effort to silence the unwanted acknowledgements and also to reacclimatise himself with the keyboard. Mitchell hesitates. He looks at the audience. Compared with the bright fluorescence of the vestry, it is incredibly dark and he can only make out faces in the first few rows. *Who is out there?* It has also gone quiet and there is a stillness which heightens his nerves. He proceeds to the stage with his back turned to the audience. Someone on the front row says *Where's Mitchell?* Mitchell then turns and tries to survey the audience again, this time with his hand sheltering his eyes from the bright stage lamps which almost blind him. Frank plays the famous chord from the *Rite of Spring.* Its dissonance serves the purpose of gaining Mitchell's attention in rehearsals and it does now. It also makes a few in the audience jump. Frank after smiling at Mitchell, plays the opening bars of Mozart's Catalogue Aria from *Don Giovani.* There is applause. Audience members who have been watching Mitchell's TV performance on playback know the aria well.

At first Mitchell performs the first line of *Madamina* in English. It is not showmanship which makes him decide to venture down the aisle singing out the Don's successes. It is the combination of confidence and the paranoia kicking in - thanks to the extra coke supply he managed to get on further tick earlier. His situation urges him to undertake some reconnaissance. He wonders if somewhere in the darkness XL and his associates could be seated. Yet somewhere in the gloom could also be the source of those unnerving messages. He sings the aria, pausing by members of the audience to recite the facts and figures of the Don's exploits.

Further down a pew he sees a movement. It makes him recoil slightly but then realises it is just someone giving him a thumbs up. He walks further down the church declaiming how every type of woman has fallen prey to the Don. Then he pauses as the aria turns back to the beginning. He grabs a service book and opens it as if reading from it the statistics of the Don's conquests, ensuring everyone can see him licentiously lick his finger before turning each page.

The song pauses as Mitchell announces it is in Hassledon (not Spain as the original words state) where the Don has had over a thousand women. This makes the audience laugh. But then he feels someone grab his shirt underneath his open hoodie. Mitchell feels it being twisted hard. It pulls on his neck. Mitchell wonders if this is the first of many women whose actions he might have to get used to. It is not. He looks down at a pair of eyes, staring with an intensity he has never seen before. He decides they do not like him, at all. Mitchell, wearing a smile he hopes will tell the audience everything is fine, tries to free himself from the grip, but it tightens on him in his efforts to put a face to the emotionless eyes. At last the grip loosens and he sees a grin emerge. He is pushed back. After saving himself from falling over backwards, Mitchell returns to the stage and closes the aria to huge applause. But as he raises himself from a bow, he looks again in the direction of where he was grabbed. The person is now applauding with his hands in the air. What is going on? He tries to keep calm knowing that fans can behave in the most peculiar, if not the most worrying and creepiest of ways to show appreciation. The cavatina commences which Mitchell sings from the safety of the stage. He is pleased to see his father and especially his friend Les sitting nearby. Les however has his arms folded. He is bored and tries to open another can without making a sound, but fails – to a big *hush* from someone behind.

The rest of the concert goes down a storm and two encores are delivered. He duets another number from *Don Giovani* with Portia. Maisie finds Portia's acting a bit too convincing. She takes every opportunity to embrace Mitchell right before Maisie's eyes. At the end they bow. Portia clasps Mitchell's hand tightly and then she kisses him. *The cheeky bitch.* Words will be had with Mitchell – probably not immediately, but soon.

The house lights are turned on to encourage people to start leaving. Mitchell now looks at the spot where he was grabbed. The seat is vacant. Bunny Lawford rises to the stage. "Ladies and Gentlemen, may I say something. When I first saw Mitchell arrive this afternoon, I could not believe he would be the wonderful singer we have all just witnessed. And I think we can all agree on that." Applause erupts. "Well, I sincerely hope we will have Mitchell and his friend…"

"Frank," says Frank from the piano.

After Bunny finishes her speech, she reminds everyone once again to take their *rrrubbish* with them as she leaves the stage. A small crowd of autograph hunters accost Mitchell as he tries to reach the waiting arms of Maisie, standing with her mother. Mitchell signs another programme a girl thrusts in front of him with the words "You're great but why can't you sing proper music?" He has no answer but signs his autograph anyway. Les who by now can hardly walk, agrees. Ryan pushes through the gathering crowd and falls at Mitchell's feet. "Don't know what that bitch of your mother thinks but I thought you were fucking great son," says Ryan. He is heaved up again by Les and the two stagger out of the church much to the bemusement of all present.

Mitchell wishes he could enjoy this moment more, signing the programmes and basking in every shower of praise, but he cannot stop looking around him. He is worried. He notices his signature, rather than displaying the curves and flow Maisie made him practice, has become jagged, resembling barbed wire across paper. Paranoia kicking in again. But at least Mitchell feels safe with everyone around him. He begins to wish they could stay with him all night, and then wonders if he could smuggle himself out with Maisie. In his mind's eye he keeps seeing the eyes of the one who grabbed him. He hopes it was just one of the weirdos Frank had told him opera often attracts.

On tiptoes he sees some people standing on the perimeters of the crowd closest to him. They look different. Their clothes seem sleeker and they are obviously not in a hurry to get his signature. They are in a group engaged in casual chat, probably about Mitchell. Are these XL's people – or someone else? Drug suppliers make huge amounts of cash and often spend it on cars and clothes he thinks. One of them pushes though, apologising in well-spoken tones: "Hi, XL would have loved it. Here - you can make an appointment with his secretary and talk with him on this number. Don't be surprised if he asks you how much you want," The gathered people look at the man relaying the information and then again at Mitchell. "Thanks" says Mitchell. He glances at the person who holds up a phone, saying: "I've got all your show, on here. I'll post it to XL later tonight." Mitchell has never felt so elated and worried at the same time. He should be reaping and savouring the results of what felt like endless rehearsals, by signing programmes in a far more gracious spirit.

Maisie elbows herself to Mitchell while apologising to those she disturbs. "Mitchell, mum thought it was excellent and she is having a chat with your mum," says Maisie. Mitchell peers through a gap in the faces around him and observes the chalk and cheese of the chattering twosome. "We're going to leave now. As my mum came on her own tonight, I'm going to walk her home. So, we'll see you later, okay?" Mitchell, still busy scribbling signatures on programmes gives Maisie a brief nod. Mitchell then nods at his own mother who approaches but gives up when she sees the amount of people around him. She just waves and tries to catch up with Maisie and her mum.

Eventually, Bunny Lawford approaches. She has never seen this picture of fandom before, even though there are not many people left. "It's a shame you are not signing CDs or merchandise people might have bought," says Roger "Look. Will be back to speak later. Just need to go and do something." He walks off with the cash box tucked securely under his arm. Vicky and Portia join him. The daughter turns and blows Mitchell a kiss which seems to happen in slow motion as Mitchell drinks in every guilty moment.

Minutes later, there are now only a few still waiting for autographs. Bunny reminds them she will be closing the church soon, while stacking chairs with a pronounced clang when dropping each one onto a mounting stack. People get the message and leave. She pauses and, quite out of breath, comes to say: "Wonderful, simply wonderful, one of the best concerts we've ever had. Now look young man, if I close the main door all you have to do is give the vestry door a jolly good slam as you leave, okay?" Bunny waits until Mitchell nods. "Did you hear that too Mister Accompanist?"

"Loud and clear," says Frank "Give the door a good firm slam."

"Good," says Bunny, returning to an elderly gentleman who has almost finished helping her stack the chairs. Bunny's peremptory voice and demeanour have as usual, done the trick and cleared the church of nearly everyone in no time. The place is almost empty. Frank watches Bunny and her elderly colleague head towards the door. It is much darker in the church when Bunny turns off all but one light and the venue becomes somewhere else entirely. There are stone plaques on the wall commemorating the dead and gone. In the dull light the carved stonework is eerie. The tombstone curves hanging on the walls make the place feel like an indoor graveyard.

"Mitchell, look, sorry but have you been paid yet? The place was packed but I haven't seen Roger. Did he leave you with the money?" says Frank.

"No. No dough yet," says Mitchell. Both turn towards the sound of the front door being banged shut. The ominous noise reverberates throughout the whole building. "In that case, I've got to go now to catch the last bus. We can sort the money tomorrow," says Frank with a holdall of music in his hand.

The euphoria of the concert seems to have vanished into the dull grey and cold atmosphere of the cavernous surroundings. Frank without the cash in hand also dreads the bus journey home. No doubt he will be rudely recognised by kids he meets on supply who should not really be tearing around the town at such a late hour.

Mitchell does not want to be on his own and wishes he had enough money to stand Frank's taxi fare. With all that hard cash no doubt present only moments ago, Roger could have at least subbed their share of the door money. "Frank - Roger said he would be back. Maybe if you hold on..." says Mitchell. He sees Frank put his music down and begin to wander around the church, studying the stone plaques hidden in the darker enclaves of the old building.

Mitchell feels his phone buzzing. It is Maisie: *Left a magazine in the vestry – on the old chair I think. Ta MXXXX. Ps. Epic gig XM.* Mitchell, feeling more confident and not being on his own, heads into the vestry to make sure he too has not forgotten anything.

The vestry feels much chillier than the main part of the church and the water heater roars louder but he can see Maisie's magazine half open on the chair they were sitting on. He knows straightaway it is a girl's read as a page dangles over the arm of the chair displaying an advert for tampons. Even without anyone present he feels embarrassed on Maisie's behalf and quickly closes it. He turns to leave the room and sees someone he has never seen before standing at the door. The stranger just stands solid with his arms folded. Mitchell knows it would be futile to try and get past him. His barricade of a body comes complete with a face which says *no entry* and his hairless skull spells the word *harm.*

Chapter 22

Turning towards the fire door Mitchell sees another man enter. Those eyes he remembers all too vividly from the concert are locked on him again. This time instead of pulling on Mitchell's shirt, the man yanks the panic bar to close the fire door. For Mitchell, it feels like the cabin door being shut on a passenger plane. He dreads to think where the destination might be.

The two stare at him. Their faces suggest they are rather fond of the sun but not of Mitchell. "Yes?" says Mitchell. They do not reply. Is this the reason Mitchell might find the church *a good place for prayer?* The man by the fire door coughs, a smoker's cough.

"You did well tonight Mitchell," says the man at the other door. "I presume with such a packed crowd you must have some readies available."

"I've not seen a single penny of it so far - honest," says Mitchell worried that his only escape from these two is to have cash, now.

"Well, you'd better find it because you owe us. Owe us big man."

"Owe you? What do you mean? I don't even know you."

"Okay, as a bit of an introduction, we've taken over from

your Raza Man. I'm afraid our credit terms arc not quite as generous - or as downright sloppy," says the first man. He crescendos on the last few words, his voice turning from calm to fierce. Before Mitchell can begin to realise how terrified he is, the man by the fire door grabs him from behind. Mitchell shouts "Frank."

The other man stands a chair up against the other door. He then produces a knife, and taking hold of Mitchell's hand, twists his palm around to reveal veins. He hovers the blade over them. They carry not just blood but also fear. The man pulls Mitchell by the finger to a bare white wall and twists Mitchell's wrist again. He seizes his forefinger, cuts the tip open and squeezes it, using the oozing blood to write digits on the wall. "Call me Scribe," says the man who dashes Mitchell's bleeding hand downwards. The other man comes from behind to restrain him again. Mitchell does not want to see what is on the wall but the man behind him pulls his hair to jerk his head up and his eyes wide open. Mitchell sees the faint digits as the blood starts to trickle down the wall. He cannot believe he is in his own horror film. He cannot believe he owes the amount on the wall. Not that much, surely? Has the Raza Man given the wrong person the wrong information?

The vestry door to the main church is rattling. Mitchell guesses it is Frank but dare not say a thing. This is followed by attempts to push the door open. Mitchell half hopes Frank stops trying to enter. "Censored," says Scribe. Frank gives up on the door while Scribe writes something on a piece of paper, this time with a pencil he finds on a table. "Okay, this address - you know it, don't you?" Mitchell nods. "Good. Well - see the amount on the wall?" Mitchell makes no reply. He does not want to look. "See it?" But Mitchell is forced to look at it again, when his head is jerked back into position. "That's what *you* owe *us*, Okay?" Mitchell gives no answer. "Okay?"

"Okay," says Mitchell.

"Bring it to this address by four tomorrow or else there'll be more than your finger cut," says Scribe. He waves the address directly in front of Mitchell's eyes and strokes the knife across Mitchell's throat. He turns the knife and presses the knife point just enough not to penetrate Mitchell's skin and make no injury. He knows exactly how much pressure to apply. "Got it?" Mitchell nods. "Oh and DO NOT even think of getting *Noddy* involved. Okay?"

There is a knock on the fire door. Scribe nods to his accomplice who lets go when Mitchell's name is called. It is Roger. Scribe goes to the door and gives the panic bar a sharp kick. This flings the door open with such force, it sends Roger backwards to the ground. The two men leave. Roger picks himself up and brushes dirt from himself. "Who the hell," says Roger inspecting a grazed palm. Mitchell stands frozen, his face is white. Roger looks Mitchell over and sees the blood around Mitchell's hand. "Shit, are you okay?" Roger now feels a cold nausea within him. "There must be, must be a first aid thing in here." Roger locates the green first aid box above the sink next to the water heater that continues to hiss. "He finds a box of bandages. "Here puts this on it," says Roger. He has to direct Mitchell's other hand to hold a gauze over his bleeding finger. "What's been going on?" Roger can see Mitchell, shaking, obviously in a state of shock. He turns to see the blood on the wall. "Bloody hell. What's that?" says Roger. He closes the fire door and gets a chair for Mitchell. "Sit down." Mitchell collapses onto the chair. "I suppose that's... your... blood?" Mitchell just stares at the wall.

Roger contemplates handing over the cheque, leaving straight away and washing his hands entirely of Mitchell. But a mixture of fear and curiosity keeps him where he is. "Think we'd better..." Roger gets his phone out but does not dial. The other door rattles again stirring Mitchell.

"Don't," says Mitchell. "They'll kill me."

"Don't do what? Who they are *they*?

"Dealers."

"Oh Mitchell, don't tell me you're involved with drugs...shit. You didn't tell me about this, did you?

"Thought..."

"Sorry Mitchell but I'm off. In fact - " Roger starts to stab at his phone and heads towards the fire door. Mitchell gets up and grabs Roger's phone, flinging it to the floor. The phone's screen cracks. The vestry door is knocked at again - Frank. They ignore him. "So that figure on the wall is what you...owe those two who were in here just now?" says Roger picking up his shattered phone. "Fuck, you are in trouble, aren't you Mitchell," he says. Something tells Roger the police ought to be contacted – but something tells him perhaps not – a broken phone for a start.

"Mitchell are you okay?" says Frank from behind the door. Mitchell takes the chair away, opens the door and begins pacing around the room. Roger imagines he is trying to work off his nerves and fear. The first thing Frank sees is the wall. He asks no questions. Mitchell continues to hold the blood-soaked gauze round his finger tip. Frank looks at Roger, who drops himself in the old armchair. He sits thinking with his fingers formed into a tent which he continually taps against his beard.

"Right Mitchell, if we're going down the DIY route, by which

I mean not getting the police involved and paying that," says Roger pointing at the wall. The blood is beginning to dry. Some of it has nearly reached the floor causing one of the zeros to transform into a gruesome looking bubble blower. "...there's one or two provisos we're going to have to make."

"Can I just have my share of the takings?" says Mitchell who wants to get out of the place and straight to Maisie's. He fears the two he owes might have second thoughts and decide to write off the debt and himself with it.

"Yes certainly Mitchell, you may, but your share of what you made tonight will not cover what is on the wall."

"What?"

"Look, let's get scrubbing. That Bunny woman would have a heart attack if she saw this. Wait. Have either of you got a phone? I suggest we take a pic before we get rid of it," says Roger. He looks around the sink for cleaning materials. Frank points his phone at the wall. As he focuses on the subject, it disturbs him and he finds it hard to keep the camera still so takes several pictures. The heater thunders when Roger fills a bucket with water and detergent. "Pics okay Frank?" says Roger, steadying Frank's phone to see the images. "Fine. Here, take this," He gives Frank a sponge. They wipe the wall. At first a faint red blur is left, but as they scrub harder it begins to disappear. Mitchell, can only look on as they wipe away at the wall. He is too weak to do much else.

Eventually the wall is cleaned. "Okay Mitchell, we need to talk about this and get a few things straight," says Roger "For now, let's just get out of here."

They depart. Roger first takes Frank back to his lonely flat where a night of triumph turns back into the realisation that he has no money and will have to return to the DDJ Monday morning. He turns the light on, wondering if Mitchell's dealers know he is associated with him. Might they turn on him too as a joint accomplice?

Roger walks Mitchell to the door of his Mum's house. Do *they* know where he is? Perhaps he has been followed. He cannot sleep. His bandaged finger is a constant reminder as he listens to every sound coming from outside and inside the house. For once his mother and Gavin are helpfully quiet.

But each movement might be something made by *them.* He does not know *them.* All he knows is they can harm him. At the same time his performance is replaying in his head. But the eyes of his new dealers keep punctuating and marring all the good moments. What have they done with Raza Man? He can still feel himself being tugged at – the twisting of his top as his torso was throttled. Then he remembers XL. *Don't be surprised to be asked how much you want.* He will be calling him on Monday. But first he needs to keep alive. Can his new dealers wait? No chance. They will find him if there is no money. No promises – no deals. The knife stroking on his throat sealed that.

Would Roger help him pay his drug debt? What will his proviso be? He thinks about Portia and how much chemistry there was between them. She has certainly lit a flame inside him. Would an affair be possible without hurting Maisie? But the word *hurt* and all its connotations brings more desperate and worrying issues to mind. How much pain or worse would *they* inflict on him if Roger changes his mind and wants nothing more to do with a drug addict?

Mitchell has too much to think about to be able to sleep

213

much. During the little sleep he does get, he dreams of a wall protecting him from all these nasty creatures he combats in *KillaTeds.* As time continues, the wall begins to crumble and each passing minute sees another line of bricks removed...

Maisie also lies awake. She thought Mitchell would be back with her by now as he is fully accepted into the Moore's household as family. She has not heard a thing from him. She tries to gain solace from the thought that Mitchell's mobile has died. But nevertheless, where is he? The way he looked at Portia while he did the duet with her keeps worrying Maisie. The way he allowed her to keep folding into his embraces so readily. Is he with her? Is Mitchell safe? Please call, Midge. Her phone buzzes. She grabs it.

Chapter 23

Mitchell answered Maisie to let her know he was okay but did not tell her about the incident in the vestry. She would know straight away he was involved with drugs – let alone potentially suffering the worst consequences.

There was probably someone outside watching him. This assumption was shared by Roger who texted him to suggest they should meet somewhere other than his house in Hassel on the Hill.

But Mitchell also felt an overwhelming sense of come down. Depression and general malaise began to take hold of him. He knew how it could be put right. If only.

Up until a day ago the arrangement was cool. He would have taken the money he made from the concert and paid what he owed the Raza Man. The Raza Man would have renewed confidence in him and his remedy would be secured. Now it was different. He realised more and more he was being used as a weapon for extortion. He wished he had never touched drugs, ever. Could those guys not hold on for just a few more days? He might get some kind of advance from XL whose crew appeared massively impressed. It was all happening at the wrong time. His new found talent, XL, Maisie, Portia, drug addiction. Everything.

At Enrico's the sound of someone talking far too loudly behind him, teaspoons endlessly stirring, cups, knives and forks forever scraping and clanging on china, are all too much for Mitchell. He never realised before how irritating cafes could be. Then there is Brady with his high-pitched whistle, whistling to every hook he catches from what Mitchell considers the worst radio station in the world: *Hassledon FM – The hits you love.* "No I fucking don't," says Mitchell to himself. He and Roger order black coffees.

Roger notices Mitchell is not at ease. He cannot blame his agitations. He looks at the bandaged finger which makes Mitchell keep forgetting to pick up his cup with the other hand. It seems his dealer has been taken over by ruthless gangsters who do not make empty threats. He knows Mitchell needs the money and the ball is firmly in his court.

"So what you are saying is that you will give me what should be mine anyway, if I agree for you to be my manager?" says Mitchell.

"No. What I'm saying is this. I'll advance you the extra money on top of what you earned, so no harm will come to you," says Roger. Mitchell knows if he signs with Roger as his manager, it will blow out any chance of working with XL – even if XL might match what Roger is offering. "It's not only because I want your..." Roger lowers his voice and looks around *Enrico's.* He leans over to Mitchell and almost whispers "– physical welfare intact, which I'm sure you do too." Roger sits back again. "But it's because I believe in you and already have plans for you. Great plans. And the sooner we can get cracking and put what I have in mind into operation, the better for us all." There is no response from Mitchell. "Mitchell – you are going places. Get these arseholes off your back, then it's onwards and upwards."

Mitchell had toyed with the idea of getting a loan from Roger on the premise that he would be able to pay him back as soon as he could receive an advance from XL. But Roger's words have just dismissed the notion outright.

"This sounds like effing blackmail to me."

"The world into which you invited yourself could not be any darker though, could it? I could recommend you getting a loan but with what? I imagine your wage to be, well..." Mitchell looks at Roger and then at the clock on the wall. 12.40. Maisie will be arriving soon to start her 1pm shift. He wonders if Roger's daughter Portia has ever had to work in such a place. What is she doing now? Thinking of him? Has Roger told her to keep well clear of a drug addict involved with dangerous people? Most likely not, or Roger would not be here now.

Then Mitchell considers the more immediate concern of time. Three hours and twenty minutes to go before...? His imagination has played through various scenarios and none are good. They all terrify Mitchell. It's a no brainer. He has no choice but to say "Yes, okay." Roger holds out his hand but then withdraws it leaving Mitchell's hand suspended over the table. "There's something else Mitchell."

"Yeah, what's that?"

"If we enter this agreement, I want your word that you will never touch drugs again. If I discover you do, I'm afraid I'll go straight to the police with absolutely zero hesitation. Understood?" Mitchell cannot stand the noises around him as he tries ponder over this additional condition. There is someone behind who is really annoying him. They seem to be taking their food on a grand tour around their dish. The scraping sound is becoming unbearable for Mitchell. He tries to drown it out by tapping his teaspoon on his cup and saucer with such force it seems as if is trying to crack the china. He is locked in a cutlery combat. "Are you okay Mitchell?" asks Roger. He sees the person sitting behind Mitchell now turn around with a quizzical brow. "Yeah, just need to get out of here," says Mitchell. He gets up as Maisie enters *Enrico's*. She is in her work clothes and all ready to serve tables. The couple dash to each other and embrace. "You were just so amazing last night, Mitchell but get this, Mum was really disappointed you didn't come to ours," says Maisie.

"Sorry, had loads to see to."

"Hey but cool, hey?" says Maisie.

"Again, sorry Maze it was really late by the time we left." Mitchell points at a pretend watch on his hand, forgetting how this could bring Maisie's attention to his bandaged finger.

"What happened to your hand?"

"Oh, just an accident, cut my finger on something as we were packing away last night."

"Do you want another bandage? It's looking a bit soiled. I could do that. There's a first aid box through there."

"Oh, leave it Maisie, you should be starting your shift now."

"Okay. But by the way, mum is convinced you're the next Darius Dalloway."

"I think he'll do better than that. Or at least I sincerely hope so," says Roger overhearing from the table.

"Maisie," says the proprietor pointing at the clock on the wall. Both Maisie and Mitchell look at it. Five minutes past one. Maisie is already five minutes late and Mitchell calculates two hours fifty-five before his fate. They give each other a final hug and Mitchell departs with Roger following.

"So, Mitchell is it a deal?" says Roger holding out his hand again. Mitchell wishes he could ask Maisie's opinion on Roger's offer but he sees she has disappeared around the back of the cafe. He hesitates. Roger takes out an envelope which Mitchell knows is his passport to a pain-free evening and most probably beyond. He has worked out he will probably not get killed - just taught a lesson most likely digested from a hospital bed. "Before I shake, can I make a phone call?" Mitchell walks further down the pavement and reaches for his mobile to try the offices of what he presumes is XL's management company. It is the same answerphone message together with the uplifting music bed of XL's latest release. Mitchell regrets he has no choice but will have to kiss goodbye to being a part of *Team XL.* "Okay Roger. Deal," says Mitchell. Their hands finally shake.

"You realise what I'm giving to you will be using up all of Frank's share of the takings as well? Would you like to tell him or I?"

"No I would not like to tell him, but I will," says Mitchell.

"Fine. Now we'd better go to the truck for you to sign something, then the money is yours."

"Okay," says Mitchell, already seeing the cash turning into coke. He looks at the document. The title reads: *An agreement between Mitchell's Music Management and Mitchell Woods.* He then turns to the page that matters: the advance. Above the figure, is a clause beginning with the words *In consideration...* He takes a deep breath and then signs his name on the last page. Roger does the same and tells him he hopes he can trust him that his wife will sign this paperwork as a witness later.

Chapter 24

Too scared to go to see his new dealers completely on his own, Mitchell gets a lift from Roger who parks around the corner. Roger does not want to be seen, but accompanies him far enough to ensure the money he has given Mitchell will be spent to end his drug taking and all business with his dealers. It is agreed that if Mitchell does not return within a certain time, Roger will call the police.

Mitchell feels his phone buzz. *U no wear we r - 4.* Mitchell wonders if he should just not pay his new dealers. Instead, he could pocket the money, run away to some far-off destination where no-one can find him and give up his performing career which has only just begun. But already as a public performer, it is so easy for anyone to find him. If all goes successfully, he could become an extremely well-known figure. Maisie's mum - and now his own - will expect absolutely nothing less.

At the same time, he is craving like mad for what his nasty new dealers have. And they seem to be the only game in town for supply. He is so wanting *it.* Mitchell hopes as soon as he settles up, he might be able to get more – on tick. But he tries to fight this thought. He knows all too well how dangerous they are, and keeps trying to combat his craving by reminding himself why he needs to get out.

Poor Frank. Mitchell knows he will not be pleased. Frank's job is not just hard work, it must be thoroughly demoralising too. Yes - poor Frank. Hadn't he already told Mitchell he hoped the concert and its revenue would buy him a few days sanctuary from the dreaded day job. He said he gets paid to be abused. Now next week will be no exception.

Mitchell turns the corner on to the street where his now ex-dealer lives. Walking around with the amount of cash he has on him is like carrying a bomb. A mugger is all it would take. They have the uncanny ability to sniff out the best target, knowing exactly what fear and desperation looks like.

The Raza Man's house looks much the same as most of the other properties on his road, and Mitchell considers it in a better state of repair than some of the neighbouring houses. The garden seems tidy with a recently mowed lawn. For the Raza Man, dealing is as much a business as any other. The only difference is down to legalities. Mitchell sees the Raza Man's white Merc parked outside and is about to admire its usually pristine condition but instead notices scuffs and dents. It has most probably been driven by someone else.

He feels his phone buzz again: *Ent, thru bak.* He is being watched. Without looking around, he goes straight around the side of the house and sees the back door ajar. He cannot decide whether to let himself in or not, but halts when he nearly steps on a mound of brown and black fur. Is it a bear? No, it is a large dog which looks like combination of canines – a dog to the power three. A dog which Mitchell supposes can do some serious damage - a helpful accessory against those who do not honour exploitative drug deals or who might start dealing on its owner's turf. The dog springs up. Mitchell springs back. "Bitch Sit," says a voice Mitchell recognises from the night before. The dog pauses and Mitchell can feel it panting on him. The voice belongs to the man who in those tense early hours referred to himself as *Scribe*. He takes hold of the dog and heaves it back. Both man and dog cannot take their eyes off Mitchell. No words of invitation are given but Scribe flicks his head back to indicate Mitchell is to enter. The dog tugs even harder as Mitchell steps over the threshold.

The place is noticeably different. Though the Raza Man's name might suggest a residence full of torn *Rizzla* booklets or ashtrays overflowing with roaches, Mitchell had previously found no such evidence. In fact the interior of his house would normally put most house husbands or wives to shame. But now, instead of polish, the odours are a nauseating combination of grease, smoke and stale tobacco. This inhalation could define the phrase: *slumming it*. Takeaways sprawl around the once clear and shining table. They are on the floor too, with half demolished silver containers and half eaten bones and ribs - presumably by Bitch. "Got it?" says Scribe restraining the dog with increased effort. If Mitchell were to answer 'No' he would probably let go of the dog and that would be just the first ferocious part of Mitchell's imminent death. There is no sign of the Raza Man who would normally be in this room to conduct business.

Mitchell takes out the envelope with as much calm and control as he can muster. He thinks any erratic moves will excite the dog which is tugging against its collar. Why can't Scribe just put it in another room? Intimidation, Mitchell realises, is the answer. He presents the envelope. On seeing it, to his relief Scribe finally takes the dog away. A brief conversation can be heard. Scribe re-enters with Raza and the door is firmly shut. Raza has a blackened eye and a scarred cheek, he gives Mitchell the briefest acknowledgment as if barred from having acquaintances. He is not in a good way at all and does not say a word. "You might want to clear up all this shit, especially with my guest present," says Scribe. Raza immediately sets about gathering up the assorted debris. "Oh and don't forget the floor," Scribe smiles at Mitchell and seems to enjoy controlling Raza. It is obvious to Mitchell, that Raza has become Scribe's personal slave. "And when you have done that maybe you could make a brew." Raza nods and gets on all fours to tackle the floor, taking on the role of work dog - no questions, no complaining.

"So," says Scribe, looking at Mitchell and the envelope. Mitchell takes the money out, stack by stack on to the table. Scribe reaches over for it and after a moment of hesitation, can see the amount is right. He does not need to count it. "Well, I'm impressed. I want you to see something." Mitchell wonders what. Then the sight of Raza reappearing from behind the table brings back a Pavlovian reaction in Mitchell - the familiar expectation of a craving about to be satisfied, like an alcoholic might feel when stepping into a pub.

"The tuck shop has re-opened" says Scribe. Mitchell looks at what Scribe has just put on the table, all bagged and ready. The drug has already performed its alchemy on Mitchell - intimidation has been transformed into temptation.

"But I can't afford it."

"It's okay. Now we know you're not the type who reneges... and have a dazzling singing career – just see me as someone who would like to be a part of it, you know. With you all the way." Scribe grins, pushing a bag towards Mitchell, who knows that he should not even touch it. He turns to the back door. It is open and for a moment Mitchell tastes the delicious breeze of freedom. Instead, he turns back and looks at the table where a different sustenance lies waiting...

Chapter 25

I t only took a few weeks for Mitchell's brief Top Vox fame to evaporate. Roger saw this coming and had a game plan for him. It would exclude the need for any kudos from his TV appearance and the immediate media aftermath - which had died almost as quickly as it arrived.

Mitchell was not happy, however. The day after he visited the Raza Man's hijacked home, he decided to call XL's office again. As soon as Mitchell mentioned his name to XL's secretary he was put straight on to his hero. While briefly on hold, he could hear XL's latest release - which just heightened his disbelief when he heard his idol shout "Mitchell" as if greeting a long-lost friend. "So, what's the situation? Perhaps I'm too late. I imagine you've probably been snapped up by now. Or maybe you're calling..." He also could not believe XL's huge sigh of disappointment on hearing that he had just signed a management agreement with Roger. "Who did you say?"

"Roger Masters."

"Never heard of him, but whatever - I hope he knows what he's doing," said XL, more tersely. "What a shame." He hardly gave Mitchell a chance to speak "Was hoping to get you singing on my next release. Was also thinking of taking you on my next US and European tour – San Fran, New York, Chicago, Rome,

Paris, Amsterdam - Oh, and a beach festival down in Rio de Janeiro - all those places playing massive venues. Was hoping to introduce a whole new audience to opera. You would have been the perfect person. But there we are. Never mind." This roll call of famous cities was a different world from what Roger had so far booked. At each place name, the salt and vinegar was rubbed deeper and deeper. A lunchtime concert in Harwich Library could hardly compete with a festival appearance on a South American beach.

However, there was a modicum of hope when XL said "Can you please post me a copy of whatever it is you signed with this Roger whatever person?" Mitchell agreed - pleased there was still some possible liaison open.

Frank listened to Mitchell's regrets but said XL was probably trying to make him feel pissed off. He told Mitchell that so much bullshit existed in the music industry you should never believe what anyone said they would do for you until they were actually doing it. It was like the reverse of the very paranoid imagining the worst possible outcome when facing adversity. "The saying *Cheer up, it might never happen* could be flipped to *Cheer up it might never have happened.* Besides, maybe this might teach you not to indulge in class A drugs. It's drugs which forced you into a no choice situation. They're also probably wrecking your voice so slowly you don't realise it. Such is their insidious effect," said Frank.

Mitchell knew every word of Frank's was true. He only had himself to blame. There was a price for everything. At last he'd finally realised this and wondered if he ought to take steps before it got worse.

"But how did you feel after you called XL?" Frank continued.

"Gutted," said Mitchell.

"Do you really want to go to bed, so to speak, with someone who can gut you in just one phone call?"

"No."

Roger's plan was to start doing concerts and hopefully gain further bookings from the merits of Mitchell's singing alone rather than any previous hype. Following Portia's example, Mitchell produced a CD (very cheaply - all recorded at Frank's home) to be sold at gigs. But, alas, Mitchell's delight on seeing hard cash and notes handed over in return for his discs soon turned to disappointment when the money went straight into Roger's pocket instead of his. He was told everything made from these sales went towards paying back the cash Roger had advanced to Mitchell - the cash which, if his new dealer Scribe had not received, would have made Mitchell's singing career rather more difficult. Frank however, was able to keep his share of the proceeds. He was also pleased to see he could receive money from performing rights. But alas it was a rather meagre amount - still not enough to allow him to become a full-time pianist. He continued to curse being unable to spend the day practising and composing. Mitchell continued to curse the early morning alarm.

Roger's other plan was to enter Mitchell into singing contests. This meant most of the door money made from performances went towards entry fees, travel expenses and hotels in various towns and cities where competition heats were held. These were not paid performances, so it was an expensive business. Luckily Mitchell won more times than he lost and often walked away with nothing less than a highly commended.

However, whenever he received a cash prize, the money

would be handed straight over to Roger. Once after Mitchell had victoriously left the podium, Frank echoed under his breath: "And the winner of the contest is...Roger Masters," when Mitchell passed a not insubstantial cheque to his manager. Roger tried his best to pretend he had not heard Frank's comment.

Despite successes and re-bookings, Frank and Mitchell were yet to see clear light at the end of the tunnel towards becoming full time musicians. So far there were no significant offers from music agents - the gatekeepers to larger venues which might enable either of them to change their life styles significantly. Frank was still dreading most weekdays. He would often come home feeling thoroughly wasted in every sense and have no wish to hear any noise whatsoever, including his own piano practice – even more vital now.

Mitchell knew he would be a great deal better off if he discontinued his addiction. But now he was in a such a state before a gig that he could not get himself into the right mood or even contemplate performing without resorting to chemicals. He still lived at home with his mother and stepdad Gavin. He would, however, spend nights on the chaste sofa at Maisie's home. How they both wished Maisie's sister had chosen to study somewhere other than Hassledon College, and vacated the room she still shared with her sister. Job-wise, he was lucky to be able to work on site as and when. Much to his father Ryan's surprise, Mitchell's foreman was pleased to help the fledging opera star.

Meanwhile, Maisie was certainly not happy about the increasing presence of Portia. Roger had to keep his accountancy practice going, so he often let Portia and her mother Vicky handle arrangements for concerts and competitions some distance from home. Like Roger they tended to book nothing less than the best hotels, thus increasing Mitchell's expense account. "I personally didn't mind staying at budget chains when touring. A posh hotel is nothing more than a budget one with biscuits and a chocolate on the sheets," Frank would remark, while watching their luggage being taken up to their rooms by a porter. They also seemed to eat at restaurants with no less than two stars in the Michelin guide. "I'm off to the takeaway. It's much better grub than this shit," said Mitchell frequently, to the horror of the Masters. But Mitchell had a soft spot for luxury hotels. He imagined they were the sort of places stars like his idol XL might stay at and who knows, where they might meet.

Touring also yielded a further advantage for the Masters. Portia was still very keen on going to study singing at either a university or music college. Therefore the family often went to view prospective properties which, it was envisioned, Portia would manage and let out to fellow students. On one occasion, when Frank had nothing to do in a town with precious few sights to see, he accompanied Portia and her mother to view a potential property. It was in an area considered to be one of the most run down parts of the country, though speculators were beginning to edge in. They saw the area as another variation on a very lucrative theme, similar to The Isle of Dogs.

Frank learned the property had been nicely done up by an existing tenant in return for a rent concession. The floor had been retiled, the kitchen and bathroom were brand new and the whole place had been transformed. Little did the tenant know he was not making the property more attractive for himself but for his landlord. After the very last lick of varnish had been applied, the property was immediately put up for sale and the hapless tenant given notice.

Frank, being a renter himself, felt for the poor tenant, who while serving the notice, had to watch a procession of interested parties, including – Vicky and her daughter – remark on what a wonderful investment the property was. A bidding war ensued. Each comment made about a positive feature of the property seemed to make the pricing gun click and cash register ring. They were not looking at a home but a fully furnished money box.

Frank realised many other properties in the area were also undergoing conversion. The existing tenants, who knew where they lived was not the most glamorous place in the country, nevertheless still had a certain pride in their neighbourhood. They were also worried that the money being chased was the same money chasing them out. Unlike mining communities destroyed by political dogma, no police intervention was required to facilitate the destruction of these communities. Enough greed and ambition from the speculators did the trick very nicely – *thank you very much.*

Maisie was not happy to hear Portia was *on the road* again with Mitchell. Unfortunately, she could neither afford the time or the money to join him on his travels. She still remembered vividly how they had performed the duet together at the church concert. It was plain that Portia was keen on Mitchell. Many nights Maisie would lift her mobile wondering and waiting, waiting and wondering when he would send her something or even call. She knew Mitchell was busy but sometimes too many hours would pass before a single text. Despite being keener on texting, she began to realise how very covert such a method of communication was. When you spoke with a person, there was a sort of vocal body language. Even if you only knew them a little, their tone, their fluctuations, their pauses would give away so much more than plain text on a screen - no matter how warm the words or how plentifully added were upper case Xs. At the least, talking required the graciousness of someone giving their time to you. Maisie wondered just how Mitchell did use his spare time. Yet the word *Hi* at the beginning of Mitchell's texts, worked like the symbol of a chemical which could cure her anxiety in an instant.

Chapter 26

Frank compares how he feels with being prone to seasickness. He imagines that just the thought of boarding a ferry could be as nauseating as the actual voyage itself. As the ship heads out of harbour and hits the swell, those afflicted soon wish they were back on dry land. There is no control. Those waves, the dark grey restless monsters mean business when their venomous spray spits at the ship's windows. Unpredictable and tireless, causing furniture to move, doors to slam, drinks to slide and fellow passengers to turn green. Vibrations imitate nerves. Nautical poltergeists.

Victims are powerless against forces far beyond their control, as simultaneous feelings of hopelessness and dread take over in equal measure. Until the voyage ends – in one way or another, they are prisoners with the added chance of being drowned. Yet the ship's crew behave like super beings. How can they act so normal amidst such turmoil, some passengers might wonder?

Eventually, the calm of the destination port brings some solace. Victims of the angry sea can at last return to the people they were once before and no longer feel possessed by Neptune's less forgiving spirits.

These same tumultuous and very physical responses are experienced by Mr Frank Peters. As soon as Frank wakes up to another school day, he feels a failure - a failure for feeling the same nausea as those embarking on a dreaded sea voyage. He, unlike the sailor counterparts, the *career teachers*, has no sea legs for the teaching vocation.

He cannot even listen to the morning radio, especially programmes featuring chatty and eager presenters, evidently happy with their lot even when they broadcast the more depressing news stories. The only bad news for Peters is that he, once again, must go and teach at *that* school. Switching off the radio and, in turn, his envy for presenters who so blatantly love their job, Peters instead listens to music.

Leave, some will quite rightly say to Frank. But Frank has spent many a time searching for other jobs. All the other positions he has seen advertised, even if he were a successful applicant, don't pay enough to meet his outgoings. He has also discovered that any in-work benefits he is entitled to won't make up the shortfall either.

He also wakes up to the continued disappointment of re-alising his performing career is still far from being back on track.

The school reception brings to mind a more convivial hotel reception. He is asked to present paperwork again, with documents to inform the school he is not a criminal. How many adolescent criminals will he be facing today, he wonders? Do they show their credentials too? He signs the visitor's book again. After being given an ID card with PETERS printed on it, he leaves the last bastion of civilisation the school provides, the lavish decor of the reception. Now he is in a corridor with graffiti-strewn walls and scuff-marked floors.

Peters enters the heavy swell caused by the movement of vast swathes of kids. Teachers stand at intermittent points, their cruel and serious faces devoutly intent on spotting the slightest misdemeanour from the students. When they do, they shout with a clout-like force which makes him jump - probably more than the kids who are plainly well used to such verbal affronts.

At last, after almost fighting his way up the staircases to a third floor lobby, Peters finally finds the room which agrees with his cover schedule. There are students clustered outside, creating enough noise to make anyone think they are trying to increase the sale of aspirin. "Are you taking this lesson?" shouts one of them. Peters nods to a gleeful "Yesss." He is well known around the school for being lax. He hopes for a brief moment of tranquility in the classroom before the students are officially allowed to enter, but the door is locked.

"Does anyone know who has the key to this room?" he asks. Without having been given express permission, two boys scatter off back down the staircase which is now clear of students. Their footsteps and loud words echo around the stairwell. Another crowd of students also waits to go into the adjacent room. For Peters, their sound hitting and rebounding off the hard stone walls of the lobby area is almost unbearable.

More students arrive. Some tower over Peters and all keep asking him the same question: "Are you taking this lesson?" Peters stops bothering to reply. Another just says *him again* with a regretful voice. Eventually a person comes along. She is wearing a white coat suggesting she may be a lab technician from the science department but she presents a key. Under her arm, there is a pack of A4 paper.

Students enter the room. The woman tries to admonish

those who push straight past her but is ignored. The sound of chair legs being scraped off the tops of tables adds another layer of pain to Peters' encroaching headache. He now enters to see the woman reading the instructions taped to the desk. "Year Ten. *Social Histories*, read pages fifty-two to fifty-four and answer questions one to five on page fifty-five. Those who finish can do the extension activity at the bottom of the page. All work to be done on paper NOT in their books," she reads, tracing every line with her index finger. "The books are there." She places a firm hand on the books "And the paper is here," she says, leaning her other firm hand on the paper. "See you later. All the best."

"Thanks," says Peters. The woman approaches him again.

"I noticed this class is 10X4. It has two main troublemakers, but so far neither seems to have turned up. Hopefully for everyone's sake, they won't," says the woman in a quieter voice.

"Yes, we live in hope," says Peters with the first smile he has made all day.

"We do indeed. But if Damon and his friends give you trouble, under no circumstances challenge them. Try discreetly to get a student to fetch a member of the leadership team," says the woman exiting the room. Upon hearing this information, Peters feels out of his depth again. *Why does this school keep booking him?* he keeps asking himself. He is aware of the students the woman has described. He knows Damon's younger brother and recently had to have him removed from a class.

There is still kerfuffle outside in the lobby so Peters closes the classroom door. He stands and waits before taking the register. On the register are photos of the students. But their mugshots look like they were taken when they were much younger. They hardly resemble what he sees in front of him. He is still waiting for the vast majority to settle down. There is shouting and laughter. Peters feels he might as well not be there. He tries to put names to the few faces he sees waiting quietly. *Thank you to...* but this technique of positive reinforcement does not work. He cannot even hear his own voice. A sympathetic student who nevertheless has been nattering with her friends comes over. "I'll tell you who's here and who isn't," she says. She takes the sheet, snatches the pen out of Peters' hand and starts ticking the names of those present. She pauses at Damon and points at the picture of his smirking face "He's mental. Luckily for you he's not here - yet. Probably been excluded, again." She finishes the register. "Want me to take it to the office for you?" she asks. Peters says "Okay." He realises nothing is for free when she makes a gleeful exit dragging along a friend.

Having given up trying to command the students' attention, Peters turns to the white board and writes the instructions straight from the cover sheet on to the board. Doing this makes him feel he is helping the students' learning in *some* way.

"More book work. When are we going to get a proper teacher?" protests one of the more biddable students. Her voice indicates she is fed up with supply teacher after supply teacher. Peters is about to apologise and tell the student it is not his fault, when the door springs open and slams against the wall. Peters hears a few students say the name Damon. "Who the fuck are you?" says Damon to Peters. The latecomer stands at the door with his hands in his jacket pockets. The rest of the class have gone quiet. Damon's jacket looks as if it might be about to fall apart any moment with his large muscular frame bursting to get out of it. In moments like this Frank Peters realises what a frail figure he is. "Can someone get a senior member of staff please," says Frank to one of the quieter students. No one moves. Damon grins.

"If you could ask me in a more polite tone I might answer your question," says Peters.

"I'll talk to you how the fuck I like. What are you going to do about it anyways?" says Damon walking towards Peters. He grabs Peters' ID card on a lanyard around his neck. "Mmm, Peters, another poxy sub." Peters does not know what to do. In front of him he can see Damon's eyes are full of hunger and anger. Two boys enter the room who he presumes are also late arrivals. Despite the brutal voices of other teachers in the corridors earlier, the school still has a large pocket of anarchy. Peters remembers he should avoid any confrontation with Damon.

"Hold on. You're the one who had my little brother removed from class last week, didn't you?" says Damon taking hold of Peters' ID badge again. "He came home well upset. Peters." The whole class has gone silent as if anticipating the next moment in some high drama.

"Can you get senior management, *please,*" says Peters to one of the students at the front of the class with half an eye on her text book and half an eye on the proceedings. She does not move and neither does anyone else. Peters wishes the girl who took the register would return. She would probably not be too intimidated to go but it is obvious she and her friend have decided to bunk off the lesson.

Peters can sense fear and hate developing in the room. Hate for him not being a *proper* teacher who should be able to do what a teacher should be able to do - take control. The only thing he can control is the piano keyboard. "Oh dear me Mr Peters, seems like you'll to have to deal with this yourself." The voice has a cockiness which reminds Peters of another voice. He attempts to divorce himself from the situation by puzzling where he has heard this voice before. "So what ya gonna do then, eh?" Peters knows the voice. It is the same tone as his agent at the supply agency who booked him into this school – into this classroom, into this danger. *What ya gonna do?* were the hurried words of the agent, when Frank could not decide whether to risk another day where he is right now. He felt rushed into making up his mind at the words "It's all we've got mate, I'd take it if I was you." Peters held the phone away from his ear because his agent spoke so loudly. He knew it was one of the toughest schools in the area. "Go on. You'd be doing me a massive favour mate," said the agent. Peters still could not reply. But then he saw in front of him an envelope with a window. Another bill. "Oh...okay then," he'd reluctantly agreed. But now he wished he had just slammed the phone right down.

"Can you leave the room please, Damon?" says Peters looking around the room. Everyone is watching him. Damon does not move, he still stands with his hands in his pockets "No, I think you ought to leave the room...please," says Damon. The whole class laughs at him. Then Peters is surprised to see the boy go and sit at a spare seat by the window. He folds his arms and instantly looks the picture of obedience. Peters, content he has got his way, lets the matter rest and picks up the last text book of *Social Histories* from the front desk. It has no cover and there is only half of the first page. Overall, the book is tatty. He takes it over to Damon and opens it at the relevant page. Damon picks up the book as if it was something the cat has brought in. "You expect me to use this?" he sneers.

"Sorry Damon, it's the last one. If you could have arrived earlier..." Damon opens the window he is sitting next to. The window would normally only move so far – but the steel holder to restrict it is no longer in place, so he can push it wide open. "Can you leave the window alone, please", says Peters.

"No," says Damon as he gets up and holds the book out of the window. The whole class remains silent to watch the altercation go up a gear. Damon suspends the book with one hand and holds the window with the other as he smiles at Peters, who pauses. If he tries to grab the book, he knows Damon will just snatch it back or drop it to its destruction three storeys down. But he notices the book is now being held by just a single page. Damon starts to swing the book causing the page to slowly tear. Peters comes closer to the window while Damon now stands to be able to hold the book at arm's length out of the window. Peters lunges for the book but then feels his shirt collar tightly gripped as his head is shoved out of the window. Peters clutches the window frame with both hands but Damon has the advantage and is too strong. Then he feels his belt being taken hold of.

"Oi, you two - over here," says Damon. Peters can hear scuffling from behind him and still tries in vain to get up. "Grab his ankles." Peters in a panic starts kicking but it is no use. He feels a firm grip on each ankle. His legs are off the floor and he is now halfway out of the window. He looks down. From three storeys up there is a huge drop to a gravel path below. "Let me back in - now," says Peters with all the breath he can muster in his lungs.

Behind him, Peters can hear students saying "Stop it." interspersed with "Bring him in, bring him in." Peters replies with "Someone go and get somebody, *now*" But Damon replies with a further shove. Peters' eyes are no longer transfixed on the hard gravel below. He jerks his head up a bit to see mist-shrouded playing fields. There is no activity on pitches; distant soccer nets sag. Nearer to him, Peters is shocked to see the tips of rugby posts all too sharply. He wonders if this is all real. More a nightmare. He still grips the window frame but, having been pushed this far he wonders if Damon might be psychopathic enough to shove him all the way. "Say sorry Mr Peters," says Damon. These words are perversely reassuring. There seems to be room for negotiation now.

"Okay sorry, sorry - just bring me in," says Peters still clinging for all his life on to the window frame.

"I can't hear you. Speak up teacher," says Damon. Peters sees what looks like the caretaker walking along below. He shouts as loud as he can.

"Sorry, I sincerely apologise. Okay, just bring me in." The caretaker looks up, his mouth open, aghast. He immediately reaches for his VHF radio which blares out a crackled conversation. Peters cannot decide if he hopes Damon has heard the radio or not. The expression *in for a penny in for a pound* comes to mind which he hopes is not transmitting itself into the lunatic's thoughts. The pound in this case would be the one great pound his head would get being cut open on the stony path.

Peters' body is still out of the window. Anything could happen. His arm aches and he wonders if he can hold on to the frame much longer. If he loses his grip it would be so easy for Damon to push him to his death. The caretaker ends his conversation, gives Peters a nod and walks back the way he came. His disappearance makes Peters more nervous. At least he was a sane face for the insanity he is at the mercy of. Peters can feel himself being pushed further out of the window and his arm on the frame feels like it is about to give up. Peters has no choice but to gamble. "I'm not sure if you are aware but the caretaker has seen me and has just radioed for help."

"Fuck. Drag him in," says Damon. He is relieved to be pulled back through the window. Touching his feet on the floor again has never felt so good, *terra firma.* He straightens himself up. "You don't say anything. Okay?" says Damon as he sits at his desk managing to be the model of decorum again. Realising he has no book, he snatches one from a neighbouring table and opens it at a random page. The door opens.

"Is everything okay Mr Peters?" says a teacher standing by the door in a very smart suit. The teachers Peters had at grammar school used to wear gowns. This one, who he presumes is a member of the school's senior management, appears more like a company executive. He also wears a lanyard but on him it has become a medal of honour. Peters turns to Damon whose eyes look up for only a second. But in that moment, they stab fear straight into Peters' chest. "The caretaker tells me you seemed to be half out of that window," says the teacher pointing at the window. There is silence in the room. The senior teacher stands with his hands in his pockets, staring at Damon who has his head down immersed in his book. "Are you sure everything is okay Mr, err? Sorry, we have a lot of supply teachers here, what's your name?"

"Mr Peters," says Peters noticing Damon writing something on his cuff.

"Are you sure everything is okay? The caretaker was extremely concerned." There is no reply as Damon once again looks straight at Peters.

"No," says the girl who earlier complained to Peters about not having anything but supply teachers. "Everything is *not* okay. When a teacher you expect to give us a safe environment ends up being shoved through a window by one of the students, it isn't okay is it. Not okay – at all."

"Oh really. Is this true Mr Peters?" says the teacher who comes further into the room and sits on a spare desk, his leg dangling. At last, he removes his hands from his pockets and folds his arms waiting for an answer from Peters. "Yes," says Peters who realises he cannot remain silent.

"So, who was it?" says the teacher. Peters can see half the class's eyes are on himself. The others glance at Damon who looks up from his book at Peters. "Oh, for heaven's sake," says the girl again with a sigh. "If you can't tell him, I will. It was Damon and he was helped by those two." The girl stands to point at the two who were grabbing Peters' ankles. Damon looks at the girl and she, unperturbed, turns away. The senior teacher rises from the desk. "Mr Peters, is this true? I just need what is a very serious incident, confirmed by yourself... the teacher supposedly in charge of this lesson." The last few words confirm to Mr Peters that his services as a supply teacher at the school are now terminated. He has nothing to lose. "Yes, it was Damon," says Peters.

"Damon and you two. You'd better come with me," says the senior teacher now standing by the door again.

"You just made the biggest mistake of your life Mr Peters," says Damon, standing up and kicking his chair over. Peters moves away, anticipating he will be kicked too. But instead Damon leaves the room with his face fixed on Peters. *Is this really the end of the matter?* Frank asks himself. *Is this really the last time I will see Damon?*

Chapter 27

Frank Peters arrived home and was not in any mood to do or try anything. He could still see the long drop to the gravel path, the playing fields covered in a grey blanket of mist, feel the grip of his ankles locked, unable to move and the clutch of Damon's hand on his collar.

The last glance Damon gave him was unsettling. No other word for it. It meant business. Even though he was not hit in a physical way he still felt assaulted - manhandled against his will. Paradoxically, it was times like this when the need for being touched was so great. He missed so much the arms of someone who understood him. A person who could envelop his troubles and absorb them from himself - to share his burden of shame and anguish. It was in these times, and there were too many, when Frank realised just how lonely he was.

On his way home he kept looking around, wondering if Damon or one of his associates might be following him. No doubt the school would exclude Damon, if not permanently - at least for a very long while. But what would Damon do with all his free time? Peters pondered over what *he* was going do too. No way, after today's episode, would the school want him back. There was too much embarrassment on both sides. Before Frank left the school, the teacher who took Damon out of the room invited Frank into his office. He was so apologetic about the whole experience. *Never in all my time as a teacher...* going on to say he would not attribute the incident to any shortcomings with Peters' professional conduct. It was plain however that Peters would not be returning to the school – even as a cover supervisor.

Frank wondered if he should take steps to sue the school for his traumatic experience. With better safeguarding for teachers, it might not have happened. Instead, as he was not going to return there, he decided he wanted as little as possible to do with the school and not least, Damon.

It was all too apparent, work-wise, that his options were beginning to diminish and he was not in a good place. He recalled the days when the only way was forward for his career as a concert pianist. And then, to think his partnership with Mitchell might have got him back on track but so far had achieved little. Playing provincial concerts only reminded him of his early days as a recitalist, waiting for the break to come. Maybe Mitchell, for his own sake, should have taken up the chances offered on *Top Vox*. At least he would be off the dreaded building site.

He kept looking out of his window. It did not seem long since Mitchell had appeared before him at that same spot. Who would it be this time? Damon? The thought made him retreat to his bedroom where he lay on the bed. He could feel his phone buzzing, but was reluctant to respond. It would most likely be one of the agencies asking if he was available for supply the next day, nothing concrete, just checking his availability. In all fairness Peters did ask his agencies to phone him strictly mornings only. Otherwise the contemplation of covering another school day could lose him an entire night's sleep. The phone remained on the bed but moments later started its continual buzz again. It was Mitchell.

"Hi Frank, you okay?"

"Besides thinking life is a totally overrated affair, I'm fine, I suppose."

"Well, guess what."

"What?" Frank knew it would be more tiresome news of another booking playing to people who had nothing better to do than munch away to the tunes of a midday concert. A concert where praise would be given mainly to Mitchell and a fee which would maybe excuse him from supply teaching for no more than a day or two.

"We have been entered into a contest."

"Here we go again, another Roger non-starter."

"No this is different. This is for singers who have to include a mainly modern programme. It will mean performing a couple of your songs Frank." This information lifted Frank's spirits. Playing classical favourites over and over was getting as tedious as he imagined playing pop standards again and again might be.

"So what's this contest called?"

"Singer of Today."

The organisers of the *Singer of Today* contest were trying to make the whole competition experience different. In front of Mitchell and Frank was a panel of judges including not just singing gurus from the classical world but also representatives of other idioms. Mitchell was doing very well and Frank's compositional skills and playing were at long last, being given due attention. One of the judges who caught Frank's eye, when not adjudicating contests was a female jazz drummer. Even better for Frank, she was particularly impressed with his musical abilities. He, in return, was impressed by how such an elf-like figure could play drums.

When Karen Timms, the drumming judge, asked to see a copy of the music, there were no pages to show. Instead, it emerged Frank performed not from a complete score but - like one of his heroes, Mozart - from a shorthand version of his composition. This was a series of musical signposts rather than having every note written down. It was like being able to recite a whole chapter of a novel from just brief notes.

"Frank," said Karen, "It's great to see a classical musician using the same performing techniques as jazz players. I do similar. You too have found a way to release music from a straitjacket." Frank was flattered by the comment and liked the way Karen compared herself with him. She was smaller than Frank but her physique had a dancer's fluidity. After meeting Karen for the first time, Frank went backstage and immediately looked up Karen Timms on *YouTube* on his mobile. It was a delight watching her play her drum kit as if she was dancing around it with such lightness yet full of intent. Karen and Frank soon found themselves deep in conversation and he was very pleased to find her appearing at their non-contest concerts too. They talked together after each performance - sometimes at great length and eventually with great laughter. Mitchell was soon referring to the girl as Frank's groupie, much to his accompanist's embarrassment. Karen also healed him of his recent humiliation with Damon.

Mitchell was pleased for Frank, especially when he saw them beginning to bond as a couple. He knew Frank had so far led a solitary existence. He would often see Karen in foyers after their concerts tapping away at anything she could find: table tops, walls or even using cafe cutlery as drum sticks on glasses. For some it was annoying, but not Frank. Mitchell guessed her vibrant activity was to dispel her excitement on meeting Frank again. Eventually, Frank and Karen would greet and depart with a kiss and a hug. Was this just the behaviour of two luvvies? Mitchell asked himself. No, it was plain there was more than professional interest developing between them. They were slowly becoming an item. Being a professional drummer Karen also had engagements to perform so when they could meet, they would make the most of their time together.

But Roger was quick to notice how Frank and his new friend began to make their own hotel arrangements and was annoyed to find he had paid for unused bookings.

Meanwhile, Mitchell was becoming an unstoppable winner of each stage of the *Singer of Today* contest and Roger became increasingly concerned that for whatever reason, Frank might not always be able to accompany Mitchell. He wished he had the same financial hold over Frank as he had with Mitchell.

Despite this, Roger, of course was delighted to see Mitchell winning the heats. These would culminate in a televised final on the *Fine Arts Channel*. At the same time, Mitchell and Frank were getting more bookings. Supply teaching for Frank was becoming an increasingly unnecessary source of income but, alas, he was not able to give it up entirely.

Remarks of praise were now printed on concert posters as Mitchell began to get his first serious reviews from the press: *A revelation, a voice which simply demands to be heard and a great direction for contemporary lieder.* The latter remark delighted Frank. Of course, to keep audiences satisfied who were less inclined to *get with it*, Frank and Mitchell continued to perform arias from operatic classics. Everything was going forward.

However, Maisie's studies were going backwards. She hated Mitchell being away nearly every weekend and now, many weekdays too. She enjoyed joining him for the occasional weekend but with her exams pending, she knew from experience being with him was too distracting, especially when it came to her studies. Maisie found touring not that glamorous. It was ninety percent plus sitting around and waiting, with only a very small percentage of time actually performing. The majority of moments were spent in transit, and she could not read while travelling in Roger's car. She was not at all happy to see Portia and her mother sometimes acting as joint road managers. Maisie thought Portia took advantage of Mitchell by performing arias in the middle of his concerts as a 'special guest.' Portia also used the concerts to sell her albums – off the back of Mitchell's growing reputation, Maisie suspected. Apparently, Portia was still keen to have another try at securing an unconditional place at her first choice music college and believed that gaining performing experience was as valuable as attaining high grades in her exams.

Maisie also was concerned by how Mitchell and Portia got on together, not just musically. They had become friends - rather firm friends. Friends who laughed at in-jokes only Mitchell and Portia understood, often referring to past incidents and people from previous concerts Maisie did not know a thing about. She witnessed the pair of them seeming to be able to mind read and anticipate what the other was thinking or about to do. Just simple things like Portia having a bottle of water ready for Mitchell, and Mitchell automatically carrying bags for Portia as they left hotels and venues. Maisie noticed Portia gave no thanks for such kindnesses from Mitchell. She seemed to expect it with no word of gratitude.

She also found Portia's privately educated voice annoying. *Stuck up bitch* Maisie would often remark to herself. There was certainly chemistry developing between Mitchell and Portia. Maisie was worried. What helped confirm her worries was during her closer moments with Mitchell she would turn to see Portia looking on. What was she doing? Comparing herself with Maisie?

Conversely, seeing Frank with a woman made Maisie so happy for him. The first time she had stepped into his solitary flat she felt very sorry for him. She could tell immediately he lived the archetypal bachelor life in an archetypal bachelor's pad. Writing him off as a lifelong singleton, she could not think of any kind of woman to suit him. A girl drummer in the shape of Karen hadn't come to mind as she vainly scrolled down her imaginary list of possible partners for Frank. Maisie found the pair's love of music more like the fondness for a mutual relative or friend. It would spawn endless conversation and laughter between the two of them. But this caused a very loud red alert to go off in Maisie's head. People and relationships could change, and surprises, sometimes not pleasant ones, could be sprung without warning.

As a result, she could not stop texting Mitchell when back at home. She worried herself with the thought of becoming too much of a pest, too interfering, too obsessed, too crowding. But she could not stop imagining what Mitchell and Portia might be doing, despite Mitchell's assurances that nothing besides shared musical interests went on between the two of them. What initially attracted Maisie to Mitchell, his roguish ways, might become the very thing which would not only hurt her but destroy her. Was Portia also attracted to rogues? The two of them represented opposites so great. Too great. She simply could not imagine life without Mitchell.

She was also concerned Mitchell had next to no money coming in so far, from singing or the day job he was on the verge of losing. He was hardly ever on the building site. He often travelled long distances the night before and after a concert many miles from home.

Maisie wished Mitchell could be like Frank who made sure he was paid for the concerts on a per appearance session basis. She heard Roger trying to contest this with Frank, saying the concerts he was playing not only promoted Mitchell but were also giving Frank exposure as a composer.

Unaware Mitchell had no choice but to keep his day job to afford the habit she had no idea he still indulged in, Maisie was confused. Despite Mitchell's great strides in the singing world, rave press reviews, interviews on radio stations, records sold at concerts, he was still pretty well broke and moody. She also watched his appearance change. He sometimes resembled something half dead, but she attributed this to burning the candle at both ends.

Now Frank was making his own accommodation arrangements with his new-found drumming friend, Roger started booking Mitchell into single rooms instead of the doubles he previously shared with Frank. This made Maisie worried. When Mitchell was miles away she felt confident there would be no hanky panky between him and any other woman, on the assumption Frank was sharing a hotel room with him. Mitchell told her that no way could he do it with anyone else in the same room. Of course, Maisie agreed. She could not imagine such a situation either. But she did wonder if she was being naive. She pondered on a plan to surprise Mitchell and turn up at a hotel unexpectedly but she was too busy with her pending exams and could not afford it either.

Chapter 28

A t the end of the semi-finals for the *Singer of Today*, the judges are unanimous, Mitchell Woods is "A singer, not only of today but of many tomorrows to come," says the chairman of the panel. The finals are to be broadcast on the *Fine Arts Channel* and Mitchell is beginning to regain major press attention. It is very unusual for the tabloids to rave about the attributes of a serious classical singer, but Mitchell is different. He refuses to wear ties and tuxedos, garb which helps further the notion that classical and opera is entertainment purely for the elite.

Frank is thoroughly flattered too. His songs are hailed as having that rare gift only the truly great composers have – of being able to please the ear of both novice and connoisseur alike. A music publisher has also approached Frank, much to Roger's chagrin. Frank is not signed to Roger like Mitchell. The mention of advances offered by a major publisher makes Roger wish he had signed the two of them as a duo.

On a glorious mid-week night, from his piano Frank can see Portia sitting with her mother, Vicky in the front seats. A smile beams across her face. Has something changed? She often sits looking bored during competitions. Unlike non-competitive performances, there is no opportunity for her to take part and slot in an aria of her own. Or is she suddenly pleased to see Mitchell doing well and is realising she plays a part, albeit a small one, in helping a new singing phenomenon to success.

If so, Frank can empathise with Portia. His protégé is now a finalist in a national and very prestigious competition. Not so long ago, who would have believed this might be possible? Frank cannot detect any sign of envy in Portia's smile or demeanour. Most singers would wish Mitchell's unstoppable rise could be their own. Is there something going on between the two of them?

He admired Mitchell's brazen frankness when his once-nightmare school student reminded Portia of the first time he saw her. She was seated in her father's large truck which, due partly to Mitchell's fault, nearly ran over a young girl. Portia remembered the child's eyes staring directly at hers as Maisie managed to grab the girl and pull her to safety just in time. Portia, despite her horror at realising it was indeed Mitchell who shared responsibility for the near miss, nevertheless liked the way he was so ready to admit his role in the incident. "Yes, I was a complete arsehole then and should feel very lucky the girl was not killed or even injured. You were right to tell me to *toss off*."

"Is that what I said?" said Portia.

"Yes. Maisie and me thought those words a bit unusual at the time. That's why they've stuck." Portia was impressed. Just those two words showed how much detail he could remember about her.

Despite Mitchell's erratic behaviour and mood swings, Portia found herself warming to him more and more. In fact the word *fond* would certainly not be redundant. She always felt she should maintain a professional distance. But that same distance did not close the gap filled with envy for Maisie, which seemed to widen every time Mitchell mentioned her name.

Portia watches Mitchell come forward to acknowledge his tremendous applause as winner of the semi-finals. She has never been so delighted for him. He smiles out to the audience – his face shining at no-one in particular. But then he readily allows the chairman of the judges, a lady in late middle age, to take him in her arms. Afterwards the chairman delivers two kisses on each cheek. To Portia's amazement, Mitchell turns his head towards her and winks. Straight after the wink, Portia finds Mitchell's face has transformed into a smile, directly at her. This final gesture lights up her very soul. She covers her returning smile with her hands which are applauding more wildly than anyone else in the audience.

Straight after the performance and brief ceremony, Portia watches Mitchell signing copies of his album and programmes. They all want a piece of Mitchell but Portia wants nothing less than the whole of him.

Finally, after the entourage has departed, partly ushered away by Vicky, Portia goes straight over to Mitchell, and hugs him as if letting go of him might put her life in danger. He is her life raft in a tumultuous sea of emotion. Eventually she releases him. Then as usual following most liaisons with Mitchell, her thoughts return to Maisie and more specifically a conversation with her only a week or so ago.

"So what have you been up to?" said Portia, sitting with Maisie before the start of the concert. It was the biggest venue

Mitchell had performed in yet. Maisie had made a special effort to come, sacrificing valuable revision time. Unusually, Portia's mother was not with the two girls. She was sitting with her husband to support him as he sat next to agents. "I certainly know what I would do if I had a hotel room with only myself and Mitchell in it. Lucky you is all I can say. You young rascals you," said Portia pushing hard at Maisie's shoulder. Maisie turned to Portia not quite knowing how to answer. Portia's tone was confident, too confident for Maisie's liking. Was this how people with money spoke? In a rather raw and condescending way? Maisie felt like telling Portia it was none of her bloody business what she might or might not have done in the company of Mitchell. "Oh, watching TV at the hotel. And what about you?" said Maisie.

"Mum and I went to look at a couple of properties. But neither seemed suitable."

"Oh really? Are you thinking of moving to this town? It's got a lovely concert hall that's for sure."

"Er...no...Why do you ask that?" said Portia as if correcting some ignorance from Maisie.

"Well, sorry to sound confused, but why were you looking at property. Just out of sheer curiosity perhaps?"

"No, I was thinking of *possibly* coming to this town to study at the music college here. Do you know, this venue belongs to the college? said Portia waving her arm to the surroundings.

"No I didn't. So are you buying a place especially so you can study here?" said Maisie pointing to the floor.

"Yes, and I'll be letting it out to other students as well. Dad doesn't want me to go to uni or college unless there is an earner in it for him - and me." On hearing these words, Maisie felt a modicum of pity for Portia. But this was instantly dispelled as she noticed her grin on the word *me*. She was not just grinning, but gloating at Maisie and all her colleagues who could not afford such a privilege.

"Got to keep on the right side of exploitation, I suppose," responded Maisie as Mitchell came on to the stage and applause began. "Pleased my Mitchell managed to do it without having to go through college. But there's talent and then there's the rest of us."

"Indeed, there is." The applause completely faded to silence and no more words were allowed - especially as Maisie caught Mitchell looking in their direction. However, she could not be sure if Mitchell was looking at her or Portia.

After the semi-final, Mitchell, finds himself alone in his hotel room. With the euphoria of his success and with what he has become, he cannot sleep. He knows he will be up all night. Waking tomorrow morning will not be easy. He knows his entire body and soul will feel it has been sapped of everything. Another text message buzzes into his phone. It is from Maisie telling him, yet again, how she still regrets missing him on such an important night, but tomorrow she has a crucial exam *because some have to work through life* - not be transported along on a cushion of privilege. Mitchell pauses at those words but then sends a reply to let Maisie know he is thinking of her. He puts the phone down to find he is also thinking of Portia too.

Until this evening, the closest she would physically allow herself to be with Mitchell offstage, was a quick peck on the cheek. A luvvies answer to *see ya* which even the chairlady of the judges allowed herself. Yet earlier in the foyer, after Mitchell's crowd of well-wishers had dispersed together with

Frank and his new found drumming partner, was the first time Portia had hugged him. He can still feel the contours of her body to be very different from those of Maisie. They represent territory he would be keen to explore.

Mitchell lies on his bed and turns on the TV which is mounted on the opposite wall. The news is on. Mitchell presses the remote to find a foreign language film with subtitles. He nearly presses again but then a girl appears on the screen not dissimilar to Portia with long black hair and thick eyebrows. She is dressed in a suit, closes a door in what looks like her residence, gives some letters a cursory look and then discards them. Mitchell is about to press the channel button again but then the girl on the film begins to take off her clothes. Every move she makes is full of suggestion. She is what Mitchell and his friends would call a *prick tease.* He is beguiled by the woman who has removed her clothes and, shot from behind, now steps into a bath. Mitchell wonders if this is what Portia would look like doing the same thing. The image arouses him.

There is a light knock. Mitchell cannot decide if it is his room door or if the sound is coming from the television. He reaches for the remote again to mute it. There is another knock. It is his door. He puts on a t-shirt and a towel over what is still erect. Through the spy hole he sees Portia. He opens the door and as soon as she is in the room, she closes the door. She pauses in front of Mitchell and in the faint light coming from the TV, unties the belt of her dressing gown. It drops to the floor as Mitchell's towel does likewise.

The following morning Mitchell wakes to find Portia is no longer with him. Most probably she has returned to the room she shares with her mother. There is a text from Maisie *You*

can wish me good luck in my exam today, if you like! XXXXXM
He notices there is a stream of texts preceding the current
one from Maisie. Mitchell remembers last night. He has no
regrets about allowing Portia into his room. It does not mean
he has allowed her into his life, does it? He too is realising,
as his dad once warned him, *You're too young to be getting
serious.* Of course at the time Mitchell dismissed this comment,
when he wished his dad could have taken his relationship with
his mother more seriously. But then he realised his steadfast
commitment to Maisie was maybe one big act of rebellion –
trying to set an example to his dad and not deciding to *play the
field,* so to speak.

*Sorry Maisie, wishing you every success with your exam. If you
are as clever as you are gorgeous – you will piss through it easy. Luv
U! XXXXXM.* Mitchell looks at his clock. It is now ten o'clock.
The hotel kick out time is only an hour away. Another text
arrives. It's from Roger. Mitchell at first wonders if Portia's
dad has found out about last night. *Great news. Guess who's on
the panel for the final of the contest? Yes – it's your hero XL!*

"Fucking hell Wow, fucking Wow!" shouts Mitchell to
himself. But then two things dampen his excitement. Would
XL fail to turn up at the last minute as he did on Top Vox?
And secondly, even if he was to impress his idol with his
performance, would XL still be put off by the fact he was
already signed to Roger? He had recently learned that most
acts were signed up to companies on what was called a 360
deal. This meant ownership of absolutely everything the artist
had to offer: songwriting royalties, income from performing,
spin offs like appearing in TV ads, sponsorship etc. etc. Not
forgetting the good old fashioned but almost negligible income
from record sales. Besides, any income from composing

belongs to Frank anyway. So in all too plain English, unless a company can own you lock stock and barrel, they will not be interested because you would not be commercially viable.

The fact that XL has not been in touch himself makes Mitchell wonder if he has forgotten him. It doesn't seem long ago that XL was sending Mitchell messages direct to his mobile. This information coming via Roger feels very second hand. There again, Mitchell consoles himself that Roger's discovery is public information. He worries however, as when it comes to contests, soliciting between judges and competitors is not done – usually.

Nevertheless, maybe after XL sees Mitchell perform live in the flesh, he might at least give him another chance to work with his hero. His hopes escalate once again. Then he remembers tomorrow he will be back having to endure the drudgery of sweeping up the mess made by his dad in almost-finished new builds. So far he has managed to keep an *only have what you can afford* arrangement with his new dealers. Recently, with his increasing singing commitments, mainly for prestigious but non-paid contest performances and not being able to earn hard cash from his site work, Mitchell realises he is starting to accumulate another drug debt.

Having already experienced what Scribe did to him, he dreads to think what else might follow. Is this why Scribe so readily gives Mitchell what he wants on loan? Is he setting him up ready to exercise his sadistic ways on him? He tries to calm himself by thinking that he has, so far, been a good client. Surely they want to keep a good client, especially one who is going places?

Chapter 29

Despite still being a learner, Portia's ability to drive is another secret she has so far kept from Mitchell. She seems quite proficient at the wheel, unlike Maisie. From the back seat diametrically opposite to Portia, Mitchell compares the two. Maisie's mother will sit by her side in the front passenger seat, pre-empting every possible mistake, which only serves the purpose of causing Maisie to make those very mistakes. "Change down gear *now* Maisie. Remember to signal *now* Maisie. You'll need to get yourself in the right lane *now* Maisie. Oh, no it's *too* late," which would invariably be followed by the hoot of a horn. With Portia, her father Roger sits in the front and does not say a word. Roger has learned to be confident with Portia as she drives the four of them swiftly out of town. Her driving abilities are adept enough to allow herself the occasional coy smile at Mitchell who can't stop looking at her reflection through the driving mirror. By his side, behind Portia, is Vicky - busy reading a magazine supplement she picked up from the hotel lobby before checking out.

Mitchell's phone buzzes. It is Maisie telling him how much she looks forward to seeing him later. After last night, Mitchell doesn't know if he can face Maisie so soon. So he texts her back, telling her that he must first go round to his mother's to pick up some music he left there.

He then receives another text. *Where is it?* Mitchell knows exactly what those three words mean. He has a good idea what he needs to pay but cannot afford to. He tries to ignore his phone until it buzzes again. Another text is abruptly delivered with an amount which shocks him. He can't believe he owes so much. This is way beyond what he can afford. The word NOW added straight after the amount is ominous. Portia winks at him again, then her face changes to one of concern. Mitchell hopes she has not noticed his sudden change in demeanour. He tries his best to pull a grin at her, then turns towards the window and sees members of the suburban populace going about their business. Mothers pushing pushchairs while checking their phones (have they just received notice of a debt requiring immediate payment from someone they wish they had never met?). A postman who seems to be whistling as he delivers letters. A garage where someone looks like they might be in a dream as they fill their car. A man behind the kiosk laughing at a joke. Mitchell wishes he could be any of those people rather than himself at the moment. Yet he is being ushered away from their world towards a place he dreads – his home town.

He remembers how Scribe so easily handled the knife to slice his finger with such alarming alacrity. Mitchell makes a rough mental inventory of his financial resources. Even if he were paid tomorrow for the days worked on site, there would not be enough. He knows he cannot appeal to Roger to lend him anything. Roger had made it very clear he would go straight to the Law if drugs were involved... but would he? Mitchell would not be able to appear in the final or on TV if he was in custody. Could he not be given a bridging loan? But then maybe Roger would contact the police straight after Mitchell had performed or even won? He tries to think of a plausible debt he could claim to incur which Roger might believe and forward a loan to clear. But nothing workable comes to mind. Could he invent a debt where Frank owes his landlord rent and is about to get evicted? No; even if Roger believed that story, he would transfer the money directly into Frank's account and the whole thing would take too much time.

"Stop biting," says Vicky, admonishing Mitchell who only now realises he has been gnawing at his nails. He feels a sudden change of inertia when his seat belt stabs into his chest and his head is tipped forward.

"Idiot. Use your bloody mirror," says Portia, managing to avoid a car which tried to cross into her lane. "You anticipated that well Portia," says Roger.

"Thanks Dad."

"Are you sure you want one of *those* as your first car, Portia? It's not the first time I've seen someone in one being an absolute fool. Look he's almost on your bumper now," says Roger. Mitchell turns to look at the offending car again. It is certainly not cheap-looking. Sportiness at a price. "When are you buying it?" he asks.

"Oh, as soon as I pass my driving test."

"When's your test?"

"Next week. It will be a present for myself, if I pass."

"You will," says Roger.

"Was wondering whether to spend my eighteenth birthday money on seeing the world. But thought now, a car would be a better idea," says Portia. She directs the word *now* with a smile through the mirror at Mitchell. He turns again to look at the car still on Portia's tail. He tries to imagine how it might accommodate the two of them, but forgets any further and more enjoyable thoughts as he remembers his debt. More importantly, would the car she wants to buy be worth enough to cover it?

Mitchell puts the key into the door. He looks around him. He knows someone may well be watching him. They probably found out where he lives some time ago. Opening the door, he sees his mother in the hallway. She looks at him and says "Hello stranger".

"Smashed it didn't I," says Mitchell.

"Smashed what?" His mother looks nonplussed.

"Mum, I'm through to the finals. I'm going to be on TV next week."

"Really? The last time you were on telly you blew it."

"Oh, don't try to sound too pleased, will you mum? It's different this time." His mother embraces him as Gavin appears.

"What's different?" says Mitchell's mother while stroking her hand through her son's hair. It is a gesture which brings Portia back into his mind again. She too could not leave his hair alone. He can still feel the pain of her tugging.

"The *Singer of Today* finals."

"Never heard of them," says Gavin.

"Look Mum," says Mitchell turning to Gavin, "Sorry to be so unsociable but do you mind if I just go upstairs and crash for a while, I'm knackered."

"No problem, Mitch. Are you sure you don't want a drink or something?"

"No - fine Mum, thanks," says Mitchell. He heads up the

stairs to his bedroom wanting something his mother cannot provide. Alone on his bed he receives another text from Maisie wondering when she can see him. He worries whether his dealers know where Maisie lives too? They will most likely follow him if he goes to hers. He does not want to see her being dragged into this sordid business, or hurt. They would stop at nothing. His mind flips from Maisie to Portia. She has the cash which can help him but would this require more than a one-night stand on his part? Yes, and probably more.

He looks again at the text sent to him earlier. The amount they demand tells him they are not just supplying drugs. They're operating an extortion racket. He sends a text asking "Are you getting me mixed up with someone else?". For some reason this makes Mitchell feel better. He is taking action - not taking potential crap. He waits for a reply and is pleased there is nothing. Maybe they have mixed him up with someone else. Then their silence makes Mitchell wonder if he has insulted them by daring to question their - or most probably Scribe's - judgment. What will they do?

Mitchell feels so tired but he cannot sleep. He Googles for information about what drug dealers can do. The knowledge he gains is not helpful. It terrifies him. He pieces together details to form his own horror story. Windows smashed, bullets through letter boxes, bullets through the skull or if the dealers are merciful, through the leg. All methods of fear and violence are listed too vividly. But Mitchell tries to console himself by realising what he is reading comes from a police site. Are they trying to frighten people purposely to prevent anyone taking up drugs?

In an effort to empty his mind of what he has learned, he tries advancing to a higher level in *KillaTeds* but can't concentrate.

His hands have not got the necessary control to beat the enemy. Nerves are playing up. He puts the game aside and lies back. Ideally Mitchell wants total silence. But the sound of the TV downstairs cheers him a little when he imagines that same TV – like many other sets around the world – will be booming his own voice out next week. But will it? He listens to every move, wondering if each sound might be announcing the beginning of the end. His end. He can feel Scribe's knife stroking his throat. Was that the door? From his bedroom he can hear footsteps outside on the pavement; they pause. Mitchell breathes again when they continue along the road. Next, he hears people speaking. One of them could be Scribe. Are they talking about him? He is sure he can hear the name Mitchell in their conversation. No, he tells himself, it is paranoia creeping up on him and he is hearing things. But is he?

A message from Maisie: *Home safely? I finish work in about twenty minutes, mum wonders if you fancy being picked up? XxxxxM* Mitchell replies: *YES XxxxxM.*

A faint thud. Yet an unmistakeable thud, followed by his mother shouting, "What the hell was that? The glass." Her shrieking voice pierces through the floor, causing Mitchell's pulse to sky rocket. Red alert. The word *Now* from Scribe's last text forces Mitchell to spring from his bed. Which glass? The hall door has glass panels. Have they smashed one of them and are now reaching for the latch? He stands for a moment, not even considering going to the window. With caution he heads down the stairs. To his relief there are no footsteps or anyone in the hall – except Gavin, standing there with his hand pointing towards the living room.

"Mitchell's only been home less than an hour and look,"

he says. Mitchell wishes he could sacrifice Gavin instead of himself to Scribe's sadistic cravings, and enters the living room without saying a word. From what he can see, he now knows his text has been replied to.

The sofa by the window is strewn with glass. In front of it, on the floor, is a brick. Gavin is looking out of the bay window, trying in vain to see if the culprit is still out there. His mother looks at Mitchell. She knows it is something to do with him. He can't hide the fear on his face because he knows beyond all doubt, this is the first salvo from his dealers.

"Mitchell," says his mother. Gavin also turns to look at him. "I think we'd better call the police," says Gavin reaching for his mobile, resting on the arm of the chair. Mitchell starts to rake the splinters of glass on the floor into a pile. "Don't you think you ought to leave it as it is until the police arrive?" says Gavin, searching for the number. "What the fuck will they do?" says Mitchell. His abrupt tones make Gavin put his mobile down.

"Well unless you want to live with that" says Sandra. She points at the hole in the window. "The insurance company will want to know that we have at least reported it."

"Okay, but don't expect the Fuzz to do much," says Mitchell continuing to brush shards of glass into a heap on the floor. "Mitchell - people don't throw bricks through windows without a reason," says Gavin, holding the phone to his ear. Mitchell can hear the ringing tone.

"Are you trying to blame this on me?"

"Pranksters? Nah...Shush," says Gavin as he takes his phone from his head to press a number. Mitchell can feel his phone buzzing. He looks at it, two words: *Got it?* He knows for sure this was not a couple of pranksters. This was *them.*

"Well great. Guess what?"

"What?" says Sandra"

"As we haven't been burgled or had anything stolen, they suggest we go online to fill in a form."

"Are you sure that's all they can do?"

"Yes, seems like it"

"Told you they would be useless," says Mitchell looking out of the window.

"But we need a crime number for insurance purposes. What do we do then? Do they want photos of the damage if some-one's not coming round?" Mitchell, on hearing these words gets out his mobile and is about to start taking pictures with it when it buzzes. He is pleased to see it is Maisie. Taking the pictures makes him feel less responsible for what has happened. He is doing *something.*

"They say after we've taken pictures we should make sure the window is secure," says Gavin, evidently listening to a recorded message. Sandra hugs herself as the cold draft through the window begins to establish itself. There is a loud rap at the front door. Mitchell looks out through the crack in the window and is more grateful to see Maisie now than ever before. The other two alternatives, the police or Scribe would not be a welcome sight. "Got to go. It's Maisie waiting." She waves at Mitchell and it's obvious she has not seen the damage done to the window.

"So, you're going to just leave us to pick up the pieces, literally?" says Gavin, who has been surfing for as much information possible on vandalised windows. He has already started making a note of glaziers who can put up temporary boarding. "Sorry, Maze is waiting," says Mitchell, heading to the front door.

As soon as he opens the door, Maisie greets him with a

hug. "Well Done, Midge. We're so proud of you," she says, but Mitchell shuffles her hug away. He sees Maisie's mother waiting in the front passenger seat waving and smiling at him. "Anyone coming?" he asks, starting to look around him from the doorway. He wonders if his house is being watched. "What do you mean Midge? No, it's just us."

"I mean down the road Maze," says Mitchell looking both ways along the pavement. Maisie steps back and does the same. "There's no-one. What's this all about?" she asks.

"I'll tell you when we get to yours. Can we just move it?" Maisie hesitates … "Can we just go please," says Mitchell, ushering Maisie by the arm to her car. He sits in the back, trying to decompose the fear from his face to return a smile at Maisie's mother, Mary. His phone buzzes, then continues to buzz repeatedly. He knows this will either be Frank or Roger. They seldom send text messages. To use Roger's words, they are both *old school*. Mitchell crouches down as far as he can and looks at the caller. It's Frank. "Hi Frank," says Mitchell getting even lower down. "Maisie, eyes on the road," Mary says, noticing her daughter twisting her head round, wondering why Mitchell is answering the phone curled up like a hedgehog.

"Mitchell, can we meet up tomorrow to go through a couple of changes I've made?"

"Round yours?"

"I can hardly hear you. Is it a bad line?" Mitchell realises he has been whispering as well as crouching in an effort to further conceal himself. "Sorry is that better?"

"Much. Yes - meet round mine."

"Yeah okay, but working tomorrow. How about half five?"

"Perfect. I'm working too. Amazing the life all this success we're having provides, hey?"

"Too right mate. Oh well yours at half five. See ya."

"Mitchell – can I ask you why you had to take that call bunched up like you were?" says Mary. She turns to look down at Mitchell now sitting or almost lying along the back seat. "Oh, er, don't want to disturb Maisie's concentration."

"I'm sure Maisie will be fine." Mary glances at Mitchell again. "Oh well – please yourself. Now Maisie, don't try to jump through these lights, it's not worth it." To Mitchell's regret they slow down. He hates not moving. Will *they* come and do something while the car is stationary and he is the proverbial sitting duck? He looks up at the locks on his door and finds it is hard to decide whether the door is locked or not. Maisie nearly stalls the car as they begin to move on, but Mitchell is relieved they are underway again. Normally he would be playing *KillaTeds*. Instead he listens and realises how noisy other vehicles are when you cannot sync the sound with their movement.

Finally they arrive at Maisie's home. Mitchell is now beginning to gain an element of confidence, figuring that if Scribe and his associates wanted to intercept him they would have had ample opportunity to have done so by now. With his renewed confidence, the guilt of the night before returns. He feels an imposter walking into Maisie's household. Then more immediate concerns for his personal safety remind him to get inside her family home as soon as possible. Are they following, or would the brick through his mum's window be enough for now? He is scared. He will tell Maisie it's the recent busy schedule and the idea of appearing on global TV soon that makes him uneasy. But how much time have they allowed him to borrow. An hour? A day? A week?

Chapter 30

Frank returns home from the only supply teaching day he needed to do this week. As far as school supply days go, it has not been too bad. Very little abuse from the kids and unlike most other times, it is no minor miracle he has not got a headache. At one point during a lesson he even found he was enjoying himself. Was this the effect of his new-found partner Karen? She, together with the success he was having with his music, was making him feel a great deal better about himself. He could look towards the future with relish and not see his life as some sort of drawn out punishment to be endured till death.

He sits on his worn settee and on opening his phone, is even more pleased to get an email from the *Performing Rights Society.* It informs him he has received royalties from the compositions he and Mitchell have been performing over the last few months, which makes this Tuesday afternoon feel even better. Thanks also to his earnings, no more supply work is necessary this week. If that is not enough good news, there is a text from Karen, whose loss is most certainly Frank's gain. She tells him she has *a gig cancellation. Would it be possible to come and visit tomorrow?* "Yes, Yes, and Yes" is what Franks shouts out to himself, showering his text reply with expressions of delight, love and affirmatives.

Looking around his flat, Frank decides he should dedicate the rest of the afternoon to sprucing the place up. He also remembers he arranged for Mitchell to come and rehearse alterations to the compositions they are due to perform in the contest finals. Maybe he should ask Karen to arrive later? Then he thinks, if she is present she might offer useful suggestions. Everything is falling wonderfully in to place.

The state of his flat however brings Frank back from this rush of ecstasy. The place is fine for when Mitchell visits but not for Karen. They have so far only enjoyed intimacy in the sanitised and rather impersonal environment of hotel rooms. Good first impressions are vital. The thought makes him nervous and he starts picking up clothes from the floor with gusto. For Karen, he relishes turning his bachelor pad into something more resembling a home. A place which might make her pleased to visit and revisit again and again. A tune comes to him. He wants to go to the piano but all such creative endeavours must be put on hold while he attends to the dishes and pans which have been sitting in the sink for several days – or more.

As he puts on the kettle for hot water, he hears the loud clatter of his letter box. It is the local free-sheet, *The Hassledon Advertiser* being delivered. The kettle is still boiling and despite the need to impress Karen, Frank uses the arrival of the paper as a perfect excuse to give domestic chores a break. He doesn't know why he bothers to look at it really. There is hardly any editorial worth reading but nevertheless, he turns over the front page and - to his astonishment - sees a picture of Mitchell and himself standing together. He cannot remember when this picture was taken. Its slightly blurred definition suggests it was taken on a mobile phone - and pre-haircut (another recent change for Frank, thanks to Karen entering his life). So therefore a few weeks ago, at least. He does not like the look of himself, especially when up against Mitchell, who nowadays always appears immaculate. He wonders how many of the kids who know him as a supply teacher will see it and ridicule his rather dishevelled visage...

Remembering his duties, he puts the paper down and decides to go out and buy polish, some new washing up liquid (he really has squeezed and rinsed out every last molecule some time ago) and air freshener. But the power of his own prevarication hits him again. He sits down to take another look at the picture and read the accompanying blurb. *Mitchell Woods and Frank Peters are now in the final of the Singer of Today contest. Mitchell, who readers may remember caused a stir when he snubbed all four judges on Top Vox last year, says: "Getting to the final has not been easy as there have been some great singers I've met along the way but I hope to smash this final."* Frank is slightly peeved that there is no mention of his input towards Mitchell's success. Without his compositions, Mitchell would probably not have got anywhere; not in this contest anyway. However, he is even more surprised they have included him in the picture.

He puts the paper aside and gets up. There's a knock on the door. Usually, before opening it, Frank checks through his front window, which is at right angles to the front door. Without wanting to procrastinate any further, he goes directly to the door. He supposes it must be Mitchell, more likely than not - the only person who regularly visits him. Twisting the latch, he is shoved hard against the wall and for a second his vision is gone. He hears the door being slammed and the next thing he sees is the face of Damon who head butts and then knees him. Frank falls to the floor.

Mitchell, is not having such a bad day at work. The site feels relatively safe, especially with those around him who would not shy away from defensive combat. At the same time, they would probably be useless - Scribe is most likely to have a gun - but Mitchell tries not to think of that, and keeps in mind the macabre but comforting thought that if Scribe kills him, the debt is cleared. He also knows that even if he doesn't win the contest at the weekend, he will most likely make enough of an impression to advance on to better things – and the vague possibility of working with his hero, XL. All this makes the day go faster.

He still worries, like his mum and Gavin, about the brick through the window - but his dad says his mother has mentioned it to him and blames the incident on Mitchell. "That's bollocks. Who's to say it is not someone who has something against Gavin? How well does he know you? How well do you know him?" says Ryan. "No, you can throw the ball back in his court – or maybe the brick back through his effing window."

After finishing for the day, Mitchell gets a lift to Frank's and upon arrival, as usual, takes his boots off before knocking at the door. He looks at the clumps of dry mud Maisie's mother has had to put up with on occasion – along with the work shirts she has so kindly laundered for him for weeks now. He is slowly becoming part of the Moore family. He thinks of Portia again and his night with her. Guilt floods into him as he realises how much he has betrayed Maisie, her belief in him and the formidable tolerance she has shown him. Above all her kindness - not just her but her whole family. Then he thinks of Portia, the moment he touched her lips; even kissing was

273

taken to another level. From the first time he saw Portia he could not rid her from his mind. As he got to know her, he soon became aware she was not the goddess anyone who first saw her would think she was. But he had come to know Portia, the person. By acquaintance and familiarity, he was able to unveil her mystique. Finally she had revealed herself to him. Mitchell tries to maintain this thought.

He approaches Frank's flat and notices the curtains of his living room are closed. This inhibits him from appearing at the window, where Frank would anticipate his arrival and let him in straight away. He wonders if maybe Frank's new drummer girlfriend has something to do with the drawn curtains. An act of discretion to keep passing eyes - his included, from seeing the amorous goings on in Frank's ground floor flat.

So instead, Mitchell presses the bell. He cannot hear any-thing. No ringing or any kind of sound whatsoever. This is an occurrence (if he lives long enough) he will grow to hate. Door bells that do absolutely nothing, no matter how hard or how frequently they are pressed - only to be assured that they *do* work. He resorts to knocking at the door and waits. No reply. Maybe Frank and Karen are in the middle of making themselves decent. He waits and knocks again. No reply. He checks his phone to see if Frank has left any messages to forewarn he might be late. Nothing. Mitchell knocks at the door harder this time yet there is still no reply. He turns to the window and notices a small gap in the curtains. He is sure he can detect the slightest movement, so bangs hard on the window this time, as if admonishing a pair of selfish lovers. Mitchell waits again but this still proves fruitless, so he assumes the slight curtain movement must have been caused by the movement of an insect or maybe a draught. He walks around the back of the flat to see, like the front, all curtains are closed.

Meanwhile Frank is on his bed. With a tissue he dabs at the bleeding wound on his forehead caused by Damon's head butt. He can hear footsteps on the gravel outside his window and sees Mitchell's silhouette through the closed curtain walking away. Damon and Scribe are on each side of him. Scribe knows Frank will not call out in reply to Mitchell's previous knocking but holds a hand over his mouth anyway. "Well done," says Scribe after he is satisfied Mitchell has gone far enough away. "Why did you not just talk to Mitchell directly?" says Frank.

"Because he will be texting you soon, won't he?" says Scribe. Scribe is correct: *Where are you?* Is Mitchell's message. Scribe asks Frank to find him Mitchell's number. He uses Frank's phone to reply: *Firstly, congratulations on getting to the finals of the singing contest. I've just read about you this morning in the local freesheet. Unfortunately we have a debt to settle so please pay. No cash means no Frank and no contest. It's that simple. Money through Frank's letter box. Thanks.*

"Well there we are. Your colleague Mitchell should hopefully be freeing you soon if he cares enough about the contest."

"He'll just get another pianist. He'll get the police."

"We'll see shall we? Damon can you go and get some grub?" says Scribe holding up a twenty pound note. Yeah the usual, cheers." Damon departs but Frank realises that Mitchell knows he needs him to play if he is going to be able to compete. He is the only one who can play his own music. Frank also is beginning to feel hungry and is not pleased Scribe didn't ask him what he wanted. Maybe he will just have to get what he is given – if anything at all.

Mitchell reads the message. They are holding Frank hostage. But then the realisation and bitter disappointment of having to cancel his appearance at the finals begins to kick in and worry him. The vision of performing and impressing XL in person begins to disappear. A dream so close has become a dream so far. He realises any other pianist would have been fine had Frank written out the music, but he hasn't ... Mitchell is stuffed. He remembers Roger badgering Frank to do this rather than playing from a half-scribbled manuscript. Then Mitchell thinks beyond the contest; his debt to his dealer will still be there. He needs the money, contest or no contest.

Mitchell feels bad. He has only himself to blame. Does he really need substances to perform? No. Does he need them to live? No. Does he need the money? Yes.

He knows he can't ask Roger. Roger would be shrewd enough to lend him the money but then, straight after the contest, win or no win, he would probably go to the law so they could arrest the dealers and Mitchell with them. But would he be given a suspended sentence with rehabilitation? That thought is immediately dashed when he remembers reading that dealers can still operate perfectly well from inside prison. They will interpret Mitchell approaching Roger as harshly as if Mitchell had called the police himself - especially as during the court case it could well emerge that Roger had warned him he would go straight to the law if he discovered Mitchell was still taking drugs.

Once, all he ever wanted was Maisie. Now he has cheated on her. Why did she have to have this geek-like side to her making exams so important?

He thinks of Portia. That car she hopes to buy will cost her a fortune. Could she lend him the money? She knows full well his performing career is on the rise. Would she make him pay interest if she was to lend him the cash? If she has enough of her dad in her, probably. He wonders if she still has his number. Was it meant to be a strict one off? The way she kept grinning at him through the driving mirror on their return might suggest otherwise. Would she care for him, Mitchell the person, as much as Maisie has done all these years?

Frank is confined to his room. His phone has been confiscated. A piece of pizza lies on the floor. It was flung there by Damon who told him to help himself to the left overs. He can hear new voices coming from his lounge. They must be Scribe's associates or clientele. Frank realises he has become the victim of cuckooing. He puts his head round the bedroom door and sees the person who had their hand over his mouth earlier stashing notes into their pocket. Someone else is there. A client? Damon opens the door to let them out. Frank wonders if Damon has become the bigger person's butler and errand boy. "I need my phone," says Frank to Scribe. Scribe comes straight towards him and pushes him back into the bedroom. He then knocks Frank back onto his bed. "First you stay in this room. Second, we will decide when you can ask for whatever. You wait until me or Damon comes. You got me?"

"Got you," says Frank.

"Why do you want your phone?"

"Because I'm expecting someone who is meant to be coming to stay with me this evening." Scribe stands by the door and looks at Frank. "Damon, this guy needs his phone." Damon comes in again with Frank's phone. He presses the power button. "Yep there's some juice in it," he says, flinging the phone at Frank, only just managing to miss his head by an inch.

Frank surveys Damon. He looks more adult than he did only a month or so ago when he shoved Frank halfway through that window. He seems to have grown into his role and is no longer just the school thug. He has developed a quiet confidence about him. At school he was always brash and a loudmouth. Now he knows there is no need for that kind of display; he has become a more efficient criminal.

"Text this person, okay," says Scribe.

"What do I say?"

"Anything, as long they don't come round, okay? By the way let me see what you've wrote before you send."

"Okay" Frank puts down his mobile and considers the whitest lie he can think of. He does not want to make Karen feel let down. *Sorry Karen, something's cropped up. Urgent business I'm afraid so will have to postpone our arrangement. So sorry Karen. Would not do this if it wasn't so serious. Will explain next time I see you. XXXXF.* Frank hands Scribe the phone. He also shows it to a curious Damon who cannot help but grin. He says "Can't imagine you with a woman but whoever it is, I bet she isn't that fit." Damon puts the phone in front of him and Frank taps the screen to send the message. Damon takes the phone away. There is a knock at the door, another visitor. Frank still lying flat on the bed, turns himself over and is greeted once again by the sight of the leftover pizza. He wonders if this is the only sustenance he will get from his captors. Maybe he will have to eat this before he is offered something else. Its cheesy odours are already beginning to compete with the unwashed socks on the other side of the bed. The cheese wins. He turns over towards the socks – socks he was about to launder especially to impress Karen, the girl he had been waiting so long for. A tear drops on to his bed sheet

– another item he meant to clean.

Chapter 31

"Well Done Portia! Only one fault did you say? Well the main thing is, you passed," Portia's mother approved as she drove back from the test centre. "So I suppose, like me you'll be wanting your own motor now."

"Yes Mum," said Portia.

"Well try and factor in the cost of insurance before you make your final choice."

"Yes Mum." Portia has it all worked out before they park in front of the car of her immediate dreams.

The seller, a youngish man called Marcus, watches the potential buyer, Portia, shuffle out of her stilettos. Portia gives Marcus a stiff smile in return – *this is strictly business – okay?* Her mother Vicky is in the back reading about the latest Royal mishap in *Le Gen'd Magazine*. She has come along because *you just never know with blokes these days.*

They set off. "You'll know if I want to buy it or not, simple. If we end up at my home, it means I want to buy the car. If we come back here, no sale. Yes?"

"Er, okay," says Marcus. After making this clear, Portia now begins a game of hotter and colder. She drives all around Hassledon, venturing into housing estates on the edge of the town centre she has always been curious to see, but then keeps

Marcus wondering by cruising back towards their starting point. Portia likes the way the car responds. She has already fallen deeply in love with the dashboard's colourful lights and meters telling her the state of the vehicle's whole anatomy. She knows this is the car for her and feels very lucky to find one locally in her favourite colour, red. Yet she doesn't tell this to the man selling the car. "Yes – handles well. When did you say it's due for its next MOT?"

"You have a whole eleven months left on this."

"That's good. The only snag I have is that I really would have preferred one in blue." The hopeful seller in the passenger seat has been too busy sneaking glances at Portia's legs. His awe for them has rendered him colour blind to her red dress. "You can always get a respray. They're not that expensive. In fact I know someone who could do it at mate's rates."

"Mmm and how much do you reckon your mate's rates might be?"

"Can't give a precise figure."

"Mmm." Marcus is a little disappointed with Portia's response but is encouraged as they are now finally heading out of town. With ease, the car negotiates the steep rise towards Hassel on the Hill, a good two miles from their starting point.

He is even more impressed as they turn into the long gravel drive towards what he assumes is Portia's house. Marcus is reassured she has the money. Portia loves the car with its very low mileage and *like new* condition. As far as second hand cars go, it is immaculate. They park behind her father's wagon. "Okay, here we are. Yes, I'm very keen but if you don't mind waiting here?" says Portia. She smiles at the man while slipping her shoes back on. He smiles back, but it is rewarded with a slam of the door. Portia and her mother head towards their front door. Portia cannot get to her money fast enough, but decides to contain her excitement and walks away at a measured tread.

Marcus sits in his car. Knowing he has probably sold the vehicle he looks at the dashboard, the steering wheel, and even opens the glove compartment for what he presumes is the last time, to check there is nothing of his remaining. He is also tempted to turn on the car's music system for the last time but thinks better of it. She might not like his taste of station "Big Beat FM". He must keep the customer happy – and knows she will try to knock him down on the colour. He hears footsteps coming from behind him. Looking back, he is sure he has seen the person before. A man in his late teenage years.

Mitchell pauses by the passenger door. He looks at the car and then the vendor, whose hopeful face takes on a different demeanour when Mitchell's expression turns from curious to one of alarm.

At last Portia reappears from the house holding a brown envelope but she is accosted by Mitchell who comes over to the car and opens the passenger door. "Do you mind?" says Mitchell. Marcus knows this is his invitation to get out of the car, which he does. "Sorry mate, just need to talk," says Mitchell. Portia gets into the driving seat again. "Portia, I'm in trouble, big trouble."

"What do you mean? Big trouble. What big trouble, Mitchell?" Portia turns to Mitchell trying to read in his face what this might all mean. He looks at her. The only clue she can see is a face which seems to have lost all colour. His hands are shaking.

"Okay, I'll confess. I'm in debt to dealers." Mitchell can feel

Portia's eyes on him. He turns to them, "Yes, drug dealers."

"Oh fuck."

"Oh fuck, that's putting it mildly. They are now holding Frank hostage and will not let him go if I don't pay."

"Should we not get the police involved, you know, like... now?"

"No, these guys are extremely well organised. They're holding Frank in his flat. If there's any kind of raid they will more than likely break his fingers to make sure he doesn't play the piano again. Trust me Portia, this lot are seriously nasty."

"So what do you expect me to do?"

"Give me the money that's in the envelope."

"What?"

"I'm serious."

"Have you not tried to get the money from somewhere else?" Portia rests her brow on the steering wheel trying to think of possible lenders. "Maybe even my dad could lend it to you?"

"If he finds out he'll go straight to the police."

"How do you know?"

"Because he knows about this already. Well not all of it. But he's already bailed me out with these guys some time ago; He paid them off before in the form of a golden hello when I signed to your dad as manager. He said that if I ever got involved again, he'd definitely call in the old bill."

"No he won't because, A, you're so close to the performing at the finals of this extremely prestigious contest and B he'll want to keep you out of the nick to protect his investment." Marcus now walks in front of the car and gives the couple a wave. Portia raises her finger in the air to signify one minute.

"But he has met these and he'll see me as a useless, can't win, never ending deceiver – a useless cokehead whose debts

283

will just escalate. If he doesn't go now, he'll go to the cops eventually. Probably straight after the competition. Look - the solution is in your hands Portia, literally," says Mitchell pointing to the brown envelope on her lap.

"No but Mitchell if you did end up in court, I reckon the judge will be very sympathetic to you being a classical singer whose career has only just begun. I reckon you'd get a suspended on the condition you went on some rehabilitation programme."

"Then the dealers would find me and probably kill me. They're more than likely part of a much bigger network where prison is no obstacle. No - surrendering to the law is not an option Portia."

"Mmmm. Have you tried your dad?"

"No bloody point."

"What about Maisie's family. Surely they must have something stashed away for when she goes to college?"

"No, I absolutely don't want to let them know about this. They wouldn't have the money anyway and I've already dragged them through the dirt." Mitchell wonders if he should make a grab for the envelope, but realises he would not get very far.

"Well maybe you haven't got *that* much respect for Maisie, have you? Remember the other night. You certainly didn't tell me to go away, did you? In fact, after that night, if you want the truth, I'm...I'm, jealous of her. Why should I be your bit on the side?" Marcus now knocks on Portia's window. She raises her thumb this time and smiles. Marcus raises a thumb in return and also smiles.

"Right Mitchell as you can see, I was about to buy this car. I love it to bits. I had set my heart on this model quite a while ago and I was about give this chap his cash but then you pounce in and tell me how much danger you're up against. Okay. Here's a quid pro quo deal. You leave Maisie for me and the cash is yours. Well, yours on loan." The car door opens.

"Excuse me, but I'm meant to be meeting someone in the next half hour who's also interested," says Marcus tapping his watch. Portia turns to Mitchell while closing the door. "Mitchell?"

"I have no fucking choice really, do I?" he responds, taking the envelope which Portia snatches back.

"Yes you do. You either continue fucking Maisie or you can carry on fucking me."

"Ha, ha very funny." Marcus now tries to open Portia's door but it is locked.

"Excuse me," says Marcus knocking on the window. Portia opens the door.

"Sorry but I'm not going to buy."

"What? has *he* talked you out of it?" says Marcus pointing at Mitchell who is still in the car. Mitchell gets out and raises his hands as if to say *not guilty.*

"Is the price too much? I can let you off a couple of hundred if you want. You did say you weren't fond of the colour," says Marcus, sitting in the driver's seat with the door ajar.

"No, sorry. Sale off I'm afraid. But would you like some petrol money for bringing me here?" says Portia dipping into the envelope to present a twenty pound note.

"Better than nothing, I suppose," says Marcus taking the note. Portia and Mitchell stand side by side watching him drive off. Vicky and Roger come out.

"Oh, so you decided against it?"

"It wasn't for me. Decided to wait. Only just passed my test. One thing at a time."

"Oh well, I'm just nipping off to get my motor back. Thought we'd do a few errands. Anything you want?"

"No fine, thanks Mum"

"Mitchell, do want a lift?"

"No, he's staying here. We're going to do some practice Mum"

"Okay, be good."

Mitchell turns to Portia who has the envelope clutched against her chest. She waves her mother off. Mitchell cannot stop looking at the envelope. "Best take this back upstairs to dad's safe. Quid pro Quo. Yes?"

"Yes, bitch." Portia, pausing in her steps, turns back to Mitchell and winks at him. "Perhaps now is the perfect time to make sure I really have made the right choice."

"I thought I'd passed that audition."

"No – let's call it continuous assessment." Portia walks back into the house. Mitchell follows her.

Chapter 32

Frank wakes up to the dim light trying to penetrate through the curtains. The flat is quiet - he can no longer hear voices coming from the lounge. He is thirsty and wants to use the toilet. Getting up from his bed and opening the door, he is greeted by a heap of fur looking like a species somewhere between bear and dog, lying motionless on the floor. By the way the animal raises its head to display a hint of fang, it clearly has enough potential to do some serious damage to anything of flesh. Particularly strangers like himself, Frank presumes.

Its bodily mass dominates a kind of no man's land in Frank's flat - a functional piece of floor joining all the rooms, including Frank's bedroom...

Except for sitting up briefly to acknowledge him, the dog's head sinks down and lodges between its paws with their sharp protruding claws. Frank tries to step over the beast but stops when he hears the faintest hint of a growl. He retreats back into his room and closes the door with care. He wishes he could lock himself in. Visiting the toilet or having a drink have lost their urgency. He lies on his bed, then hears a sound similar to brushes on a snare drum and the door flings open. The dog parades itself into his room, obviously keen to get to know Frank. It advances towards the bed, taking sniffing seriously. Its snout investigates Frank's head, the only visible part of him emerging from the duvet. His limbs don't feel safe with merely the flimsy protection of easycare cotton and a layer of stuffing. The dog moves away and sniffs at the still discarded pizza box but as there is no trace of anything to suit its carnivorous appetite, it exits the room, pawing its way into the neighbouring living room.

There is a thud and Frank presumes the dog has lodged itself against the front door. This is confirmed when he very quietly gets up and peers round his bedroom door. By closing the lounge door left open by the dog, the toilet and a drink of water are now possible whilst there is at least temporary safety to get to both.

After welcome relief, he can hear scratching at the lounge door. He knows that given sufficient time, those claws could quite easily create a big enough hole to reach him. Frank considers how he might escape. The windows. He has tried them once before in a mock fire drill shortly after he began his tenancy, but the gap is too narrow. This memory in turn prompts him to remember his rent will soon be due.

His landlady is a reasonable person. If he is slightly behind, she will allow some leeway, but Frank wonders if he will ever be able to pay her again. He has not set up any kind of automatic transfer and makes a manual payment at the end of each month. He imagines what would happen if he fails to pay - which under his present circumstances is not unlikely. His landlady would try to phone him. He would not reply because he has no phone. She would eventually visit to see if he was all right but there would be no answer to the door. He has discovered the dog is trained not to bark. She would follow up with a letter which would not even be acknowledged. Then a court order, then the bailiffs and then...

Would the bailiffs, for once, become saviours and great redeemers? That would be a first, thinks Frank.

If the landlady has a key, she would be shocked. The toilet is disgusting. Does Damon and the other person know how to use a flush? He had to hold his breath and avert his eyes during his visit. The clawing continues and the sound changes as the dog starts scratching slowly through the door. Frank turns to look into the kitchen and is greeted by a bigger mess than before he decided to tidy the place for Karen. There are takeaway containers strewn all over the work tops. The place smells of fat and grease. In the sink, the pans lie amongst mugs in a brown coloured liquid with specks of gristle. This diminishes Frank's desire for a cup of water or anything to consume whatsoever.

The scratching stops followed by the sound of the front door opening. Damon's voice can be heard. Frank doesn't try to dash back into his bedroom - he freezes. The lounge door opens and he sees Damon's larger colleague now standing on the threshold allowing his hand to be licked by the dog. He steps towards the kitchen where Frank is standing. "Pleased you found your way in here. As you can see, this place could to do with bit of a clean up, so ... when you're ready...eh Frank?" Frank wonders why he has been chosen as their victim. Then Damon's smirk provides the answer. No doubt he knew Frank had a special kind of vulnerability. Not the fragility of a junkie, no, but Damon knew he was a total soft touch as a teacher. Someone who could be walked right over. "No time like the present, hey Frank?" says Scribe as Damon laughs.

Meanwhile, Maisie is opening the front door of her parents' place to Mitchell. She tries to hug him but all he can offer in return is a quick peck on the cheek. He turns left to walk – without invitation – straight into Maisie's family lounge. She pauses, trying to decipher his unusual body language. "Midge we can go up there," says Maisie standing by the door looking towards the top of the stairs. "Mitchell, everyone's out. They've gone to see my brother in a show at school and they won't be back for at least an hour or so."

"Which show's that?" Maisie is surprised Mitchell doesn't take up the invitation more readily.

"*We Will Rock You*, was well tempted to go myself but then thought this would present an opportunity to... you know." Maisie pulls at Mitchell but he remains stationary.

"Maisie, can we sit down?" Mitchell perches on the sofa. "Look I'll come straight to the point." Maisie now sits on a chair opposite the sofa underneath the window where Mitchell sits. There is the dim glow of dusk behind him as the velvet curtains are yet to be drawn. "And the point is?" Maisie sits back, trying to read Mitchell's face. It has a reticence causing her to sit up again. "Come on Midge, the point is."

"Okay it's the least you deserve." Mitchell looks at the photographs displayed around the lounge. The images reflect a sense of general order which does not want to be broken. The history of the family to date. The pictures of Maisie's Mum and Dad on their wedding day. Maisie and her siblings getting bigger and changing uniforms as they progress through school. Even a picture of Mitchell and herself – evidence he is finally accepted into a family where words like sever, split or divorce are not part of their emotional currency.

Maisie lifts a hand to her mouth. "Are we a bit young to be

this serious?" says Mitchell.

"What?"

"Aren't we a bit young to be a – you know, item?"

"So, you're saying you want to finish this. You know, you and me. Come on then - that's the point isn't it."

"Maisie, look we're young. Life is just beginning for both of us." Maisie pauses and looks away from Mitchell. Her life with Mitchell is passing through her mind's eye from the first time she put her hand through his hair to only earlier today when she was sharing her pride in him with her mother.

"Oh, I get it. Now you are on the verge of taking off as a singer, you want to play the field, as they say"

"It's not like that."

"Well what is it like then?"

"I just want to have a breather I suppose."

"Oh and I suppose your first *breather* will be with that stuck up bitch Portia."

"Portia?" says Mitchell.

"Yes, her. I've watched you two. Don't try to tell me there's nothing going on because I watched you *and* her."

"Well what's wrong? We just get on really well."

"Yes - I've noticed that. So, what are you saying?" says Maisie as if she is trying to make light of the words said so far. "I mean we get on. And that's that".

"That is not that at all, is it. I can see it all now. The point is, you're dumping me for *her* aren't you and that's the point you haven't even got the fucking guts to mention." Mitchell can see the anger rise in Maisie eyes and notices the door is shut. He stands up. Maisie is turning red and looks as though she is either about to burst into a flood of tears or explode with rage.

"Look, Maisie, you've got it wrong. I'm sorry, really sorry

you see it like that."

"There's no other way to see it as far as I'm concerned. And you wouldn't do this if you were sorry."

"You'll just have to believe it, I am. Truly sorry.''

"I can't believe I'm hearing or even seeing this. I think I'd better go and dip my head in the sink or something to make sure I'm not dreaming this." Maisie rises but Mitchell holds her.

"Look, Maze, in a few years you'll see this as a favour," says Mitchell squeezing Maisie's shoulder.

"Get off me. See what as a favour? This? Fuck favours." Mitchell now looks at Maisie and just about manages to repeat the "This."

"Yes. Talking of favours, all those countless favours and cover ups I've done for you over all these years and now this. Wow you sure know how to repay."

"Look be honest, we're different types, aren't we Maze?"

"And that stuck up tart is, what? The same as you? Really? She's just like her mum. She's a user Mitchell and she's using you."

"No, leave Portia out of it. She has nothing to do with it."

"Well she is and she's using you."

"I think I'd better go."

"No hold on, maybe you're right. Maybe there is something more to this than just me, you and her. It's so sudden. There's something else I can't quite put my finger on, isn't there Mitchell? Mitchell stays silent. "By the way, have you fucked Portia?" Mitchell remains silent.

"You have, haven't you?" Mitchell still gives no answer. "Your silence Midge is yelling out the answer "*Yes* isn't it? Can you just get out. Get out now."

"Look believe me Maze. Again, I'm really sorry."

"I don't want to hear you say that word. It's so fake. In fact I don't want to hear any more words from you. All I want to hear is the sound of you going. Go on. Go."

"Look Maisie - as I said, not now, but in years to come you will see this as the best thing that could have happened. And you'll be glad, honest." Mitchell retreats from the door watching Maisie's temper becoming dangerous.

"Just go Mitchell and make me glad I didn't kill you here and now...go." Half way down the driveway Mitchell wonders if he ought to wait or even return to make sure Maisie doesn't do something silly. The door flings open and he only just misses the flying framed photo of the pair of them.

Chapter 33

In the afternoon before the televised contest, interviews with all the contestants are recorded. Before Mitchell's turn, the other entrants say more or less the same thing: How they love their repertoire, how such and such a composer or songwriter writes so wonderfully for their voice, how great it was to be in the finals, how they worked so hard with their singing exercises and scales. This last point made Mitchell laugh – "If you want to know what really hard work is, try shovelling rubble all day. Stuck up ponces the lot of them... especially the tart who says she appeared in a TV ad as a child and now wants to star in musicals. I can see her parents from day one - push, push, push."

When it comes to Mitchell, he is fed up with all those other squeaky-clean interviewees so (to Roger's chagrin) decides to revert to his old self again. Soon into the recording they ask Mitchell to bear in mind that the footage will be broadcast before the watershed but he replies: "Do you want to interview me, or a pretentious prat?" Taken aback, the interviewer rises from her seat and has words with the Director. But with zero control over who can end up as a competitor, they are obliged to continue with the material (contestants) present and the programme editor is alerted to the beeper.

The interview recommences: "I was a complete (beep) arsehole at school, particularly to my music teacher Mr Frank Peters, who is now not only a fantastic composer but a brilliant accompanist. Back at school, I used to think he was such a sad (beep) fucker and thinking about it, so was I. But now it's like we've helped each other to get where we are and to be honest, I'm (beep) bloody proud about that. Without him, I might have ended up a complete and useless (beep) shit."

When it came to Frank's turn he just said what a waste of time music college was and that he'd found the experience one of the most confusing episodes in his life. "Now I just write what I think sounds good. I don't write notes only to impress intellectuals who treat a piece of music like some sort of notated brain-teaser, not to be listened to but looked at. No, I write notes intended to communicate with as wide an audience as possible and hopefully serve the wonderful poetry of *Attila the Stockbroker*."

Evening. In the purpose-built concert hall sit Mitchell, Portia and Frank - who is sorry to see the empty chair where Karen should have been sitting by his side, but she had gig commitments.

Only a minute to go before the first half of the evening is due to start, Mitchell can't stop looking behind him towards the judges, just a few yards away. Two so far have taken their positions. "Where's XL?" says Mitchell to Portia who is holding his hand. "Hope he's not going to blank this too, is he?" Portia also turns to see a rather officious -looking person come over to speak to the panel members present. What is he saying? *Our other panel member is not able to come this evening.* Mitchell turns round again to watch the activity on the stage.

A choir is assembling. It reminds Frank of a school assembly. Procedure is all. They seem to know exactly where each of them should sit. Their dress code, black, is worn by all its members. Their music too, like the agreed attire, is bound in black folders. They all sit up and very few are talking with each other. Frank wonders what some are saying. Did any have a story like his to tell?

Well, last week my flat was taken over by some drug dealers and a rabid hound that I'm sure is the cousin of a werewolf. I was held captive until a debt was paid. How am I? You ask. Well still a bit shaken up but I think I'll be okay to perform this evening. Can't let the side down can you? How are you? Fine? That's good. You want me to tell you more? How I got away?

Okay, I was lying on my bed, there was little else to do. I began to lose count of the days, well, not days but certainly hours. It seemed all I could do was doze off. I kept waking to that odd feeling you get when you fall asleep during the day – you wake up, it's still light and you think it's morning – but it isn't.

Then I heard speaking and my hopes raised as I was sure it was the voice of Mitchell – I'd got to know every nuance of his voice having worked with him for some time. The talking continued. I couldn't make what they were saying but then the bedroom door flung open. There was Damon (my abductor – a person I had the misfortune of trying to teach once) with Mitchell standing behind him. I sprang out of bed, almost wanting to hug Mitchell, then the door shut. I felt like that girl trapped in the well in Silence of the Lambs where she sees Starling and pleads with her not to go. However, cupping my ear to the wall, I could hear him telling them he needed me and the words "You've got what you wanted so can I have Frank?" But there was no reply, just another door shutting and a mumbling through the wall, followed by a slam of what sounded like the front door. I couldn't make anything out. Was that it? No more Mitchell?

With nothing else to do, I just collapsed onto the bed, this time not with self-pity, more with anger. So, I got up again and stepped over the dog which didn't even growl – perhaps it was getting to like me. I could see Scribe counting money in the lounge while Damon was watching something on his mobile I'd rather not describe. Scribe paused and looked at me in a way I suppose was meant to make me feel as miserable as possible. "Back" was the only word I needed to make me retreat to my room. Feeling powerless and helpless I fell on the bed again; then I figured maybe they were counting my ransom money. In a way I felt great. If it was, perhaps my release (well freedom to wander around my own flat again) was imminent. Then I began to feel not so great with the thought that I had put Mitchell and maybe others through such a lot trying to raise my release money. However there seemed to be hope and with that hope I began to experience a surge of excitement which, like a sugar rush, eventually only made me feel weary again. Eventually, after what seemed like hours, I fell asleep or I suppose I did. Next thing I knew, I heard banging on the window and shouts of "It's me, it's me. You're free." It was Mitchell. Not once but twice my redeemer. Those words "You're free" sounded even better than Haydn's 'Rolling in Foaming Billows.'

Most choir members sit in silence awaiting their next instruc-tions. Frank expects that these will be perfectly executed without question by this small army with sensible faces. They seem to manifest in the discipline required and all look like they probably excelled at school. Their choir is no doubt an ideal vehicle to continue to relive and act out a tribute to those halcyon days which allowed them to get where they are on their respective career ladders.

Finally the lights dim and so does the audience chatter. A conductor appears, smiles and takes a bow. Members of the choir - folders already open - also applaud. Silence. The conductor raises his arms and the choir levitates as one. The sopranos all watch the conductor - whilst holding their music in a very upright way. No slacking; obedience is all. Mitchell is sure he can see his old English teacher amongst their number. She is the very model of protocol with her eyes fixed on the conductor as he brings her and her fellow sopranos to the end of a phrase. They can now breathe – quietly.

"Thanks," says someone from the middle of the auditorium. The voice bites through the gentle tones coming from the choir. Half the audience, including Mitchell, turns to see XL entering the hall. There are sighs and clucking as if XL is something the cat has just dragged in. He mouths the word *sorry* while making his way to the judges table escorted by an usher. Sitting, he catches sight of Mitchell, gives him a faint nod and an even fainter smile. Mitchell is euphoric. The choir no longer bores Mitchell, though the item they are currently singing really annoys Frank. He can tell a mile away it was written by some ex-college student. Like the members of the choir, the piece itself sounds like it is trying to tick all the boxes of some rigid strictures.

The interval. Frank so wishes Karen was with him. She has, however, sent him a bottle of champagne with a note saying *To be opened after you've won – or what the heck, whenever you feel like it but please don't damage those fingers again - you need them.* Frank turns away from the bottle in a silver bucket full of ice and looks around him. He has always thought there is something very odd about dressing rooms. Tomatoes grow in greenhouses as sure as nerves flourish in backstage rooms. He looks at the champagne again. If he were female, the gift would probably be a bouquet, nothing quite as dangerous as alcohol. *Would one small glass be too much?* Frank has an odd but disturbing vision of the dressing room being invaded, like his flat, by Damon and his colleague on unfinished business. He ignores the bottle but as he tries to button his shirt, realises how unsteady his fingers are.

Looking through the door to the ensuite toilet, Frank wonders - as he begins to feel queasy - how much vomit has been retched down the convenience, thanks to stage fright. The room is beginning to take on an awful familiarity to the room he was sitting in before he went out blotto and ruined his career by damaging that most important tool, his hand. He can't stay inside there any longer so ends up wandering the passages behind the stage, where he can hear the first contestant. She is singing something from a musical. He wonders what she looks like, so returns to his room where he can watch her on a TV monitor. She knows how to flirt with the audience but also owns a confidence and smile Frank absolutely hates. For him it is so fake and superficial - just like the music she sings: *quite* clever rhymes but set to a melody which would challenge the range of even the most gifted singers and would probably end up wrecking their voices.

Portia is watching the same performance in the stalls, now joined by her parents. Her mother is tapping along to the music and smiles at the attractive singer. She whispers to Portia the name of the musical the song is from - *Actz*, a sequel to *Jesus Christ Superstar*. Portia thinks Mary Magdalene has never presented herself so glamorously, then she remembers what her singing teacher said about musicals *It is the look of the thing that matters above all else.* At the end of the song *Now I Know How to Love Him*, the audience, like her mother, loves it and the performer takes her curtsies. Portia sneaks a glance at the judges. One of them, a middle-aged woman wearing a frock more befitting a ballroom, is giving the performer a standing ovation. XL looks up at his colleague with a most quizzical face, mouth agape enough to say the word *What?* Portia is pleased when the cheers and clapping finally die down. Mitchell is next.

She watches Mitchell from the seat she supposes Maisie would have been sitting in, feeling guilt and envy in equal measure. Envy for not being a finalist in such a prestigious competition and guilt for using her financial power to take Mitchell from Maisie. Yet she quickly reconciles herself with the knowledge it is not her fault Mitchell fell victim to a drugs gang. She tries to rid herself of such thoughts by acknowledging that the person on the stage performing brilliantly is now *her* man. She is also pleased her parents have not probed too much into why she turned down what was meant to be her dream vehicle.

Someone behind her is chatting and another has decided to open a bag of sweets. Portia wants to get up and tell them to be quiet. Luckily someone beats her to it and says *Excuse me, we are not at the pantomime now.* She stares at Mitchell and wonders if Maisie is sitting back at home with her family, watching her ex sing so fantastically. The first song finishes. As a new composition unknown to the audience, it only receives a muted applause. She turns round to XL who is busy writing something with a smile illuminated by the glow of a table lamp. The woman next to him in the ballroom frock is looking bored with her arms folded. Portia is sure chewing gum is being tossed around behind those vividly rouged lips.

Mitchell's next number is a great deal more up tempo and the cross rhythms Frank generates between both his hands seem to command more attention from the audience. It is a perfect piece for the two of them: Mitchell's soaring vocals glide over the infectious and propulsive accompaniment. There is also audience participation in the middle section where the listeners are invited into a game-like call and response. The piece ends on a crescendo and Portia cannot believe the reaction. She turns to look at the judges again. XL is not up from his seat but his heavy clapping seems to be annoying the one who chews on her gum with far less discretion and gives Mitchell nothing more than a few light claps. The judge on the other side of her is craning over to nod in agreement with XL.

After all the contestants have sung, the compere comes on to introduce a pianist who will play while the judges make their final decision. Portia sends a text to Mitchell telling him how brilliant he was and how, whatever the result, his career is made. But before he has a chance to read it, the finalists are summoned back to the stage. Mitchell stands with the other contestants, trying their best to look as humble as they can with their heads bowed low.

The three judges mount the stage. The chair is the woman in the ball gown who has now removed her chewing gum. She goes to the microphone and in a voice Frank associates with royal commentators says "May I first of all, on behalf of the panel, thank the organisers and everyone behind the scenes for making this magnificent event possible." There is a round of applause. "Also, of course, the four finalists, who I have to admonish for being so amazing and making the job of we

301

judges a very difficult task indeed." She shakes an envelope at them as if she a primary teacher telling off young miscreants. Even louder cheers are heard. XL shrugs his shoulders. It is obvious he is in disagreement to the chairperson. "Well, we have come to a decision and the information you've all been waiting for is as follows." Portia sits in her chair clutching her mother's hand. They both hold their breath. "The winner of *The Singer of Today* contest is -." XL cannot stand still. "Daphne Hughes." There is a loud applause. XL gives the winner a token handclap and starts to shuffle towards the side of the stage but is grabbed by the chairperson and dragged back centre stage. There is laughter as XL cups his mouth. She then lifts up a gold cup mounted on a podium and presents it to the winner. Mitchell, who has been watching this small pantomime between the chair and XL catches a grin from his hero.

"Well ladies and gentlemen," says Daphne "I really can't believe it. Am I really here receiving this awesome trophy?" she gives her face a quick slap. "Yes, it really is me and this really is my hand holding this awesome award, right here. But you know what? I still can't believe it." There is further applause. Mitchell turns to XL who flings his head back but then grabs the microphone.

"Can't believe it? Would you like me to pour a bucket of water over you - just to make doubly sure Daphne?" says XL. The chairperson gives him a forced grin. Daphne continues "No thanks XL, this is definitely reality. So can I first of all give the biggest thanks ever to my mother and father sitting down there somewhere – go on show yourselves." Her parents stand to more applause, "Particularly my mother who took me to all those singing lessons with my wonderful singing teacher,

Toni Farr." More applause erupts. Her singing teacher also stands and is mouthing something at her protégé. "Lastly all I can say is, well, you know - thank you. Oh and thank you to the writers of the musical *Actz* who provided me with such a great and wonderful song to sing." A young girl comes onto the stage to give the winner a bouquet. Then after one final applause, the finalists prepare to leave. Mitchell hangs on and sees XL give him a smile and a thumbs up. Mitchell holds his hand out to him. He returns it with the words "Bad luck," then leaves the stage. Mitchell tries to see where he went, but XL just disappears through the doors he'd entered by. "So that's that," Mitchell says to himself. He walks off stage, watching Daphne being interviewed by a TV presenter with a whole pack of photographers and reporters around her.

Disappointed XL did not have further words with him, Mitchell is about to enter Frank's dressing room. He is at rock bottom and knows exactly what he needs to pick himself up again, then he feels a hand on his shoulder. "Hi Mitchell, at last we meet," says XL shaking Mitchell's hand. "As far as I'm concerned the real winner tonight by a mile is you."

"Thanks," says Mitchell.

Through the open door, he catches sight of Frank battling with the champagne bottle, then he turns to see Roger, Vicky and Portia coming towards them along the corridor. XL sees them too and says "Look, I have to go. Give me a ring first thing next week. Just say it's you." He is about to go but Roger takes hold of his jacket sleeve.

"Hello, my name is Roger Masters, I'm Mitchell's manager," says Roger, holding out his hand towards XL.

"Oh, Manager. Great. Well good to meet you. I've got to

303

dash I'm afraid."

"Was wondering if you and Mitchell might work together."
XL fumbles in his pocket and gives Roger a card. "Here, give me
a ring - sorry, as I said, must dash. Well done again Mitchell."

Roger watches as XL walks away and then looks at his
card. "Must be busy," says Roger examining XL's card. "Oh
well." They enter Frank's dressing room. He has already half
demolished the champagne. "More of where that came from,"
says Vicky holding up two more bottles. Portia hugs Mitchell,
then steps back. "Shall we toast the real winner? Mitchell you
are just totally awesome and so much more than a tarty show
girl," says Portia.

"Now, now Portia, each to their own," says Vicky.

Mitchell would normally not mind those words. But from
Vicky they highlight what Mitchell considers the inverse snob-
bishness she carries on her person - like her overpowering
scent. He finds both nauseating and does not want to be in the
dressing room any longer. He stands on the dressing room's
threshold. He would love to be able to run off and start working
with XL immediately. Instead, Portia comes and puts her arm
round him again. This gesture just reinforces the idea that he
is locked in to the whole Masters family both professionally
and personally.

"What the fuck," says Mitchell staring at the contents of
Portia's opened handbag. expecting to see maybe a packet
of exotic condoms she might have bought from a machine in
the toilets, she shows him something else, which is all too
visible. It is white. It is wrapped in transparent cellophane. It
is gear and it is tempting, too tempting... He knows full well
how wonderful it would be to surrender to this temptation.

Portia drags him down the corridor but he holds his ground.

He realises she is using the drug in the same way the dealers might - to control him. He looks at her and in her face he does not see her gorgeous features. He sees Scribe, he sees the Raza Man turned slave and a wretched-looking Frank, so desperately relieved to see a friendly face opening his own door.

With all his strength he says "No" and walks back into the dressing room. He can still feel XL's handshake and the charisma transferring itself from his idol into his entire being. The feeling is already acting like a different, even more potent drug. He wants more of it. With it he can see another future, a better one than that which Roger might have planned - especially with Portia steering him towards drugs again. He wants out. But how? Looking at Roger reminds him of his contractual obligations - the document he signed. He rushes back down the corridor again but is accosted by a TV announcer. "Can we have a word?"

"No way" says Mitchell. Roger, Vicky and Portia stand frozen not quite knowing how to react. "Mitchell" shouts Vicky. Mitchell turns, "This is essential profile. Stop, NOW." continues Vicky. Mitchell ignores her, hoping he can reach the station in time to catch the last train to Hasseldon. He prays Maisie might forgive him. He hates Portia for her total hypocrisy, what she made him do and everything she and her family stands for.

Roger turns to Vicky as they watch Mitchell run, and says in her ear. "It's okay, we've got the bastard sewn up."

Chapter 34

Monday.

"Hello can I speak with XL?" says Mitchell

"Who's speaking?" says the PA.

"Mitchell."

"Mitchell who?"

"XL just told me to say it was me... Mitchell the singer." Mitchell can hear the knocking of the receiver being taken. "Mitchell," says XL "So pleased you called. Look - well done. You should have won. But we need to talk, preferably in person. Would it be possible for you to come here?"

"Yeah no prob. Where are you?"

"Actually, second thoughts. Before you come, I need to see something." Mitchell's drops the phone from his ear. It suddenly feels heavier.

"What do you need to see?"

"I presume you will have signed something with that manager of yours I saw the other night, yes?"

"Er, a contract do you mean?"

"Yes, a contract. Have you got it? I need to see it before we can go any further." Mitchell now takes the phone right away from his ear. He wonders where it is. He just remembers the time he had to sign it. What happened to it after that he doesn't know. He looks at places around his room. The drawers - is it in those? He checks by lifting up a pile of clothes he hasn't worn for some time; nothing.

"Mitchell, are you still there?" On hearing XL's distant voice, Mitchell grabs the phone again.

"Sorry, was just trying to find it. Look XL, it'll be somewhere."

"I do now remember asking some time ago if you'd send me a copy. Did you do that?" XL's surly tone reminds Mitchell of his past, and the language of teachers investigating missing homework. For the first time he realises those words have serious consequences. "Look, okay. As soon as you find it will you send it to me? If you just photograph each page with your phone that'll be cool for the time being. Okay?" Mitchell feels instant relief from XL's more casual voice.

"Okay."

"By the way, you can start to call me John from now on. So when you phone here, just ask for John and there should be no objections from my secretary. Sorry - should have told you this the other night."

"Okay, er, John."

Okay Mitchell, I'll pass you back to my secretary who can give you my personal email address where you can send the photos. Speak soon. Bye."

Mitchell smiles. How many others know XL is just a plain ordinary John? He looks in the drawer again, unimpeded now by trying to hold a phone at the same time as searching. Nothing. He peers under his bed. There are boxes filled with toys he hasn't used for years; boxes with projects and pictures he did at primary school. Nothing. No contract. His floor becomes a mess with the accumulated papers scattered all over the place. Mitchell shoves them back under his bed. He opens his wardrobe – nothing. Checks on top; nothing. Goes inside every coat and jacket pocket. No sign of the signed contract.

"What are you looking for?" his mother asks as he rummages around the living room lifting magazines off tables and cushions from chairs. It's not there. Bending down under the sofa – nothing. "I'm trying to find the contract I signed with Portia's dad."

"I didn't even know you signed a contract with Portia's dad." Sandra gives the room a brief reconnaissance. "What does it look like?"

"You know – pieces of paper, white, A4 size, probably looks a bit like that project I did all those years ago." Mitchell watches his mother sorting through the small book case wondering if the contract has somehow lodged itself between the oversized books: an *AA* road atlas, three *Viz* annuals, an encyclopaedia in two volumes, several cookery books, a photo album and a couple of old telephone directories – which his mother takes the opportunity to throw out.

After several minutes of fruitless searching, Mitchell begins to wonder if the contract could be at Maisie's. He's worried. If he can't present it to XL, will that be seen as signifying that he doesn't take his singing career seriously enough? Or maybe XL cannot proceed without the document. He knows Roger will have a copy or at least be able to print off another one. But if he were to ask him, Roger would no doubt want to know why exactly why Mitchell needed it.

Scouring places he has barely glanced at before, makes Mitchell realise the incredible amount of storage space in the house he's lived in for all these years. The tops of cupboards with their half-used shelves, a mantelpiece in the kitchen with two folders on top, mainly containing paid bills, interspersed with the occasional splash of colour from a postcard or sales brochure. It seems a miracle his mother discovered the note from his dad's lover with so many places he could have hidden it. But as for the contract... nothing.

Mitchell is pleased Gavin isn't in. He would have hated him finding it first. Gavin's weasel-like disposition would probably have found the contract but not informed anyone until it had been fully scrutinised and he'd seen the amount Roger had advanced. *You never told us about that Mitchell.*

This last thought makes it imperative that Mitchell should find it before anyone else. But where is it? He catches himself looking in the same places over and over again but what represents the potential key to XL's kingdom remains elusive. Having hunted everywhere around the house, he eventually concludes it must be at Maisie's.

Thinking of Maisie brings Portia to mind. Could he ask her to get him a copy? No. She too would want to know what he was up to and, especially having snubbed her the other night, would be reluctant to help. The contract is somewhere – hopefully not in some landfill by now. Or has it already been recycled into one of the many flyers his search has uncovered?

How is he going to ask Maisie? Could he get Frank to ask on his behalf? No, it's his contract and his business.

Maybe by now, like the photo she hurled at him, she has probably chucked away everything to do with him. To ask her if *by any chance you might have a contract of mine somewhere...* would take some audacity. But she could hardly expect anything other than audaciousness, if she really did know him – split or no split.

At first, Mitchell feels it will be futile sending the text to Maisie asking her for anything. Is he being a coward? Why not go and request it face to face? There is no reply to his text for a good two hours. In that time he muses on other ways he might get hold of the contract. Maybe he could think of some kind of enquiry? *Sorry Roger can I have a copy of the contract? No, I can't find mine. I'm concerned about how much I still actually owe you? The loan company needs to see it in black and white before they can make a decision.* Probably no way Roger would allow that but Mitchell decides to ask him anyway.

He can hear Roger's answerphone giving the usual spiel but it is interrupted by his phone buzzing - a notification. He cancels Roger's call just before being invited to leave a message. A text has arrived from Maisie. *Yes, I have left it in a brown envelope at the end of the drive. On top of the red bin. It's collection day so you better hurry up.*

Mitchell feeling elated, is also stunned. This action of Maisie's goes against all natural laws. As he hurries over to her house he wonders what the catch might be. Turning the corner into her road, he can feel the first spots of rain on his head and increases his pace. True to Maisie's word, there is a brown A4-sized envelope on top of the bin. He hurries as it turns darker and the faint spots turn into heavy thuds. He realises that in his haste, he has not brought anything to carry the vital papers in. Not even a plastic bag. He sees the envelope, decorated with circular spots of rain which he hopes haven't seeped through into the contents. He grabs it and walks away - knowing Maisie will be watching - trying his best not to look towards any of her windows. But he feels some kind of nod of acknowledgement towards her front door is required. The rain is starting to pour down more constantly so Mitchell stuffs the sealed envelope under his shirt, hoping to protect it. He remembers a bus stop only a couple of roads away and rushes there.

There are two people already waiting under a small canopy, barely enough to keep them sheltered from anything stronger than drizzle. Luckily a bus comes. Mitchell watches them board, but another person gets off and stands under the bus stop, reluctant to make a dash for home. Mitchell has to face them. The person at the stop is staring at him, looking as if she probably knows him. Perhaps she has seen his recent TV appearance or his picture in the paper? He gives an unreturned smile as he too shelters the best he can. The person shuffles as far to the side as the rain will allow her.

Mitchell takes out the envelope. It feels thin between his finger and thumb, but still heavy enough for the content he needs. He turns around to gain as much shelter as possible from the rain which still manages to patter onto the envelope. Reaching inside, he realises what Maisie has done. His contract has been ripped into pieces. This makes him think about the ways ex-partners' clothes are ripped up. Further inspection shows she has only torn the document into quarters; a gesture, no doubt done in haste. Why waste more effort than necessary trying to turn the pages into confetti? Confetti which will certainly not be showering the couple formerly known as Mitchell and Maisie. He waits for the rain to subside and thinks.

Chapter 35

Reconstituting the contract is the hardest and most boring jigsaw Mitchell has ever completed. But he feels lucky each page is written on only one side of the paper. Fortunately these sheets are also numbered and the whole document is only four pages long, making the task less time consuming. The trick is to make sure all the torn edges of each quarter page overlap seamlessly. Mitchell reads the text at the joins and though unfamiliar with legalese, as far as he can make out the words seem to make some sort of grammatical sense.

Having finished the contractual puzzle, Mitchell is relieved not to have to post it to XL. He lays the first intact page on his bed and photographs it. He is quite pleased with the result; except for the odd smudge, courtesy of the rain at the bus stop, the page is legible. At the top of the contract is the title *Mitchell's Music Management* (in upper case) and the other party *Mitchell Woods* (also in upper case). Finishing all four sides, Mitchell looks at the images and despite the odd blur, which could be attributed to mobile camera photography, it can be sent to XL – he should be able to understand it.

Shortly after emailing his document, Mitchell receives a text message from Roger with a string of dates he has already managed to secure. Before this list of engagements are the words: *Despite your early departure the other night and not maximising your exposure by being so rude to the presenter who wanted to interview you, I have managed to confirm the following dates...*

These are all in much larger venues than where Mitchell has so far performed. He realises all the fees attached to the dates will be money owed, not only to Roger but now his daughter too. The dates are also close together and include many week nights. This means he would not be able to make any money of his own via the job he hates but which provides an income he can keep. He will have no spending money at all and will be fed and watered via hotel breakfasts and roadside cafes where the receipts will (as always) be carefully filed by Roger.

He looks at the fees and wonders how much of those will cover the expenses, especially when he remembers the word *gross* written in the contract he has just reassembled. He knows what gross means from the invoices his dad has shown him – it means the amount payable before deductions or expenses. Therefore Roger is taking his cut before the cost of hotels and transport are considered. How long will Mitchell remain in Roger's clutches? He seems just as bad as the drug dealers. The only consolation for Mitchell is that he thoroughly loves singing and performing much more than working on a building site. So does Frank – who he presumes will be continuing to accompany him.

Another thought occurs: *Where does Portia get her gear from?* He wonders if the business with Scribe is finally over. With great effort and the prospect of joining forces with XL, he is able to get through the weekend without succumbing to his craving. The devious craving comes in waves, like some kind of dormant illness which still lurks and pounces at unexpected times but he is winning and is determined to keep winning.

Mitchell heads straight to Frank's, who opens his door with an expression Mitchell has never seen before. Frank is radiating a confidence and energy. The inside of his flat is very different from how Mitchell remembers it being when he rescued him. There is an odour which spells the word 'woman'. They both sit down.

"Mitchell, I'll come straight to the point. I'm afraid I won't be able to accompany you any more, or at least not to the extent I've done so far. My friend Karen has asked me to join her band, so I'm sorry but I'll be working with her. As you know she tours constantly. Of course, we can still perform together, but only occasionally, if you don't mind..."

"It's fine Frank, I'm really pleased for you. It probably won't matter because guess who I've been talking to?"

"No idea. Oh hang on - your hero X whatshisname."

"Yep XL. He wants to sign me. Well, hopefully."

"That's great Mitchell. Seems we're both happy and sorted then."

Roger also sent me a list of dates but I suppose I'll have to find another pianist for those."

"Yes, Karen has already got some gigs lined up, sorry. Where are these dates Roger's got you?" Mitchell shows him the phone.

"Do you know what? These look like serious venues. If Portia is going to keep making guest appearances in your shows, you would be entitled to charge her a 'buy-on'. This means you could get her to pay for the exposure to those bigger audiences you'll be getting now."

"That's a really good idea, thanks Frank. All I can say is a massive thanks for all you've done for me and I wish you all the best. You will be so hard to replace."

"Think nothing of it. It's been of mutual benefit. Oh, by the way, I've written out full versions of my music for your new pianist."

The world seems to be settling. Mitchell takes Frank's advice about charging Portia for a buy-on, and to his surprise, Roger agrees. To make the most of this, Vicky then arranges for her daughter to be followed by a writer from *Le Gen'd Magazine.* It is for a feature entitled: *Life on tour with an opera sensation.* Vicky had managed to collar the gossip mag writer shortly after Mitchell's swift exit following the contest. As part of the deal with Mitchell, it is agreed (for extra money) that Portia will join him singing duets at a second encore. Amongst photos of Portia singing solo, the magazine photographer also shoots the two of them embracing while singing operatic love duets. Despite the icy relationship that has lately developed between them, the pictures tell a very different story. They make it look like Portia and Mitchell are an inseparable couple both on stage and off. This is confirmed by a picture of Portia hugging Mitchell backstage. It is a thank you hug from Portia after her performance with Mitchell secured her a lucrative solo gig. Mitchell asks the photographer to delete this photo.

He finds working with another pianist much harder than performing with Frank. There is no doubt whatsoever the replacement pianist is good, if not brilliant but Mitchell finds him to be rather a *stuffed shirt.* There seems little rapport between them beyond the music they play. Unlike Mitchell, he is obviously a person who flourished at school – academically at least. Before concerts he usually has his head in a book rather than even trying to make conversation.

Weeks have passed and Mitchell wishes he could be touring with Frank again. He still awaits a reply from XL but tries his best not to phone him. In the same way he makes every effort to avoid taking drugs, which he is sure Portia is taking.

Morning time. Mitchell is on his own in a hotel room when his phone starts to buzz. "Hi Mitchell it's John here," says a voice. At first Mitchell wonders who on earth John can be, then realises straight away when he says "So sorry for getting back so late, I've been unbelievably busy but thank you for sending me the contract." For a moment Mitchell wonders, what contract?

"The good news is, I think we can get you out of it."

"Really?"

"Yes really. The very top line is the clue to your release. Your name is Mitchell isn't it?"

"Yes it is."

"Okay well, if you sign a contract saying it's Mitchell's Music Management, whose management do you think it belongs to?"

"Er"

"Mitchell, yourself, of course. Now if the contract had a name like Cowell or Epstein on the top, that would be a completely different matter and trying to secure your release would be futile. But as it stands there is some hope, in fact quite a bit of hope.

"Brilliant."

"Also, another thing. Did you get any kind of legal advice or representation before you signed the contract?"

"Er no."

"Well that's it. In fact what you did was in some ways illegal. In this day and age of the music business, it would not be acceptable amongst professionals. I'm about ninety per cent sure we can free you from that agreement you signed with Roger. Now if you could post me a hard copy that would be good. I've already forwarded what you sent me to my lawyer but you know - formalities are formalities. The postal address is on the card I gave you. Have you still got it?"

"Somewhere. I'm away from home."

"Look I'll tell you it again. Have you a pen and paper handy?" The address is given. Mitchell wonders if he ought to come clean about the physical state of the contract but hopes he can somehow find a way of supplying XL with an unblemished copy.

After pacing the room he phones Frank.

"How's it going? How's the new pianist? How's it going with your hero?" Frank asks.

"The pianist is a struggle. But I've hit a big snag now with XL. I have to send him a hard copy of my contract with Roger, but the only one I've got was torn to pieces by Maisie."

"What?"

"Yes, XL wanted to see it. Luckily I managed to piece it together and send photo versions of each page. But now he wants the full Monty." Frank muses on this for a moment.

"Do you know what, I'd insist Roger gives you another copy of the contract. Just tell him the truth - your ex decided to rip it up after discovering you were having an affair. Besides, he'd have to submit it if any legal proceedings were to begin. It's commercial evidence. If he doesn't know that, well..."

Mitchell endures an agonising wait, but months later, after his contract is finally secured from Roger and properly scrutinised by a music lawyer, he ends up signing with XL. He had never been completely comfortable performing in the venues Roger booked him into...

Now working with XL, his name is becoming very much linked to his hero's. His new audience is a much broader one and he begins to appear regularly in the popular press where he continues to provide enough copy for gossip columns.

On a day off from tour, Mitchell is walking towards *The Faithful Retainer* to have a drink with his dad, Ryan. He is about to enter when he feels his collar being grabbed with such force he nearly falls backwards. "Knew it all along you cheating bastard." It's the not so familiar voice of an angry Maisie. She thrusts a copy of *Le Gen'd* magazine in front of his face, open at a page with a large photo of himself and Portia in an amorous embrace. "If there was nothing going on between you two, what's this?" says Maisie stabbing the picture with her finger. Mitchell now remembers the time Portia was followed by a magazine writer. It seems so long since then. He too has had a similar experience touring with XL. Sometime a feature is written but held back until the best time to run it. *Le Gen'd* magazine interviewed Portia ages ago but has only just decided to print it now. "That's us on stage, it's acting Maisie. Can't you remember? We did it before your very eyes several times." Maisie turns the page to reveal the backstage picture of the couple. Well this is not on stage and it's certainly not acting, is it Mitchell?"

"She grabbed me, honest."

"Oh yeah, and my name's Peppa Pig. It calls you her boyfriend here," says Maisie stabbing another part of the page. "They are full of lies those mags. If you believe them, you'll believe anything. Excuse me. I was about to have a drink with my dad."

"How neat. Two philanderers toasting their conquests no doubt." Maisie throws the magazine at Mitchell's face. She walks off and feels something in her trouser pocket. It is a memory stick and on it is the footage of Mitchell in the practice room. She wonders if she should post it somewhere. Somewhere where such a video would be very welcome material indeed especially now that Mitchell has gained such a cool reputation.

Mitchell sits with his dad Ryan. They are the only two in the pub until a couple walks in behind them. "Look, I won't pretend to like opera but you're doing well with it, so each to their own I suppose. Perhaps this pub ought to have a blue plaque outside saying Mitchell Woods, opera singer, started his career here." Mitchell shrugs his shoulders and notices there is already a picture of him on a wall by the bar. "Oh, and I'll tell you something else. I suppose with all your escapades and that, you might not have been following local news. Les have you got that copy of the *Hassledon Gazette*?

"Yeah, it's here," says Les while serving the other couple. " Well, thanks to me, that kid who abducted your pianist friend should be facing a stretch inside," says Ryan. Mitchell's face turns pale. "What? What did you do?"

"This kid was in here a couple of weeks ago. Turns out he

was called Damon. He said from behind *Right what's everyone having?* I was just sitting here at the bar, like I do. But then his mate, also behind me said *I suppose we have Peters to thank for this, yeah?* Then the next thing I heard was *Ouch...Okay, sorry.* I turned around to see that lad had just hit his mate on the arm. Must have been hard as his friend was trying to soothe it better. But the only Peters I know is the Frank Peters who accompanies you on the piano. Then I remembered you telling me he was abducted on behalf of yourself. It was obvious that Damon was treating everyone with the money you paid for his release."

"So what did you do?"

"Went to the bog and called the old bill." Mitchell looks around, at the tables, at the chairs, at the walls and finally at the door. He stands up. "What? You called the old bill?"

"Yeah, I was sure it was them. Especially when that Damon character hit the other – trying to keep him quiet. As you can see, it's written here they were busted at another place."

"Well, thanks Dad. They'll probably think it was me who grassed on them. Now I've got to keep looking over my shoulder, probably forever. They'll come and find me or might have accomplices to do it for them. They most likely know I'm with you here, right now."

"I imagine they'll find it hard to get to you when they're inside."

"But when they come out? What then Dad? What then...?"

THE END

About the Author

SFP has been just about everything from a deckhand to a jingle writer for radio and TV. He is very fond of playing and listening to all sorts of music and loves sailing. In between writing, he thoroughly enjoys coaching students in Maths and English.

You can connect with me on:

 https://www.facebook.com/stephen.fosterpilkington

Printed in Great Britain
by Amazon